Praise for the Asperger's Series
—————— *The Question of the Mission Head* ——————

A Mystery Scene Best Book of 2014

"[A] delightful and clever mystery."

—Publishers Weekly

"Delightfully fresh and witty, this story about a detective who has Asperger's syndrome illuminates the condition for the reader and is also a perfect traditional mystery, told with humor and originality. You'll be forgiven for being reminded of Detective Monk, but this is a detective whose deductive methods fit right alongside Sherlock, Columbo, and, yes, Monk. Pure heaven."

—Mystery Scene

"In this well-crafted story, the Asperger's element … provides a unique point of view on crime-solving, as well as offering a sensitive look at a too-often-misunderstood condition."

—Booklist

"Copperman/Cohen succeeds in providing a glimpse not only of the challenges experienced by those with Asperger's, but also of their unique gifts."

—Ellery Queen's Mystery Magazine, four stars

"Cleverly written and humorous."

—CrimeSpree Magazine

THE QUESTION OF THE UNFAMILIAR HUSBAND

AN ASPERGER'S MYSTERY

E.J. COPPERMAN

JEFF COHEN

MIDNIGHT INK
WOODBURY, MINNESOTA

FIRST EDITION
First Printing, 2015

Book format by Bob Gaul
Cover design by Ellen Lawson
Cover illustration by James Steinberg/Gerald & Cullen Rapp
Editing by Nicole Nugent

Midnight Ink, an imprint of Llewellyn Worldwide Ltd.

This is a work of fiction. Names, characters, places, and incidents are either the product of the author's imagination or are used fictitiously, and any resemblance to actual persons, living or dead, business establishments, events, or locales is entirely coincidental.

Library of Congress Cataloging-in-Publication Data
Cohen, Jeffrey, 1957–
  The question of the unfamiliar husband/Jeff Cohen, E.J. Copperman.—First edition.
    pages; cm.—(An asperger's mystery; #2)
  ISBN 978-0-7387-4350-9
1. Asperger's syndrome—Patients—Fiction. 2. Murder—Investigation—Fiction.
I. Title.
  PS3603.O358Q48 2015
  813'.6—dc23
                            2015021914

Midnight Ink
Llewellyn Worldwide Ltd.
2143 Wooddale Drive
Woodbury, MN 55125-2989
www.midnightinkbooks.com

Printed in the United States of America

To Seymour M. Cohen and Byron T. Copperman, our dads,
who showed us what being a familiar husband should be.
And to Jessica Oppenheim, for making it a joy.

AUTHORS' NOTE

The reception to *The Question of the Missing Head* was really overwhelming in many ways, not the least of which was hearing from families of people dealing with autism spectrum disorders and from some of the Aspies and others on the spectrum themselves. It is a humbling experience to get your emails, and we appreciate all the comments (even the somewhat testy ones). We try to present as accurate a picture as we can, but we know perfection is impossible, certainly in our hands. We're going to drop the ball every now and then. Your letting us know when that happens helps ensure it will not recur.

Some of the stories we've been told and messages we've received have touched us beyond our meager powers to convey. Suffice it to say that we are happy and privileged to be on the almost-front lines with you. The battle for understanding goes on.

There are always thanks when a book is finished, and this is no exception. Even two authors can't do it alone. First, E.J. would like to thank Jeff for toning down the corniness for a bit, and Jeff would like to thank E.J. for letting Samuel go on a date.

But enough about us.

Thanks to the indispensible D. P. Lyle for Reglan, which was exactly what we needed. When you need a poison, always go to a licensed physician.

For guiding us through, we as always appreciate the amazing work of Terri Bischoff and Nicole Nugent at Midnight Ink. Thanks for taking something barely comprehensible and turning into something … comprehensible. It's nice to be treated like people and not word machines. Because we're pretty sure we're people.

Naturally, huge thank-yous to Josh Getzler, Danielle Burby, and everyone at HSG Agency not only for getting Samuel to Terri's attention, but for introducing him to the world! Samuel is now available in a variety of languages in a variety of countries, and that's because of you. Thank goodness Josh lives in a convenient apartment building in Manhattan, or none of this might ever have happened. So thanks to Chris Grabenstein.

To all who have read any of our books ever, we are astonished by you. Yeah, we know how that sounds, but the idea that someone other than close friends and family actually chooses to pick up our work and read it is an honor we do not take lightly. Thank you from the bottoms of our hearts.

—Jeff Cohen and E.J. Copperman
In the darkest corners of New Jersey
June 2015

ONE

The front door opened and a woman walked in.

I had been working on my Mac Pro in an attempt to complete the answer to the question of a client I'd taken on the week before. The question involved an asp, a high-diving board, and a quantity of bourbon, but it was not noteworthy enough to explore here. I had agreed to answer the question because I had not worked in six days and needed the mental exercise. The fee was also a consideration.

Questions Answered had been open for six months. I'd rented the storefront at 735 Stelton Road in Piscataway, New Jersey, because it was close to the house in which my mother and I live, it was adequate to my needs, which were minimal, and it was affordable. Since then, I had advertised sparingly and through that activity and some word of mouth—an expression that makes very little sense to me, since words written on paper or pixels are just as effective—I had managed to keep busy most of the time the business had been in operation.

The woman, who was approximately twenty-seven years old, five-foot-six, and brown-haired and -eyed, looked nervous as she scanned the room. It is not an unusual response among people who enter my establishment.

Before I opened Questions Answered, the building had been devoted to a pizzeria called San Remo's. The ovens that had been used to create the chief product of that retail operation were still in the room, although I had never attempted to operate them. I must admit, however, that curiosity did sometimes cause me to consider doing so.

The rest of the large room—larger than I needed, but adequate to my needs and open to the possibility of experimentation—was devoted to a desk in the center at which I was currently seated; a reclining chair to one side where my mother often sat when she visited the office; and two posts supporting the ceiling. Much of the room was empty, but it was clean. It has been suggested to me that the walls could benefit from a coat of paint, but I had not seen the utility, since there is no data of which I'm aware suggesting that people are more apt to ask interesting questions if the surroundings have been recently painted.

"May I help you?" I asked the woman. I had trained myself to ask that question. My natural impulse would be to discover the nature of the potential client's question, but Mother says that people find such directness disturbing. I never ask, "Can I help you?" It confuses me when a person at a store or business asks me that. I have no idea if that person is capable of helping me before he or she knows the nature of my interest. I am certain I can help most of the people who walk in to ask questions, but statistically, it is true that I will not be able to answer every question.

I have not yet been asked one I could not answer, but it is theoretically possible.

"I … I'm not sure," the woman said. "Is this, like, a detective agency?"

So. It would be easy to deflect this interaction, because my business is nothing like a detective agency. "No," I said. "This is Questions Answered." I gestured toward the sign I have displayed in the front window, on which I had clearly written the business name in permanent marker.

Mother says I should invest in a more professional-looking sign, and I suppose I should, since she is usually right about such things.

Instead of appearing discouraged, the woman took five more steps toward me. I stood, since I have been told by Dr. Mancuso that it is viewed as impolite to sit while a person with whom one is conversing remains standing. I held out my hand, as I have practiced. "Allow me to introduce myself," I said. "I am Samuel Hoenig. I am the proprietor of Questions Answered."

"Um … if I have a question that requires some investigation, you can handle that?" It was not technically a question, but her tone, with an increase of two and a half tones at the end of the sentence, indicated she believed it to be one.

I answered as if I agreed that she had asked. "It would depend on the question," I said. "Most questions require some research, but not all need outside investigation."

"You've investigated a crime before," she reminded me. "I read about it in the *Star-Ledger*."

I bit down on the insides of my lips just a little. It was true; I had answered a question about a murder three months earlier, but only because it has been related to another question I was attempting to answer—and because Mother had rather unfairly asked about the murder and then paid me one dollar to answer her question.

"We did," I admitted. "That is not our primary business, however. If you need someone to investigate a crime, I suggest you look for a private detective or consult the police." I thought about sitting down as a signal that the conversation was finished, but that came into conflict with the possibility of being seen as rude. It was a difficult situation, so I remained standing.

"I'm not sure I do need someone to investigate a crime," the woman said. "I'm not sure a crime has been committed at all." She took another quick look around the room and her eyes stopped at Mother's chair. "May I sit down?"

Since my mother was not in the room, nor was she expected soon, I nodded. If nothing else, the woman being seated would allow me to sit down behind my desk again. She sat in the recliner but did not raise the footrest. I reclaimed my position and asked, "What is your question?" Again, I was not certain my direct inquiry was appropriate, but I felt it was necessary to progress the conversation so I could return to the matter of the asp.

"My name is Sheila McInerney," the woman said. I had not asked her name, but she continued, as I had expected she would. "I'm a graphic artist working for an advertising firm in the city." When people from Northern New Jersey say "the city," they mean New York City, specifically Manhattan. When people from Southern New Jersey say "the city," they mean Philadelphia. Ms. McInerney meant Manhattan.

I remained silent, as she had said nothing so far that seemed to lead to a question I could be employed to answer.

"I've always enjoyed my work, but I still want to have the home and the family and everything," Ms. McInerney went on, still saying nothing I found especially useful. "I've done the usual dating things, even signed up with one of the online services, but I hadn't met the one for me, I guess."

I felt it was time for me to say something, although it would be difficult not to sound impatient or rude. I thought carefully. "How has this search led you here?" I asked. It seemed unlikely that Ms. McInerney had, through some computer algorithm, determined that I was the man of her dreams, but if she had come to that conclusion, it would probably be necessary to disabuse her of the notion.

Still, she seemed startled despite my attempt to employ tact. "Well, I'm getting to that," she said. "I wanted to impress upon you the idea that I'm not, you know, settling for just anybody romantically. I want to find a man who can be my friend and my partner, not just my lover."

The conversation was definitely going in an uncomfortable direction for me. I considered telling Ms. McInerney I was involved with someone, but that would be lying, and Mother always says lying never helps a situation. I could dispute that in theory, but in practice I am a very poor liar, so her advice is generally well taken.

Luckily, Ms. McInerney had simply taken a breath and was not expecting my reply. "What I'm saying, I guess, is that I'm not the kind of woman who just falls into bed with a guy."

I have struggled for years to establish and maintain eye contact in conversation, but when the subject matter is awkward, I still have some difficulty in that area. Now I was staring at the screen of my Mac Pro, which showed a page devoted to various kinds of bourbon. But I was not really trying to read the copy. "I understand," I said. Technically, that was true—I understood the message she was trying to convey. *Why* she might want to communicate that information was completely beyond my comprehension at the moment.

"Good," said Ms. McInerney, as if that settled something. "So we have the basis for you to understand my problem."

Certain keywords trigger responses from me that have become almost reflexive. When I hear someone refer to a "problem," I am quick with my answer. "I do not solve problems here," I said. "The business is called Questions Answered. I answer questions."

I was about to recommend several courses of action Ms. McInerney could pursue to solve whatever problem she might be experiencing, but she spoke before I had the chance to do so.

"Okay, then," she said. "I have a question for you, Mr. Hoenig: Who is the man in my bed who calls himself my husband?"

TWO

THIS TIME, I MADE sure to establish eye contact with Ms. McInerney. "Do you believe an impostor is claiming to be your husband?" I asked. "Are you married to someone else?" She seemed to have said the opposite before, so I watched her face very carefully. There was no hesitation, no flinch. She had expected the reaction, and had indeed phrased her question for the maximum effect. It had worked very well.

I was intrigued.

"No, I believe I'm unmarried. I think the man who is now living in my apartment and sleeping in my bed is a fraud."

I looked at her left hand, where a woman often wears an engagement ring or a wedding ring, or both. Hers had the simple gold band and nothing else. Neither hand bore a diamond nor any other jewelry. "How is that possible?" I asked. "Surely you would know if you married someone."

"It's complicated," she answered, and I noted that this time she was the one to break eye contact. That can be telling in most people considered "neurotypical."

"I would imagine it is. How, specifically, is it complicated?"

Ms. McInerney sucked in on her lower teeth as if trying to expel an unpleasant taste. "I don't want you to think that this is something that happens a lot," she said.

My opinion of her actions seemed to be important to her, and as a potential client (now that I was interested in the question), it was important to alleviate her concerns. "I can only imagine you have just one unfamiliar husband," I said.

"It's not funny, Mr. Hoenig."

"I was not attempting to be amusing," I answered. "Please. Tell me what happened."

She nodded and took a breath; I could not be sure if the action was genuine or for my benefit. I found myself wishing Mother were in the room, as she can often explain a gesture or signal that I will not recognize.

"It was at a party a little over a month ago," Ms. McInerney began.

"Who hosted the party?" I asked.

Ms. McInerney's eyes blinked and widened just a little, which indicated she was either surprised or irritated at the interruption. "A friend of mine from work, Jenny LeBlanc," she said. "It was a costume party, which I don't usually like. But this one was fun. You were supposed to show up dressed as your favorite character from the movies."

I took a moment to process the idea that Ms. McInerney did not mean I was intended to be at the party in a costume. "As whom did you attend?" I asked, because I believed she wanted me to do so.

"Actually, I went as Harpo Marx," she said. "Do you know who that is?"

Was it a trick question? I had seen all thirteen of the Marx Brothers films, and while some of the jokes were difficult for me to understand ("viaduct" really would not be mistaken for "why a duck," a question which itself makes no sense), I was familiar with Harpo

Marx. But Ms. McInerney masquerading as that character was confusing to me.

"Harpo Marx was a man," I pointed out. "And your hair is straight. His was very curly and unkempt. He has been dead for over sixty years. How could you have hoped to be mistaken for Harpo Marx?"

She did not stare at me but held my gaze for a long moment, as if searching for something that was not there. "I wasn't hoping people would think I was the real Harpo Marx," she explained. "I was simply pretending for the party. Other people pretended to be Spiderman and Ron Burgundy. One woman came as the princess from *Frozen*. It was a party."

I forced myself to put aside the idea of masquerading and focus on the question. "How does this relate to the husband you claim is a fraud?" I asked.

Ms. McInerney nodded, getting herself back on topic. I resolved silently not to allow for any more unproductive tangents in the conversation. "I met a man at the party. That much I remember. He had come dressed as Zorro, with a mask over much of his face."

I had never seen a film about the fictional Zorro, but I had seen photographs of actors in the role, so I was familiar with the look the character would have had. A wide-brimmed hat and a mask over the eyes would have obscured much of the man's face. "Was it the man to whom you are now married?" I asked.

Her arms flapped a little at the sides, just once. Some people with autism spectrum disorders will flap their arms in excitement or frustration, but this gesture was less severe—more like a shrug to indicate she could not answer definitively. "He says so," she reported. "I remember having two glasses of red wine with him on the deck behind the house, and then I don't remember anything until three days later. He says we were married the second night because we were so taken with each other that we couldn't wait any longer. I don't have any memory of that at all, but there is a marriage certificate and pictures his best friend Roger took at the wedding. I'm smiling. I don't know why."

"Where was the wedding performed?" I asked. "You wouldn't have been able to get a marriage license that quickly in New Jersey."

"Apparently we went to Darien, Connecticut," she said. "They don't have a waiting period up there as long as you have identification on you."

"I would have suspected Delaware, but if the person getting married is not from the state, there is a four-day waiting period there," I noted. I hadn't actually made a specific study of the delay times for marriage licenses, but I had once been asked a question about Delaware's specifically, when a man had wanted to know if his parents' marriage license was indeed legitimate. It was.

"I don't know," Ms. McInerney said. "I don't remember being in Darien, Connecticut. I don't even remember leaving the party. I think I was drugged, Mr. Hoenig."

"I am not aware of a narcotic that would erase three days of your memory, Ms. McInerney, but I will have to do some research. What do you remember after attending the party as Harpo Marx?"

Her face clouded over, as if she were being forced to recall a traumatic experience. I have seen people look that way after the death of a pet or the loss of a favorite sports team's most important game.

"I remember waking up in my apartment, like always," Ms. McInerney said. "And when I saw Ollie—that's his name, Ollie Lewis—in bed next to me, I almost had a heart attack." She was clearly exaggerating at this point, since heart disease is brought on through arterial blockages or other organic internal causes, and not by a surprise. I ignored the point. "I thought I'd done the most impulsive, ill-advised thing ever, and I was right, but I had no idea how right until he woke up and started calling me his wife."

"You had never met Mr. Lewis before?" I asked.

She shook her head. "Never. I'd never even heard his name mentioned."

I had not been taking notes, but they would not be necessary; I knew I would remember the conversation accurately. "What was his connection to your friend Ms. LeBlanc?" I said. "Why was Oliver Lewis at her party?"

Her voice sounded wistful and betrayed regret. "He was a friend of a friend," she answered. "I heard he came with Terry Lambroux."

"Terry" is a name that can be assigned to either gender. "Is Terry a man or a woman?" I asked.

"That's a good question," Ms. McInerney said. "I wish I could tell you, but I've only heard the name. I've never met the person. The only other person I met at the party was Ollie's friend Roger Siplowitz."

"The party and the wedding, if one actually took place, happened weeks ago," I said, moving the conversation ahead. "What steps have you taken? Have you notified the police?"

"And tell them what? That a man married me against my will? It doesn't make sense, Mr. Hoenig. I'm not a wealthy woman; I work for a living. Ollie can't be trying to claim he's my husband to have access to my vast fortune. I don't have one, and neither does anyone in my family."

"Perhaps he just wanted to have sex with you," I suggested. Sex is often a motivating factor in the actions of people, particularly men.

"So he married me? If Ollie slipped a date rape drug into my drink, he could have done what he wanted and then left. I hear it happens all the time." She stood up and turned away from me. The effect was similar to that in an old noir film, except Ms. McInerney wasn't wearing a trench coat and had no cigarette in her hand.

However, she was correct in pointing out the illogic of my suggestion. "Have you seen the marriage license Mr. Lewis says you have?" I asked. "Do you have a copy with you?"

The question seemed to surprise Ms. McInerney; she blinked twice and then bit her lower lip again. "No, I don't," she said. "But I have seen it. It looks official."

I ran my tongue over my upper teeth, which is something I seem to do involuntarily when thinking. Since it took me over a year in therapy to break myself of a larger gesture (wiggling my fingers), this did not seem to merit much attention. "It is not difficult to produce an authentic-looking document," I said. "I will have to do some searches in the files of the Fairfield County clerk's office." I was speaking more to myself than to Ms. McInerney, whose expression was difficult to read—Irritation? Puzzlement? I couldn't tell.

"Then you'll take the case?" she asked.

"I do not take cases," I explained again. "I answer questions."

"Will you answer my question, Mr. Hoenig?"

"First, what is your favorite song by the Beatles?"

Ms. McInerney's eyes narrowed, as if trying to see me more clearly. I have observed this reaction to that question—one I ask to help determine a person's state of mind—before. But she did not ask why I might be interested. Her lips bulged a moment, very slightly.

"'Yesterday,'" she said.

Conventional. Possibly regretful.

"That is all I needed to know," I said.

"So you *will* answer my question."

"Yes, and the one about your purported husband, as well."

She thanked me. We agreed upon a fee, and she paid half of it, as I require whenever a new client employs me. She filled out my client intake form, which took nine minutes, and then left, saying she was pleased I was going to help her. I wanted to tell her that I had not agreed to help—if she was indeed married to a man she barely knew, I couldn't extricate her from the situation as a divorce attorney could—but decided reiterating that I would answer the question was enough.

But once Ms. McInerney had left, I noticed a feeling of anxiety in my stomach. Usually the questions I am asked can be answered with some simple research. In fact, I often turn down easy questions, or answer the client on the spot and charge a small fraction of my usual fee. People could easily discover the information they believe to be elusive. Usually, coming to Questions Answered is more a symptom of laziness than difficulty.

With this sort of situation, however, I was entering into a situation that did not play to my strengths. Facts are often easy to obtain, particularly when they pertain to history or science. Determining whether the Battle of Gettysburg was influenced by one general's facial hair (as I had once been asked to do) was a simple matter of research and meteorology. A supposedly legendary trade of the Boston Red Sox slugger Ted Williams for the New York Yankees star Joe DiMaggio, which purportedly had been agreed upon and then abandoned, took less than three hours to confirm.

But Ms. McInerney's question ventured into considerably more unfamiliar territory. It would be easy enough to find out whether or not a legal marriage had been filed and recorded in Darien, Connecticut, on the date she has mentioned. But her question was more complex than simply knowing if she were indeed now a wife.

Ms. McInerney's question was more complex than that: "Who is the man in my bed who calls himself my husband?" In order to answer that, I would have to venture into the interactions between men and women, matters of emotion and expression that are not at all my area of expertise. It was possible I had agreed to answer a question that I was especially unqualified to address.

I started to do some power walking, raising my arms for extra aerobic effect, around the perimeter of the office. Since I had been advised by my doctor not to stay in an office chair for more than twenty minutes at a time, I had been very careful about raising my heart rate three times an hour. I would like to say the practice helps me to think more deeply, but the sad truth is I think at exactly the same level, but with heavier breathing and a higher perspiration rate.

Mother appeared at the door when I was on my eleventh lap around the office. She was accustomed to my exercise regimen but looked at her watch, no doubt wondering why I was doing so seven minutes later than usual.

My breath was slightly forced, but not enough that I could not tell her, "I was meeting with a new client." Mother knows I will adjust my routine when an unfamiliar person (particularly one who might become a paying customer) is in the room. For some reason, seeing me walk rapidly around the room while raising and lowering my arms makes some people uncomfortable, although it is a reasonable thing to do in terms of health. Mother nodded her understanding.

Once I had completed my rounds, I walked to the vending machine and bought a bottle of spring water. A man named Les comes once a week to restock the machine, and he gives me what he calls my "cut" of the money I have used to pay for the drinks I have bought that week. It doesn't seem a rational system, but it seems to satisfy Les and I pay only half for water all week.

"What's troubling you?" Mother is able to read expressions, particularly those on my face. It is a talent I am working very hard to cultivate, but it does not come naturally to me. Before I'd had a chance to say a word, she was already aware that I was perplexed, and possibly a little concerned. "Does it have something to do with the new client?"

I nodded and explained my dilemma. "I find myself wondering if I will be able to answer this question," I said after explaining the circumstances. "It might require an understanding of areas in which I am less than proficient." At that moment, a thought struck me which must have affected my facial expression again, because Mother asked, "What?"

It seemed the most logical thing in the world, so I was amazed I hadn't thought of it before. "There is only one way to attack this question," I told her. "I must get in touch immediately with Janet Washburn."

Mother smiled, but her tone did not communicate any joy that I could detect. "Oh boy," she said.

THREE

"WE'VE BEEN THROUGH THIS before, Samuel."

Janet Washburn sat in the living room of her modest suburban house in Cranford, New Jersey, and looked at me with an expression I read as stern. Mother, who had driven me to Ms. Washburn's home only after some discussion, was drinking the lemonade Ms. Washburn had offered, and which I had declined. Lemonade is simply water with lemon and sugar in it, and not a very healthful drink.

"That is precisely why I am asking you to come back to Questions Answered," I responded. "You understand how I work, and you complement me very well."

Ms. Washburn had been my associate for only two questions, both of which revolved around the same matter. The arrangement had absorbed only parts of two consecutive days, but I had been impressed with her ability to keep me focused and to interpret for me aspects of the question that I would have had trouble noticing or understanding on my own. I had asked her to stay on with Questions Answered on a permanent basis, but Ms. Washburn's husband had been in opposition to the idea, she had told me, suggesting the work would be too dangerous.

"I'm not reminding you that we've been through the situation before," Ms. Washburn said now. "I'm saying that we've had this conversation, where you ask me to come back and I say no, at least four times before today."

It was true. There had been, in fact, five times in the past three months when I had reiterated my offer of full-time employment to Ms. Washburn, whom I had considered invaluable in answering the question of the missing head. Each time I had done so, she had declined, although Mother often said she believed Ms. Washburn's refusals to be reluctant, based on facial expressions and body language I had not noticed or interpreted accurately.

"This time is different," I argued. "I am asking for your help with only one question, one that I believe might be outside my own abilities. I need you because you understand both the interaction between people and my own thought process."

Ms. Washburn nodded but did not meet my gaze, which I was making a point to aim at her face. "I'm aware that your Asperger's makes some things more difficult for you, Samuel, but you know perfectly well that with the proper amount of concentration and determination, you can handle yourself just fine without me."

Mother, who had taken up knitting a scarf in the armchair, did not look up. "I've been telling him the same thing, Janet dear," she said. "You know how he is when he gets an idea in his head."

To be fair, Mother has a somewhat different view of the relationship between Ms. Washburn and myself than my own. She believes I harbor some romantic feelings for Ms. Washburn and is disturbed by the thought, since Ms. Washburn is indeed a married woman. I have denied having such feelings, often and emphatically, but Mother is not to be dissuaded when she thinks she has noticed something in me.

"The idea in my head is that you can be of the utmost assistance on a question that might pose a special challenge to me on my own," I told

Ms. Washburn, not directly acknowledging Mother's comment. "You can earn some money, which I imagine you would welcome, and I will maintain my reputation as well as an unblemished record of answering all questions posed. What is the disadvantage to doing that?"

Ms. Washburn drew in breath slowly and let it out at the same pace. This appears to be a way for people to either gather their thoughts before responding, or to quell emotions they would prefer not to express, such as irritation. I asked Mother later which this was, and she indicated it was the former.

"The disadvantage is that my husband is still opposed to my working with you," Ms. Washburn said after the pause. "He still believes that your work is too dangerous, and after what happened—almost happened—last time, I can't say I disagree. I'm sorry, Samuel, but the answer is still no."

Mother put her knitting in her bag, drained the rest of the lemonade with a satisfied gulp, and stood. "I'm sorry we bothered you, Janet," she said. "Thank you so much for the lemonade."

It was odd for Mother to give up her seat and make such remarks when the conversation was clearly not yet concluded, but her thinking is not always immediately clear to me.

"There is no danger in this question," I told Ms. Washburn. "We are simply trying to determine the identity of the man claiming to be Ms. McInerney's husband and his motivations for doing so."

Ms. Washburn looked at me, then at Mother, then back at me, but she was squinting, as if I were very far away and difficult to see. "You don't recognize the potential for danger there?" she asked.

I confessed that I did not.

"Suppose this guy Lewis really is some sort of con artist and we ruin his plans by exposing him," Ms. Washburn went on. "Suppose he gets mad at us for doing that. Do you think a man who imposes himself on a woman, gets her drunk and marries her or pretends to marry her, that kind of a man would simply stand up, pat his hands and say, 'well done, you got me'? You think there is no element of danger at all? Come on, Samuel. You're a very intelligent guy. Is that scenario, as you'd put it, at all likely?"

If her concern really was that of physical danger, I could accommodate that provision. "I will see to it that Mr. Lewis never knows you are involved in answering the question," I said. "When anyone asks, you will be known as Ms. Baroni, a graduate student in neuropsychology who is"—and here I probably winced at the word—"studying me for her capstone project. Your real name will never be mentioned."

Mother, apparently taken by surprise, stopped and put her hand to her mouth. She seemed to consider the possibility.

But Ms. Washburn was having no such thoughts. "No, Samuel," she said. "I'm simply not going to tell Simon that I'm going against his wishes on this. I'm sure you can find someone else who can help you at least as well as I can." She looked at Mother. "Vivian?"

That seemed to startle my mother. "Oh no, Janet. I couldn't. My knees wouldn't allow it. And besides, it doesn't look good for a man to have his mother following him around in his business." She held her hands up as if trying to stop any words Ms. Washburn might say from getting too close. "I'm not a candidate for the job."

"Neither am I," Ms. Washburn insisted. "I'm flattered, Samuel, honestly. But I'm not that special and I'm not the only person on the planet who can take notes and run interference for you. Why not place an ad on Craigslist or something?"

"My needs are very specific," I answered, having considered the question before. "It's not the kind of thing a person finds on an Internet site. That seems to be the place to get rid of unwanted furniture and used pool tables."

This was proving to be a difficult problem to solve. I needed Ms. Washburn's help, but I was unable to convince her that the situation made her participation necessary. I decided, without a great deal of consideration, to try another tactic.

"Have you been working as a photographer?" I asked. Ms. Washburn had been a newspaper photographer whose job had been downsized not long before we met. I had originally agreed to answer her question—which was a fairly simple one, as it turned out—in exchange for some photographic work.

She looked away. When I do that in conversation, it is because I am not fond of looking at the faces of others. But I have observed, and this is borne out in the literature, that such a move can also be a signal that the person looking away is somehow embarrassed.

It had not been my intention to make Ms. Washburn uncomfortable; indeed, my thought had been to try to get her to take some photographs in connection to the question being asked. But her face reddened a bit and she had a different tone to her voice when she said, "No. Not since we saw each other."

That would have seemed to be the perfect opening for my gambit of asking for photographs during my investigation of the question, but now I was unsure what effect the inquiry about her work might have had on Ms. Washburn. I hesitated for a moment.

"Well, I'm sure Samuel could use some pictures when he's looking into this fake husband," Mother said.

Her words had an electrifying effect on the room; my head snapped in her direction, wondering if somehow she had discerned what I was planning to say. But Ms. Washburn's reaction was even more pronounced. Her eyes narrowed and her right index finger went to the tip of her nose.

She was considering.

"It would be helpful," I decided to add. "I believe some photographic proof of whatever findings I make would increase the voracity of my answer and validate its certainty."

Ms. Washburn thought longer. This time she scratched her nose, which I am informed is a "tell" for those who play poker that the player is uncomfortable, perhaps with the cards he or she has been dealt. She opened her mouth slightly, drew in a breath, and stopped. Then she turned toward me and smiled what I am sure was a very friendly smile.

"No," she said.

FOUR

My mood when Mother and I arrived at the Questions Answered office was not ebullient. I had tried every logical argument and even some devious tactics to lure Ms. Washburn back to work, and she had refused, consistently citing her husband's disapproval as the key point in her reasoning.

"You must explain it to me, Mother," I said, checking the phone answering device—I do not own a cellular phone because I am concerned that I might lose one if I did—which showed no new messages. Business at Questions Answered was sporadic most of the time, but for the past few weeks had been very slow indeed. Paying this month's rent on the storefront was going to be a bit of a dilemma if I did not answer Ms. McInerney's question quickly. "I do not understand why an intelligent woman like Ms. Washburn would allow a stranger to dictate her actions."

Mother looked at me with an expression that indicated I had said something odd. "A husband is hardly a stranger, Samuel," she said. "He is the closest friend a woman can have, someone to whom she opens up about her entire life and all her feelings. He is a partner. In a marriage, the idea is to have the other person's welfare in mind ahead of your own."

I thought about suggesting she ask Ms. McInerney about the closeness of a husband, but I realized my client's situation was not one that represented the norm. "Ms. Washburn's husband does not appear to have her best interests in mind, or he would withdraw his objections to her working at Questions Answered," I countered.

In all honesty, I should confess that I considered using my mother's marriage to my father as an example of a rather one-sided relationship, but I have learned through a great deal of experience that my father is not a topic my mother enjoys discussing, even as she will defend him in conversation no matter what argument I might bring. Besides, my parents were not the point in question.

"Every marriage is unique," Mother said with what she intended to be a gentle tone. I have come to recognize most of her inflections, although those of most others are still a challenge for me.

"I don't see how that is relevant."

"The one thing you can always know about someone else's marriage is that you don't know anything about someone else's marriage," Mother said. Her words seemed an aphorism, but I didn't recall ever hearing them before. Before I could ask, she added, "We can't know what kind of arrangement Janet and her husband—what is his name?—have. For all we know, she is perfectly happy letting him make that kind of decision for her. What you have to do, Samuel, is forget about Janet—no, I don't mean that literally. You need to stop thinking you'll convince her to come back and work here and focus on the alternatives that are possible. What are those?"

It is not atypical for Mother to ask me a question in order to distract me from a topic she thinks is occupying my thoughts too heavily. The tactic often works, as it did in this case.

"The most obvious choice is for me to answer the question on my own, as I have done with all the others except the two Ms. Washburn assisted on," I said. "I believe that is not a viable option, since my skills lie in areas opposite from those this question requires."

"Do you really believe that, or is that just something you were telling yourself as an excuse to contact Janet again?" Mother asked. Mother believes me to be more devious than I am.

"It is documented," I told her. "Interpersonal relationships are most difficult for those of us with Asperger's Syndrome. Understanding those dynamics is certainly among my most telling weaknesses. I will need someone to keep me focused on the nuances and point out their meanings. I am not without ego, Mother, but I do know my strengths and my deficits."

"So. Other options?" Again, she threw the ball into my court, an expression I struggle with, since the court for any game is a communal one, not belonging to just one player.

I thought, and found myself pacing the room. "I could try to find a permanent replacement for Ms. Washburn, but that would require a very specific skill set, and could take considerable time. It is unlikely I could find and train another associate soon enough to answer this question promptly."

"Janet just walked in the door one day as a client," Mother reminded me. "It was a stroke of luck. Maybe there are more people who could help you that way than you think."

I dismissed that; the serendipity that brought Ms. Washburn to Questions Answered was undoubtedly rare and could not be willfully duplicated. I shook my head. "The time factor is still too pressing," I said. "There is no time to hold auditions."

"So what does that leave you with?" Mother asked.

I was becoming impatient with the way she was forcing me to work through the problem. It was frustrating and forced me to consider alternatives with which I was not comfortable. "I could ask you, but I'd prefer not to."

Mother looked slightly startled. "I would turn you down," she said. "Would you?"

"Yes. This isn't my kind of work, and I meant what I said to Janet about not having your mother follow you through business activities."

I was about to counter with the obvious assertion that Mother's statement had only reiterated my need to coax Ms. Washburn back to Questions Answered when the door opened and a man walked into the office. He was large, solid but not overweight, with dark hair that had been slicked straight back on his head. He bore no facial scars I could see. His eyes were dark brown and wide, and he gave off a somewhat blustery demeanor. Both Mother and I looked over, not startled exactly, but at least a little taken off-guard. I do get some walk-in business, but usually the person with a question will call first and the in-person consultation will take place at an appointed time.

People with Asperger's Syndrome tend to dislike surprises.

My first reaction was to ask the man to leave, but that has been my initial reaction to virtually everyone I have ever met, so I have had to learn to squelch the impulse and allow each new acquaintance to be evaluated individually. It is not easy to do, but my work with Dr. Mancuso has helped.

"Allow me to introduce myself," I said to the man. "I am Samuel Hoenig."

His face did not show any expression I could discern, but he nodded in my direction. "I'm Oliver Lewis," he said. "I believe my wife Sheila came here to ask you if I am really her husband."

FIVE

I ASSESSED THE NEW visitor to Questions Answered for visual information and could find very little of help. I have read all of Sir Arthur Conan Doyle's Sherlock Holmes stories and have found the fictional detective's observational skills, if not his annoying habit of jumping to conclusions about what he has observed, remarkable. I am endeavoring to develop my own abilities in observation without deduction, since facts are the only real tools to use in answering a question. But my efforts are still in their infancy, so I am not in any way comparable to the fictional Mr. Holmes.

People believe, because of their exposure to entertainment media, that everyone with what is considered an autism spectrum "disorder" is a savant with amazing abilities. That is not the case. We are each given talents and deficiencies. Mother says people with Asperger's Syndrome are just like everyone else. Just more.

The man who claimed to be Oliver Lewis was tall, at roughly six-foot-two, with my estimation of his weight at one hundred eighty-five pounds. He wore a two-piece business suit, bought from a department store and not custom tailored, with slightly scuffed shoes, no hat, and a bright teal tie—an indication that he had not purchased his accessory recently. Observers of fashion would remind the rest of us that teal had been considered a cliché for some years now; that was a fact I had gathered when answering a question about shoelaces.

"Ms. McInerney was here earlier today," I answered the man. "But she did not ask me to determine whether or not you are her husband." That was technically true. Ms. McInerney had asked me to tell her who the man in her bed might be.

"She didn't?" he asked. His eyes widened, then blinked. I looked to Mother, who mouthed the word *surprised*.

"No," I said. "I am not able to discuss the nature of a client's question with you, but that was not what she asked."

Mother looked slightly amused but said nothing.

"That's very odd," Oliver Lewis said.

"Is it? Should she be concerned that you are *not* her husband?" If I could somehow make Mr. Lewis betray a transgression in his marriage, I might be able to answer Ms. McInerney's question without the help of Ms. Washburn after all.

But his demeanor took on a new attitude. He stood straighter, made direct eye contact, and arranged a look of slight irritation on his face. "Of course not," he said. "It's just that she's been acting strange lately."

I did not point out that the correct grammar for that sentence would have been "acting *strangely* lately," because it was not pertinent to the question, but Mr. Lewis was incorrect. I noted it and moved on. "In what way?" I asked.

"She's been … distant." He glanced briefly in Mother's direction, perhaps trying to signal to me that he was not aware who that woman was, or that he was not comfortable discussing his situation in front of her. I quickly introduced Mother so he would know who she was, and decided any reservations he had about her discretion were unfounded and therefore unimportant.

"Distant?" I said.

"He means she doesn't want to have sex with him," Mother said. She seemed to be stifling a smile, although that hardly seemed an amusing situation if Ms. McInerney and Mr. Lewis were truly married.

Mr. Lewis gestured toward the client chair, so I nodded and he sat. Mother took up her work in her seat, and I resumed my position behind the Mac Pro and my desk. "It's not just … that," he said when everyone was seated. "I know she suggested that our marriage was somehow illegitimate. I don't know where Sheila got an idea like that. She was at the wedding, after all. And we do have a valid marriage license."

"You don't happen to have that document with you, do you?" I asked.

Mr. Lewis's expression suggested that I had asked him if he could grow a third leg. "No. Why would I carry that around with me?"

"You were coming here to ask Samuel if Sheila had asked him whether you were really her husband," Mother pointed out. She did not look up. "It wouldn't be all that odd for you to bring the one thing that could prove your claim, would it?" Mother knows most people see her as a little old lady and think she is therefore either less intellectually adept than she once was or for some reason inherently benign. It seems to surprise them that she has a working mind and chooses to express her thoughts. I find that attitude difficult to comprehend, but I have seen it exercised numerous times.

Mr. Lewis took his time, but I could not read his face. He did not appear to be thinking of a response. "I know we're married. I see no reason I need to prove it," he said.

That was the position he was going to maintain, so there was very little I would be able to glean by continuing this conversation. "What is it you want of me, Mr. Lewis?" I asked, as a way of terminating the discussion.

He offered a response I had expected: "I want you to tell Sheila that I'm her husband and she should stop making these ridiculous claims."

"I'm afraid I am unable to do as you wish," I told him. "I have a client who has asked a question. I am obligated to answer it for her."

Again Mr. Lewis blinked, more than once. "But I just told you there's no question we're married."

"You could have just told us you're the governor of Utah, but there's no proof," Mother pointed out. I could tell she had taken a dislike to Oliver Lewis, although I was unsure of its cause.

Before Mr. Lewis could respond, I agreed with Mother's point, although in less colorful terms. "Even if you are not Ms. McInerney's legal spouse, you could tell me that you are," I pointed out. "I have no reason to believe or disbelieve you at the moment because I have no factual proof for either answer." Clearly, he would have to understand that argument.

Instead, he stood quickly and took a step toward my desk, then looked at Mother and held his position. Mother might have been holding one of her knitting needles with the sharper end pointed in his direction, although I think she was merely between rows.

"So Sheila *did* ask you to prove that I'm not her husband!" he spat. I was about to protest that she had asked nothing of the sort—because she had not—but he spoke before I could get the words out. "You're a crook, Hoenig! You tell people you can answer any question and then you take their money and you give them nothing!"

"I give them an answer," I said, my voice probably mirroring my uncertainty in the situation. I am not well suited to emotional outbursts. "It might not always be the answer the client wants, but it is the correct answer."

"And I say you're a con man," Mr. Lewis countered. "I say you're the same as the storefront mediums who claim to have the line on the future and can talk to dead relatives. You take their money and you tell them what they want to hear. Well, this time you'd better back off, pal. Give Sheila her money back and stop asking questions before you find yourself in a whole lot more trouble than you can handle. Understand?"

He pointed an angry look at Mother then pivoted on his left foot and walked out of the building. I found I had some difficulty summoning my voice because my throat felt dry.

"No," I said. "I do not understand."

———

There was not much for Mother and me to say after that. She went home, knowing I would want to "muse," as she puts it, on the events of the past few hours, and that I think better when left to myself. The truth is, I often have to remind myself of the social skills training I had after my diagnosis and my sessions with Dr. Mancuso to remember precisely why it is better to interact with other people at all.

The question Ms. McInerney had posed was an intriguing one, but I now had a very strong feeling that I should not have accepted it. Emotional entanglements between people are a source of consternation and confusion to me. I had accepted the question, I now realized, at least partially because I had assumed I could appeal to Ms. Washburn to help based on her knowledge of my difficulties with such matters. But that had not proven to be the case, and now the matter had been complicated with the arrival of Oliver Lewis, who had made some sort of threat against me and accused me of defrauding my clients. That could be a serious impingement on my business if he were able to communicate his beliefs on a broader scale, like an Internet site. It could do real damage.

After standing up and exercising twice, followed by one bottle of water from the vending machine, I had examined the problem from every possible angle and had concluded beyond any doubt that my first instinct had been correct—Ms. Washburn was necessary to the successful answering of this question.

Since her reticence to assist me was based strictly on her husband's objection to her working at Questions Answered, it had been a mistake to appeal to Ms. Washburn at all. I should have seen that immediately. A new plan of action was required, and I implemented it immediately.

After a quick check with directory assistance (a convenient service that still exists despite the dominance of Internet and smartphone technology), I dialed the phone on my desk. I was surprised to find myself a trifle nervous as the earpiece registered four rings. Then the call was answered.

"Hello?"

"Is this Mr. Taylor?" I asked.

"Who's asking?"

I had spoken with Ms. Washburn's husband once on the telephone, but did not have a clear recollection of his voice. I was fairly certain this was the same man, although they did not share a last name. I understand that is a convention some women observe after marriage while others do not. Because marriage is based on an archaic chattel system that made the woman the property of her husband, I can applaud those women who do not change their names; others do so out of a sense of tradition, which is more difficult for me to understand, but I do respect the decision.

"This is Samuel Hoenig," I answered.

The voice on the other end made a noise that sounded like, "pwah." Then he said, "I can't believe you're calling me."

"I do not understand your disbelief," I said. "You have all the evidence. The telephone rang, and I identified myself when you responded. Is this Mr. Taylor?"

There was a wispy, somewhat guttural tone to the voice. "Yes, this is Simon Taylor. What the hell do you want, Hoenig?"

"I wish to know why you object to Ms. Washburn working for my firm," I told him simply. "I will pay her an honest wage and her work will be both rewarding and helpful to the clients we serve. What is your concern?"

"You have a lot of nerve," Simon Taylor said. "Do you know that?"

Each human being has the same number of nerves, and the human brain has approximately one hundred billion neurons, so the number was indeed quite high. "Every person does," I said, although I did not see the relevance to the conversation we had been having. "You have just as many."

There was a pause on the other end of the conversation. "Let me make this clear, Hoenig," Simon Taylor said. "I don't like you. I don't like the idea that my wife worked for you even for one day. She came very close to getting her head cut off, and I *really* don't like that. So when you call me up with your Ass Burger voice and ask me why I don't want my wife to work for you again, I get mad. So you want to know why? I'll tell you why: because of you. Is that clear enough?"

"Quite clear," I answered. "Thank you. Now may I make my case, please?"

"I could just hang up and not answer when you call again," he noted.

"Yes, you could. But I believe I can convince you, and as a man who appears to enjoy a challenge, I am willing to presume that you think I can't." I had anticipated using this tactic. It was true that I had no evidence Mr. Taylor enjoyed a challenge any more than most men, but I was taking a calculated gamble. I waited for his response.

"You wanna bet?" he asked.

It would be foolish to include a wager in the equation; if Mr. Taylor thought there was a prize to be won by staying implacable, he would not listen to my argument. "There is more money to be made if your wife is under my employ," I said. "Wagering funds on this conversation is counterproductive."

"It's an expression," he said, I believe wearily. It's not always easy for me to gather information about a person's mood from his tone of voice. I was not familiar with the axiom about wagering, and wrote it on a pad I keep next to my Mac Pro, so I could consult with Mother later for an explanation.

I decided to press on with my argument. "I understand your objection to the danger that Ms. Washburn met with when she helped with the question of the missing head," I said. Then, leaving no time for him to interject, I added, "but I am committed to keeping any employee of Questions Answered, including myself, out of any physical peril, and I will immediately discontinue my acceptance of the contract if—and I consider this extremely unlikely—any such situation arises. In addition, I will guarantee to you that Ms. Washburn, should she opt to continue working for the firm as I would hope, would be able to veto my answering any future question posed if, within her judgment, there is any unreasonable level of danger. Is that an acceptable situation for you?"

There was a long pause on the other end of the line. "Do you always talk like that?" Simon Taylor asked.

I thought quickly. "There are times I try to sound like Elmer Fudd in an attempt to amuse my mother," I said. "Other than that, this is my speaking voice."

"You're a nut, Hoenig. You know that?"

I felt it was best not to respond. When directly challenged like that, it is my experience that I have either done something to offend the other person, or I am misreading a signal. In either case, there is no helpful response. If an apology is required, it will become evident quickly.

"I want you to know I never told Janet she can't work for you," Mr. Taylor went on. The need for an apology seemed less likely. "She's not the kind of woman a husband can just order around. But

I've told her I don't like it, and she has chosen not to work with you again. I know you've asked her a bunch of times. So that should tell you something, shouldn't it?"

It probably should have given me some information, but Ms. Washburn's explanation for not returning to Questions Answered had always been that her husband objected. If he had indeed only expressed an opinion, it could mean that Ms. Washburn had chosen to reject my offers for other reasons.

I sat at my Mac Pro and felt my left hand on my forehead, massaging the temples. It was an involuntary response, but one that had been developed over long periods of time with great effort and hours of practice, under the tutelage of Dr. Mancuso.

Before that, I had flapped my hands at my side whenever confronted with emotions I found disturbing.

"I am not sure exactly what information I should take from what you've told me," I finally said to Simon Taylor.

"Think about it," he answered. "To show you what a nice guy I am, I'm not going to tell Janet you called me."

Then he disconnected the call.

My first impulse, after replacing the phone on its cradle, was to call Ms. Washburn's cell phone number. But Mother's voice in my head warned against that. "She's a grown woman and she gets to make her own choices," it said. Even though I knew it was a manifestation of my own thoughts, I was slightly displeased with Mother for saying that.

Other people's choices make very little sense to me, while mine are completely logical and seem to confuse the "neurotypical" population. It is a very difficult concept.

It seemed that Ms. Washburn was not going to walk through the door to my office anytime soon, and that my attempts at correcting that situation had failed. The only two possible reactions I could have would be to call Ms. McInerney and rescind my acceptance of her question, or to gather the necessary data to answer it on my own.

I opted for the latter.

SIX

THE DARIEN, CONNECTICUT, TOWN clerk could not have been less helpful.

"I am sorry, Mr. Hoenig, but we do not give information about marriage certificates out over the phone," Diana Febrizzi said. "If you don't have a copy, you and your wife will have to fill out the form for a certified copy. I can give you the web address."

"I am not married," I told her.

"Then you don't need a certificate." That was technically true, but not in the least bit useful to me.

"How long should it take to receive a copy once the form is submitted?" I asked. Getting Ms. McInerney to send in the proper paperwork, while an inconvenience, would probably not be difficult.

"When did the marriage take place?"

That hardly seemed relevant to my question, but bureaucracies have their eccentricities, just as people do. I understood that well. "Within the past month," I said, not having an exact date.

"Then you can't get the copy of the certificate from me," Ms. Febrizzi said with a tone that I believe indicated I should already have known that. "For anything that took place within the past four months, you go through the state's vital records office. That should take about six weeks."

Forty-two days seemed an inordinate amount of time to generate one document through a printer, but I knew there would be no benefit to pointing that out to Ms. Febrizzi. It would likely yield nothing more than an explanation of the process, a recitation of the number of requests processed each day, or a rebuke for expecting special treatment, whereas my point would be that *everyone* should be able to obtain vital records more quickly than in six weeks.

I thanked her for her time (because effort had not seemed to be her strong suit) and went back to my Mac Pro to continue the research I'd begun before the phone call. While I prefer Internet searches to talking with other people, the official website for Darien, Connecticut, had been taken offline for "system upgrades" that morning, according to the message on my screen.

A basic background search on Oliver Lewis yielded little. The name was not an uncommon one, so the best way to narrow the investigation was to look for images of the man and match them to the person I had met the day before. The most common photo matches for "Oliver Lewis" were a magician, a model, a cyclist and a man who played the part of Gummo in a production of the musical *Minnie's Boys*, about the early days of the Marx Brothers.

(The coincidence of a Marx Brothers reference after Ms. McInerney's costume of Harpo Marx was interesting, but not as statistically unlikely as it might at first seem.)

The Oliver Lewis I had met was not evident.

Searches focusing simply on the name had come back with the same four men and a novel written in 1977 by John Fowles. Since I had not discovered what Ms. McInerney's nominal husband did for a living, it would be difficult to narrow the search by profession.

Doing so geographically, to the address Ms. McInerney had supplied on her client intake form, was equally frustrating. There were no such listings, probably because the man I knew as Oliver Lewis had only been living at Ms. McInerney's address for a few weeks.

I needed to talk to my client again to fill in more of the information I did not yet possess, but calls to her cell phone were sent directly to voice mail. The only recourse was to wait until she called back.

In some desperation, I searched marriage announcements on sites local to the area for any involving Oliver Lewis and Sheila McInerney. While such things would hardly be conclusive—anyone can *say* they've been married—they might offer some data that I did not yet possess, and that is always a benefit.

Searches of the local newspaper sites, including the *Home News-Tribune* and *The Star-Ledger*, showed no announcement. But there was one in the *Metro Jewish News*, which was surprising, as neither Lewis nor McInerney would be considered a traditional Jewish surname. I have found that it never aids an answer to assume anything without facts to prove the assumption true.

The listing, although brief, did contain some new information:

Marriages
Lewis/McInerney
....

Oliver Lewis, proprietor of OLimited Investments in Piscataway, married Sheila McInerney, a graphic designer with Hunger, a Manhattan-based advertising firm, Sunday. The civil ceremony was performed by a municipal court judge in Darien, Connecticut.

The bride's parents, Michael and Tina McInerney of Freehold, and the groom's parents, Lewis and Roslyn Markowitz, did not attend the ceremony. The couple will reside at the bride's residence in Edison.

From this copy (the only such announcement I was able to find after a thorough search), I had learned Lewis's profession and the names of his parents. Also, the revelation that a municipal court judge, and not a justice of the peace or other official, presided over the ceremony created an avenue to investigate.

I was about to look into OLimited Investments of Piscataway when the office phone rang. Caller ID indicated Sheila McInerney was on the other end of the line.

"Questions Answered," I said. Even when I am aware of the caller's identity, it is important to maintain the demeanor of a business.

The voice coming through the receiver was breathless, gasping, but definitely that of my client. "Mr. Hoenig," she said, "this is Sheila McInerney."

"I know."

"I'm at my apartment," she went on, with no indication she had heard me. "I'm in the bathroom."

That seemed an inappropriate place from which to make a telephone call, and an even more inappropriate place to announce as the location of a telephone call. I had no response, but I might have made a sound in the back of my throat.

"It's Ollie," she whispered. "He's gotten violent. He says he told you to stay out of our marriage and you refused, and he's coming after me with a knife!"

"Hang up," I said. "Disconnect this call and dial 911 immediately. Get the police there." There was no time to explain that I believed I had not provoked Lewis. The objective now was to secure Ms. McInerney. But she did not end the phone call.

"Come here," she said in a quiet, tense voice. "Come here right now."

"I do not drive," I said. "Call the police."

"You can stop him," Ms. McInerney pleaded. "Just get here. You have the address. Hurry!"

And then she hung up.

I hoped she was in the process of dialing the police, and wondered if I should do the same. Unfortunately, Ms. McInerney lived in Edison and I was in Piscataway, approximately a fifteen- to twenty-minute drive, assuming I could summon Mother soon enough to make a difference. Her need to drive to Questions Answered to pick me up would add another eight minutes to the trip.

I was reaching for the phone to call her when Janet Washburn walked through the door to Questions Answered.

"I don't know what happened, but my husband said I should make up my own mind about working here," she said before I could explain the situation. "So I'm here. You said we have a new question to answer. But it's not dangerous, right?"

Clearly, a decision had to be made. While I had promised both Ms. Washburn and her husband, Simon Taylor, that she would never be in any physical danger, there was the growing feeling that something very bad might happen to Ms. McInerney if I did not answer her pleas to come to her home quickly. I would have to choose between lying to Ms. Washburn—something I would never consider doing if I could avoid it—or endangering my client. In addition, admitting to Ms. Washburn that there was indeed a chance of violence attached to this question would likely jeopardize any chance I had of her working with me, probably ever again.

"There will be no danger to you at all, I promise," I said. "But it is very important that you drive me to Edison immediately."

Ms. Washburn searched my face for a moment, seemed to consider something, and then turned toward the door.

"Let's go, then," she said.

The trip took only eleven minutes, but while Ms. Washburn was driving, I was considering whether I had been honest with her. She followed the instructions being spoken by her Global Positioning

System device and was concentrating on the road, so there was very little conversation, which is usually my most comfortable option. But this time, being left with my own thoughts was not as desirable as it would be under typical circumstances.

Ms. Washburn had not asked for an explanation of the question we were about to research. I knew from past experience that when she was driving, her attention was very difficult to divide—she would watch the road very carefully, probably because she knows that eases my anxiety about riding in a motor vehicle. While we'd walked to the car, I had told her only that the question involved a wife who was unsure of her husband, and that I needed her help because the interactions between couples were a mystery to me, so I might miss an important fact she would easily notice.

I waited until there was a pause in the directions being issued by the device that would allow for some talk and said, "Ms. Washburn, I am glad you decided to work with me again." I was about to add that the promise of a completely danger-free assignment might have been hasty, but Ms. Washburn stopped me by putting up the index finger on her left hand.

"I'm not saying it's permanent, Samuel," she interjected. "Let's see how this question goes, and then we can talk about it after that, okay?"

That was a disturbing turn; if this were to be a trial question for her continued employment, the situation to which we were racing (at the regulated speed limit) might very well cause Ms. Washburn to decide against any future association. I was determined not to let that happen, so I returned to my thoughts as she drove.

We arrived on Evergreen Road and located the building which contained Ms. McInerney's apartment, according to the intake form. I noted that there were no police cruisers parked in front of the building, but I could not determine whether that meant that I should relax and assume there was no further complication, or be especially concerned because Ms. McInerney had not heeded my instruction to call the police.

Ms. Washburn parked the car across the street from the building, a nondescript brick-faced garden apartment building of two stories that, from the floor plans I had taken from the renting firm's website, would hold four apartments. Ms. McInerney's would be on the upper floor, on the side opposite the street. There were, therefore, no windows into which I could look from my current position to determine the situation inside the residence.

"Please stay here in the car," I said to Ms. Washburn when she had extinguished the engine. "I will investigate on my own."

Ms. Washburn's face rearranged itself; if I were reading her expression properly, she was looking skeptical. "Why?" she asked. "I'm not just the driver, am I?"

"Perhaps in this instance," I answered. "I promised that you would face absolutely no danger while finding an answer to this question. I am not able to guarantee that if you come with me to the apartment, so I am living up to my promise by asking you to stay here."

I opened the car door and stepped out, but Ms. Washburn did the same, which puzzled me.

"I'm coming with you, Samuel," she said.

That seemed unwise. Perhaps I had not explained myself adequately. "I believe there is a possibility of violence in the apartment, although I cannot be sure," I told her. "If you come in with me, you might encounter something that would controvert the promises I made to you and to your husband. And then you might leave and not come back, and I would do anything to prevent that."

I could not read Ms. Washburn's expression. She cocked an eyebrow and leaned her head toward me. "You spoke to Simon?" she asked.

Mr. Taylor had said he would not tell his wife we had spoken, but he had not suggested I refrain from mentioning it—in fact, he'd said he would conceal the fact as a favor to me. I required no such consideration, so it had not occurred to me that revealing the fact of the conversation would be a miscalculation. With that look on Ms. Washburn's face, I was reconsidering that decision, but it was too late.

"You had said his objection was the obstacle to your continued employment, so I attempted to determine the cause of it. But there is no time for this conversation now. I must go up to Ms. McInerney's apartment and I very strongly suggest you stay here."

I turned and started across the street without looking back. It wasn't until I was on the opposite sidewalk, climbing up the small incline toward the building, that I realized Ms. Washburn was walking at my side.

She had made her decision in possession of almost all the facts. She was an adult and able to make her own choices. And Ms. McInerney might very well have been in very grave peril at this moment, so I could not stop to question her decision.

We did not run, but our pace was definitely swift, so we were at the door in very little time. But it was locked. There was a buzzer connected to an intercom system and, seeing no less public avenue to take, I waited, not comfortable with the idea of touching something that had not been cleaned, and Ms. Washburn pressed the button.

She and I stood at the threshold and waited. Very quietly I believe I heard her mutter, "I can't believe you called Simon." But I was not certain of that, so I did not react. My mind was focused on the problem at hand.

"Might there be a door on the other side of the building?" I said, doing what some people call "thinking out loud," but which is really simply posing a rhetorical question.

"A back door?" Ms. Washburn responded. "It's possible. I'll check."

She had walked away before I could consider the possibility that she could encounter a negative situation at the other side of the building. If I followed her, I would forfeit the chance of someone letting me in at this door.

Then I recalled seeing a film in which a man faced with a similar situation rang the buzzers on all the apartments in a building and was admitted by someone in another apartment who did not care to screen any visitors. It was worth trying. If I could get inside quickly and there was no back door, Ms. Washburn would not be able to enter the building, sparing her from any unspecified danger.

I rang all the buzzers, which amounted to only four buttons. It was not easy for me to do so, but pressing them with my elbow proved to be the least objectionable avenue, and the process did not take long.

One unit, marked B4, squawked to life. "Who is it?" asked a voice filtered through the primitive intercom system. It took a moment to separate the voice from the noise.

I did not have to touch the unit this time, which was a help. "I am attempting to answer a question," I said. "Would you let me in, please?"

"What?"

That response left me with a conundrum. Sometimes people say, "What?" because they did not hear what was said very clearly. That was obviously a possibility through the aged intercom system. But sometimes they say, "What?" because they find what was said confusing or difficult to believe. There was no clear indicator of which meaning this person was trying to convey.

"Please," I said. "I need to get upstairs." That was true, and it seemed to make the difference, because the buzzer was activated and I was able to open the outer door.

I made sure to get inside quickly, thereby putting into action my plan to separate Ms. Washburn from the potentially dangerous situation. She did not appear behind me, and I did not look back. I climbed the stairs quickly and located apartment B2, which was the unit Ms. McInerney's intake form listed as her address.

The door was closed, and there was no sound coming from within when I stood very still and listened. Again, the question of knocking arose. If Oliver Lewis were actually inside with a weapon, would it be wise to alert him to my presence? I tried the doorknob and found it locked, so the question became moot. Short of knocking the door down—something I would not consider for a number of reasons—there was no other way to gain entrance to the apartment.

I did wish Ms. Washburn was present now, because her cell phone could call Ms. McInerney and ask for an update on the situation, something I probably should have done from the car. But Ms. Washburn had been driving, and I am reluctant to handle her phone myself.

That, too, was now irrelevant. I had not called, Ms. Washburn was not here, and the door was locked. I knocked, quietly, three times and waited.

SEVEN

No response came from inside the apartment.

This could either mean that Ms. McInerney and (presumably) Oliver Lewis had left, or that something very disturbing had occurred inside. It could also mean only that Lewis had left on his own, and Ms. McInerney, having secreted herself in the bathroom, was still behind a closed door and had not heard the knock. Perhaps I should knock louder.

I had raised my hand to do so when Ms. Washburn's voice, from behind me, asked, "Do you want me to call her cell phone?"

I turned to see Ms. Washburn wearing an expression I recognized from the last time we had worked together: It was wry. "What's the matter?" she asked. "Wasn't I supposed to come and be a useful part of the team?"

"Would you please call Ms. McInerney's number?" I asked, choosing not to answer her question. "I am somewhat concerned about her safety." I refrained from saying that I was also concerned about Ms. Washburn's safety, and perhaps my own, because it would simply have reiterated a point I'd made when I suggested she stay in her car.

"Let me see the number."

I reached into my pocket for the page of the intake form but was already reciting the number from memory before I held it out for Ms. Washburn to see. She nodded, punching the numbers into her cellular phone as I spoke. She pushed another button to place the phone in speaker mode so I could hear.

It rang twice, then we heard Sheila McInerney's voice, which sounded small and wavered. "Hello?"

"Ms. McInerney, this is Samuel Hoenig. I am outside your apartment door." Ms. Washburn, knowing I did not want to hold the phone, extended her arm so it would be closer to my face. "Is it safe for you to let me in?"

"I … I don't know. It's been quiet out there for a little while."

"Are you still in the bathroom?" I asked. I watched Ms. Washburn's face for a reaction, but did not see one.

"Yes." Ms. McInerney sounded quite afraid, if I was reading her tone accurately.

Ms. Washburn looked at me and mouthed the word, "Scared." I nodded.

"Can you open the door just a little so you can see if anyone else is there?" I asked.

"I don't want to." There was an echo effect from what I imagined was the ceramic tile of the bathroom.

"Did you call the police as I suggested?" I asked. It would be helpful to know if there were officers on the way.

"No. I thought that would make him mad. I'm going to open the door a little. Don't say anything, in case he's out there, okay?"

I said nothing.

"Okay?" she repeated.

It seemed odd that she would ask me to speak after asking me not to speak, but I answered, "Yes."

The moments that followed must have seemed very long to Ms. Washburn, because she was exhibiting behavior consistent with a person experiencing impatience: she shifted her weight from one leg to the other six times, bit down on both lips, and folded her free hand under the arm that was outstretched, holding the phone.

I simply noticed that the interval took twenty-two seconds. That is not a very long time.

After that time had elapsed, the apartment door opened slowly. Ms. Washburn ended the call on her telephone, stood straighter, and stared at the door, while I tried to maneuver myself between the entrance and Ms. Washburn. I assumed Ms. McInerney would be behind the door, but I had made a promise and would shield my associate from any potential source of danger.

Of course, I had been correct, and Ms. McInerney, face very serious, looked out into the hallway, first at me and then at Ms. Washburn behind me and to my left.

"Who's that?" Ms. McInerney asked.

"This is my associate, Ms. Washburn," I answered. "She is essential to the successful answering of your question."

Ms. Washburn held out her hand. "Janet Washburn," she said. "I'm glad to meet you."

Ms. McInerney almost flinched when confronted by the hand, but she took it and then held it. She said nothing.

"May we come in?" I asked.

That seemed to have a wakening effect on Sheila McInerney; she let go of Ms. Washburn's hand and stepped back. "Of course." We walked through the doorway and into the apartment.

It was a fairly standard one-bedroom apartment at first glance. The entrance opened into the living room, which included an upholstered sofa, a floor lamp, a flat-screen television, a large table, and an armchair. The floor was covered with an area rug that reached from the television, which sat on a table, to the couch. The walls were painted white. The effect was of efficiency. I would have to ask Ms. Washburn later, but based on previous conversations, I would predict that she'd say the room lacked warmth.

It did not lack bloodstains, however. There were a few spots on the beige rug, two on the brown sofa, and several leading out of the room toward what I assumed would be the bedroom. If someone with a weapon were still in the apartment, it was logical to assume he or she was in that room.

"Who else is here?" I said very quietly.

Ms. Washburn reached into a tote bag she carried and pulled out a notebook and a pen. She is very good about giving me detailed accounts of each interview I conduct, even if I would remember them very clearly on my own. They are useful to me because I can see what Ms. Washburn believes are the most relevant points of the conversation, which might differ from my own opinions.

"Nobody," Ms. McInerney answered. "Why?"

Feeling guilty for involving Ms. Washburn, I pointed to the blood trail. "Something has happened here, and that trail does not lead to the door." I continued to keep my voice at a very low volume in case someone in the other room was listening.

Ms. McInerney looked at the stains I had indicated and gasped. "Is that *blood*?"

"Yes. Who beside you was here in the apartment? You said Oliver Lewis was here when you called me. Did this happen when you two were arguing?"

"No. He didn't hurt me. But he did have a kitchen knife, and he was waving it around. That's why I hid in the bathroom. But he didn't cut me or anything."

I started to walk, very slowly, following the bloodstains. I was wearing New Balance running shoes, as I always do for the arch support they offer, so my steps were relatively quiet, although a few of the floorboards did creak as I moved.

Ms. Washburn, not looking up from her notepad, asked, "Do you think he might have hurt himself?" It was a very intelligent question, and it illustrated my need for Ms. Washburn in answering such questions as this. I rarely consider the idea of a person who might harm himself because the concept of doing so would never occur to me.

"Honestly, I don't know him well enough to answer that," Sheila McInerney said. "Are you going in there?" She pointed at the bedroom door.

Her behavior was not rational. She was giving any potential assailant in the other room, which was past a galley-style kitchen from which there was indeed one rather large knife missing from a block, a warning that someone might be coming. Did she want Lewis to know I was on my way? Was that so he could attack me, or escape before I could find him? Or did she simply not comprehend the situation?

"No," I said. "I'm staying right here." But I kept inching my way toward the bedroom door, which I could now see was closed.

"But you're—"

Ms. Washburn, ever useful in any situation, stopped our client before she could cause any more possible damage. "Why didn't you call the police?" she asked.

Ms. McInerney, who had seemed to forget there was anyone but herself and myself in the room, turned sharply toward Ms. Washburn and frowned. "Because I was embarrassed, okay? What was I going to do, tell the cops that a guy who says he's my husband, but I don't think so, was waving a knife around the apartment we shared?"

Ms. Washburn waited a second to see me turn the corner toward the bedroom door and answered, "Yes. That's exactly what you should have done."

Now within reach of the doorknob, I moved quickly. I noted the lack of blood on the knob, but had already taken a handkerchief from my pocket and reached for the knob with the cloth in my hand. There would be no sense in leaving my fingerprints in the room should this become the scene of a police investigation.

Cognizant of that possibility, I did my best not to wipe the doorknob clean as I turned it; I did not want to remove any helpful evidence the police might need. The knob turned and the door swung open into the bedroom.

Behind me, I could hear Ms. McInerney say, "Why are you going in there?" I did not respond.

The room beyond the door seemed empty enough, but I had seen enough films and television programs about crime to know that I should look behind the open door before declaring it so. That was made less urgent by the fact that the door swung all the way open, actually touching the wall to my right as I entered. There was no room for a person behind it.

I did look anyway, and there was no one there.

It was as colorless and plain a room as the living area. The bed, a full-size model, was neatly made with an off-white comforter and white pillowcases. The walls were painted the same generic off-white as the rest of the apartment, no doubt done by the renting company to all the units in the complex. The wall-to-wall carpet (certainly also a standard feature in all the apartments) was colored beige, and was not worn, but not new.

Also, it had more bloodstains on it.

They were little more than spots, starting at the threshold and leading directly into the room toward the bed, then making a turn toward the opposite wall, where the windows were situated. One of them was open, and the screen was raised.

"What are you doing in my bedroom?" Ms. McInerney called. I was almost certain now that she was trying to warn a compatriot of my presence, but I could not summon a plausible rationale for her doing so.

Again, I did not answer her. The carpeting in the bedroom provided enough soundproofing to cover my steps in the room. I chose to ignore the open window for the moment in the name of security, and opened the door to the single closet. Inside was a small collection of women's clothing, shoes, and a few boxes. To the far left, hanging from the bar, were three men's suits. One pair of black men's shoes was on the carpeted floor beneath them.

"Get out of my closet!" Sheila McInerney's voice was directly behind me, and it seemed upset.

I turned to see her standing just a few feet away, her eyebrows raised and her eyes wide. Ms. Washburn stood behind our client, notebook in her left hand at her side.

"Sorry, Samuel," she said. "I didn't know she was coming in to yell at you."

"I *said*, get out of my closet!" our client insisted. I have never truly understood that particular impulse. Obviously, if I hadn't heard her when she'd spoken the first time, there would be no reason to be irritated with my not following her instruction. And if she was assuming that I had heard, the reminder of what she'd just said did not seem like a strong tactic to use in getting me to obey. It had not worked the first time, and the information that she'd said it once before was not a persuasive argument.

"I was securing the area and that would certainly require me to determine whether there was someone hiding behind the closet door," I explained. "There is nothing to be ashamed of in your closet, Ms. McInerney."

She made a few sounds that fell between an exhale and a cough, perhaps to express some emotion, but I could not decipher the meaning. "I'm not *ashamed*," she said. A few more of the unusual sounds followed, but she said nothing more.

"What about the window, Samuel?" Ms. McInerney asked.

I walked toward the window, surveying the rest of the room and seeing nothing out of the ordinary, which made me uneasy. I was careful not to place my hands on the window frame or the sill.

There was no person dangling from the window, which had been a slight concern of mine. I am not fond of heights of any altitude above a few feet (although I am not clinically acrophobic), so I did only a perfunctory examination of the exterior, not wishing to dangle myself out of the window. There was no further sign of a blood trail.

"We must go outside to examine the exterior of the window," I said. "But it seems likely that whoever was in the apartment was somehow wounded, and for reasons I cannot yet explain, chose to leave via the window rather than the stairs."

"Huh?" Ms. McInerney asked, although I was reasonably sure she had heard and comprehended what I'd said.

"Someone was in your apartment, and there is blood," Ms. Washburn said. She turned toward me. "Don't you think the first order of business is to call the police?"

"I'm not sure a crime has been committed," I explained. "There is blood, but the person—"

"It was Ollie," Ms. McInerney said. "He was the one in the apartment with me. And he had a knife. That's why I locked myself in the bathroom." She seemed pleased with herself, reestablishing her role as the victim in the drama at hand despite her clearly not being the person who had been wounded.

"Did you hear him cry out in pain or say anything that would indicate he had injured himself?" I asked.

She thought. "No."

"My point was that whoever the person was—and we don't have the facts yet to determine his or her identity conclusively—could have been injured in a perfectly legal way, slicing vegetables for cooking or trying to open a package. We could call the authorities, but we have no evidence yet of criminal activity."

Ms. Washburn studied my face and her eyes looked thoughtful. "That's technically true, Samuel, but I'm having a hard time coming up with circumstances that lead to a wounded person climbing out the window unless there was some danger in the apartment."

I nodded. "So am I."

EIGHT

Over Ms. McInerney's objections—she insisted that "nobody could survive a fall like that," out a second-story window, perhaps ten feet if the person dangled from the windowsill first—we left the building and walked around to the side beneath her bedroom window.

"I don't see any blood up on the window or the wall," Ms. Washburn pointed out. "It wasn't a really a lot of blood, even upstairs."

"Probably I cut myself and forgot," Ms. McInerney said. Ms. Washburn gave her what I interpreted as a withering look, and I must have been doing the same. It was an absurd assertion. How could a person cut herself to the point of bloodshed without leaving a mark, leave a trail of blood through two rooms, and then forget?

It seemed obvious, although inexplicable, that she was somehow covering for the person who had been bleeding and then exited by her bedroom window. I could not conjure a scenario under which that type of behavior made sense, but it unmistakably fit the facts I had to work with, and nothing else I imagined could do that.

"Did you then go and jump out the window?" Ms. Washburn asked. Ms. Washburn is an excellent associate in part because she knows when it is appropriate to go outside the boundaries of what I had been painstakingly taught as polite behavior.

"A pair of binoculars would be helpful," I mused aloud. It was not a great height to the window, but small specs of blood or other physical evidence could escape me from this distance. Even with my distaste for heights, I might have considered asking the building superintendent for a ladder and then asking Ms. Washburn to climb up for a look, but she was wearing a skirt and might have objected.

Instead, she extended her cellular phone. "Take this, Samuel," she said. "It has an app that works like a zoom lens."

As I've said, handling Ms. Washburn's cell phone is not something I enjoy doing. To be candid, I am not pleased about touching an object belonging to anyone else. I am not a germaphobe, and I do not believe that Ms. Washburn is at all unsanitary. Instead, it is the prospect that I might in some way damage or lose the object that concerns me, particularly in Ms. Washburn's case. She believes in me as few people other than my mother do, and to betray her trust, even accidentally, would be very upsetting.

Nonetheless, I needed a closer look at the area underneath Ms. McInerney's bedroom window. "It's okay, Samuel," Ms. Washburn said, no doubt sensing my reluctance. "Nothing's going to happen to the phone." She smiled.

I took the phone from her hand as Ms. McInerney complained again that she saw no point to staring up at her window "like Juliet," when in fact it is Juliet standing on the balcony and Romeo at her feet in Act 2, Scene 2 of Shakespeare's play. I felt it would be unproductive to correct her, so I accepted Ms. Washburn's instructions on the operation of the zoom lens application on her phone, and aimed it at the window.

The image was not perfect, but it was a vast improvement over the view from the ground. "What are you looking for, exactly?" Ms. Washburn asked.

While the cliché answer might be that I would know when I saw it, I told her, "I am searching for anything that will provide us with information. Specifically, we need to know if it was indeed Oliver Lewis who chose to take a very unconventional route out of the apartment. If so, this exercise might prove helpful in answering the question at hand. If we discover proof that someone else climbed through the window, it will not be the least bit helpful."

"Wouldn't knowing that it wasn't Lewis point us in a direction, at least?" Ms. Washburn asked. "Wouldn't that help us take a step toward finding out what happened?"

"Certainly, but that is not the question we were hired to answer. The question is who the man claiming to be Ms. McInerney's husband really is. If Mr. Lewis were not the person leaving by the window, the incident upstairs might have no bearing on that question at all."

Ms. Washburn blinked. "Samuel—"

"Of *course* it was Ollie," our client interjected. "I told you that. He was the one holding the knife."

"Precisely," I said as I trained the phone's lens on the windowsill itself and found remarkably little. "The person holding the knife and acting violently is rarely the one who ends up bleeding." The distance and the size of the phone made it difficult to focus properly; any tiny movement of my hand was reflected in a very noticeable shift in the image I saw on the screen. But what I saw was enough to provide some information.

"There is nothing of note on the windowsill," I said. "No scratches, no blood, no torn fabric from a piece of clothing."

"That seems strange," Ms. Washburn said. "If a person were trying to escape through the window, especially a bleeding person, wouldn't they leave something behind?"

"Why?" Ms. McInerney wanted to know.

I took the phone away from my eye for a moment and faced her. "Even someone who might believe his life to be in danger would not simply leap through the window," I said. "If he did, he would undoubtedly have injured himself, probably to the point that he would not have been able to walk away from the area. Look around here. What do you see?"

Our client took a moment to scan the small shrub-lined area in which we stood. "Nothing," she said.

"Very good," I told her. People like to be praised; it gives them a sense that their contribution is valuable, even on those occasions when it is not at all. "So what does that tell you?"

Sheila McInerney stared blankly in my direction for seven seconds. That was really not a long time, but she looked as if it felt like an eon to her.

"Ms. McInerney is not going to answer, Samuel," Ms. Washburn said quietly. "She is waiting for your explanation."

Ah. "The grass is undisturbed. There is no evidence of trampling or impact at the base of the building underneath the window. In short, there is absolutely no sign of a person, injured or not, falling from the window and then extricating him or herself from this area."

"But the window was open," Ms. McInerney protested. "Why would someone go and open the window and the screen, and then walk away? And if that's what he did, then how did Ollie get out of the apartment?"

That seemed simple enough. "The most likely explanation is that he walked through the door, down the stairs, and then to his car," I said.

"But he was bleeding." Our client seemed to *want* her husband, however disputable their wedding might have been, to have jumped out her bedroom window.

"I sincerely doubt that," I told her. "There is no evidence that was the case."

"What are you talking about?" Ms. McInerney demanded. "There's blood all over the place up there."

"Well, not 'all over the place,'" Ms. Washburn accurately pointed out. "There were a few drops of blood in a trail..." She did not finish the sentence, but stood with a thoughtful look on her face for a few moments. "Samuel, did someone stage that scene upstairs?"

I nodded. "I would not rush to that conclusion based on the evidence just yet, but it certainly seems to be the most likely explanation at this point."

"But the window," Ms. McInerney reiterated. "The blood." Her hands flailed a little the way mine still sometimes do when I am upset. I wondered if Ms. McInerney had some neurological issues.

"The fact that there is no sign of disruption at the window is significant," I told our client. "If a person were indeed to dangle from the window and then drop down, it would be reasonable to expect some scratching, some scuffs from shoes, at the very least finger marks. There would be something. And if that person was indeed injured and bleeding, even slightly, it is very likely there would be some blood on the sill or the side of the building. But there is nothing, not even variations in the level of dirt."

Ms. Washburn stood, arms crossed, listening. Ms. McInerney, however, simply stared at me.

"So?" she said.

"So the physical evidence we are able to find at the scene of the incident very clearly indicates that no one left the apartment through that window," I explained, although I believed I had made my point adequately.

"That's ridiculous," Ms. McInerney spat. "There's a trail of blood and an open window, and Oliver is gone. The only explanation is that he left through the window."

I started to walk from the scene, having taken in all the information I would be able to gather there. Ms. Washburn fell into step with me as we headed toward the building, but Ms. McInerney stood still in the center of the grassy area, looking astonished, from what I could see as we retreated.

"That's it?" she demanded. "You take one quick look through a cell phone and you've decided the whole thing?"

"The physical evidence is clear." I stopped to look back at her. "This is not aiding in answering your question."

"But what about the blood?" she said.

"I do not see the blood, if it is blood, as relevant physical data," I said. "But I would like one more look upstairs. Trying to decipher this scene has distracted me from the task at hand. The key is to re-examine your apartment, which should not take long, and then we will be out of your way."

Ms. Washburn and I walked toward the stairwell that had led us from Ms. McInerney's apartment to this area. As we walked, Ms. Washburn leaned toward me, speaking softly, I believed, because she preferred our client not hear.

"What do you mean, 'if it is blood'?" she asked.

"As you suggested," I said, my voice probably somewhat louder because volume modulation is a challenge for me, "the supposed injury and flight of a mysterious person upstairs was probably staged for Ms. McInerney's benefit. It is possible that the person doing so could have cut himself to produce a few drops of blood, but the more likely possibility is that something less painful was used to create the effect."

"Why would somebody do that?" Ms. Washburn asked.

"It is a mistake to try to discern motive through raw data," I said. "We don't have enough facts yet, and the ones we thought we had are now suspect."

Ms. Washburn looked at me quizzically but did not speak as we climbed the stairs to the apartment door. We waited a few moments for Ms. McInerney to appear, assuming she had followed us. It did not seem appropriate to enter her apartment without her present, even though she had tacitly given us permission to do so by letting us in before.

She did not arrive.

"What should we do?" I asked Ms. Washburn, grateful again that she had returned to Questions Answered. Her counsel in such matters—which would be extremely difficult on my own—was invaluable.

"Damned if I know," she said.

We waited for three minutes, neither of us saying anything, fully anticipating Ms. McInerney's arrival at any moment, but it did not occur.

"The door is unlocked," Ms. Washburn said. "We could just go inside and wait for her there. It's more comfortable, and her neighbors might wonder why two people are just standing outside her door."

"I have not seen any neighbors observing us," I pointed out.

"Those are the ones you have to watch," Ms. Washburn asserted, and opened the apartment door.

We walked into the living area, and Ms. Washburn immediately turned to me and asked, "What is it we're looking for? How do we answer the original question about who her husband is, or something?"

"The question remains who the man was who claimed to be Ms. McInerney's husband," I reminded her. "We should be looking for a marriage certificate or any state-issued identification. Any photographs from the wedding of Oliver Lewis with the woman he said was his bride might be helpful."

"Where do you want me to start?" she asked.

"Please go through the bedroom a little more thoroughly," I suggested. "Don't open drawers, but see what is on display. We are technically not authorized to perform a search since Ms. McInerney is not here. So be sure not to disturb anything—just observe."

"Right." And she was gone.

I had done a reasonably complete scan of the living area when we had first entered the apartment, so I decided to concentrate my efforts on the kitchen and then the bathroom, two sections we had not examined at all so far.

The galley kitchen was fairly standard but, like the rest of the apartment, it seemed oddly underused. The built-in dishwasher was empty and showed no signs of usage. The sink was clear of used dishes, glasses, or utensils. The one knife was indeed missing from the set of knives on the counter, and was not visible anywhere else in the room.

Even a dishtowel, hanging from the handle of the oven door, was clean and folded.

My mother keeps her kitchen very carefully and I do my best to help, so there is rarely a great deal of detritus visible in that room of our house. But even when Mother is especially concerned with its appearance, as when we are to receive company, there would be no room in our home that looked this pristine.

I had once toured a model home when answering a question about the water table in Somerset County, and this kitchen—in fact, this entire apartment—reminded me of that.

It was like no one lived here.

Having had that thought, it was difficult to banish it and concern myself strictly with facts I could verify. But I have a talent for focused thought, so after a few moments I decided to look for any relevant data in the apartment's bathroom, the only unviewed area left in the unit.

Again, there was not much to see. The bathroom was functional. A plain shower curtain hung from the rod over the bathtub. There was no mildew or discoloration of the grout around the tub. There were no wet towels or anything out of place. Ms. McInerney had said she'd been hiding from her husband—if he was indeed her husband—in this room, but there was no indication anyone had been in here at all.

In hotels, the first piece of paper hanging from the roll next to the toilet is often folded by the housekeeping staff into a triangle shape. It was something of a surprise that hadn't been done here.

The immaculate condition of the apartment (aside from the rather theatrically arranged "blood" stains) was irritating. It was difficult under normal circumstances to find any relevant information simply by observing a scene. When it appeared that the area had been staged, then sanitized, there was little one could possibly discover beyond the fact of the sanitization itself.

It was tempting to open the medicine cabinet installed on the wall over the double sink. While such a fixture is usually a very fertile source of information, opening it without Ms. McInerney's permission would constitute a serious invasion of privacy. I hesitated at the thought, keeping in mind that it was still possible, even with the strong evidence that nothing criminal had happened here, the apartment could be a crime scene, so keeping my fingerprints to a minimum was still advisable.

I was mentally weighing my options when I heard Ms. Washburn's voice from the hallway outside the bathroom. "Samuel," she said. "I don't know if this is anything, but—"

She stopped speaking when the apartment door opened and two uniformed police officers entered, each with a hand on his holstered weapon. Behind them was Sheila McInerney, looking oddly pleased with herself when the officers' eyes were not focused on her.

"That's them," she told the officers. "Those are the people who broke into my apartment."

NINE

"THIS IS ABSURD," I said, power walking around the cell and raising my arms for added aerobic activity. "There is no reason for us to be held. We explained to the officers exactly how and why we were in Ms. McInerney's apartment."

Ms. Washburn, sitting on the bench of the holding cell, drew a heavy breath and made a sound in the back of her throat. "This is not how I pictured the day going either, Samuel. But they'll sort it out and we'll be out very soon. You heard what the sergeant said."

No amount of explanation, including even showing the Edison police officers my copy of the contract between Ms. McInerney and Questions Answered, had convinced them the burglary call they'd gotten was simply a misunderstanding. Of course, it was not at all a misunderstanding—Ms. McInerney, for reasons we could not begin to determine, had clearly set up Ms. Washburn and myself to be arrested at her apartment for, as Officer Duncan had explained before reciting our Miranda rights, "criminal trespass and suspicion of burglary." He had mentioned something about "theft" as well, since when they'd arrived, Ms. Washburn had been holding a wedding band that was not her own. But I had not heard anything about thievery mentioned when we were processed upon arrival at the police station at the Edison municipal complex.

The wedding band, which was inscribed "O.L. to S.M.," had been confiscated as evidence.

Throughout, Ms. McInerney had insisted that Ms. Washburn and I were unwelcome guests in her home, that we had "barged in" with a wild story about her beloved husband Oliver, and that she had asked us to leave repeatedly and we had refused. She'd had no recourse, she said, but to go outside—afraid for her own safety—and notify the police.

"How long should it take to get here from Montclair?" Ms. Washburn asked me in the cell. She had called her brother Mark rather than her husband, she said, because "if Simon hears about this, he'll never let me out of the house again."

"It is difficult to calculate based on traffic patterns, but the trip should take thirty-nine to forty-four minutes," I said, "at this time of day."

Ms. Washburn looked at me and smiled, not happily. "It's just that sort of thing I missed," she said quietly.

I did not understand, but I knew enough not to answer.

Officer Duncan and his partner Officer Patel had not been unsympathetic, but their bureaucracy had demanded we be arrested, booked, and then arraigned, which had taken two hours and seventeen minutes. We had made our phone calls, and now Ms. Washburn was concerning herself mostly with the reaction her husband would have if he were told of her ordeal on her first day back at Questions Answered.

I saw no conflict. Simon Taylor need never know that his wife had been held briefly on charges that were true from a technical standpoint—we had entered Ms. McInerney's home without her permission,

64

largely because we had been awaiting her return—but were groundless by any other measure. Clearly, we had not burglarized the apartment, nor had we any intentions other than the gathering of information to answer the question Ms. McInerney herself had hired me to research.

After my twenty-third circumnavigation of the cell, I stopped my efforts to raise my heart rate and stood next to the bench where Ms. Washburn sat, chin rested in her palms. "What I don't understand," I said, "is why Ms. McInerney would have hired us if she did not want us to answer her question."

Ms. Washburn looked up at me. "It is curious, isn't it?" she said. "The day after she asks you about her husband, she gets us arrested by way of defending her husband. There doesn't seem to be any sense behind it."

These were precisely the areas in which I most needed her help. "Could they have reconciled overnight?" I asked. "Found some common ground in whatever misunderstanding they'd had?"

But Ms. Washburn shook her head. "It doesn't fit. She never said they had an argument; she said she didn't know who he was and doubted they were really married. There's no reason to set us up that's going to help that."

"It's true," I agreed. "And even if there had been some kind of understanding reached, why would Ms. McInerney call me and say her husband was outside the bathroom door brandishing a knife? Why would she ... " My thought process began to speed up, which is what happens when I apply myself singly to a task.

Ms. Washburn's eyes narrowed. "What?"

"The only reason for Ms. McInerney to insist on my being there, if the goal really was not to determine if Oliver Lewis is her lawful husband, was that she wanted me there and nowhere else," I mused aloud.

"That doesn't make sense." Ms. Washburn stood up and tilted her head to one side, as people sometimes do when trying to comprehend what another person is saying. "How does getting you to her apartment help the situation with her marriage?"

I found myself touching my nose, which is another stimulation move I make subconsciously when deep in thought. I resolved to work harder to stop doing that, and dropped my hand to my side. "It doesn't," I said. "It is possible that none of this was ever about the marriage, if there was a marriage."

"You're miles ahead of me, Samuel. Slow down and come back to the station." My face must have looked very confused, because Ms. Washburn smiled and added, "I'm just saying that you should explain yourself more completely."

"Of course. This comes to a question of motivation." I did start pacing around the cell, but more slowly this time. "As you said, there was no reason to claim you and I had been unlawfully violating Ms. McInerney's apartment. There was nothing to gain from that. Unless the reason was that Ms. McInerney wanted to be certain I—and by extension, you, because she had never met you before—were in that apartment, and then in this cell, for a number of hours."

Ms. Washburn held up her hand. "So this was a ruse to get you to a spot where you're no longer able to leave? She wants you detained?"

"I believe so. The idea was to occupy me with the bogus notion of a man with a knife who somehow cut himself and then jumped out the window, to get me to consider that for a long period of time. When that did not work, because the elaborate scene that had been staged did not pertain to the question I'd been asked, Ms. McInerney put her backup plan into action, and that involved immobilizing us here."

Ms. Washburn shook her head again; this time it seemed out of a sense of befuddlement. "I don't get it. Why would Sheila want to keep you stuck in a cell for hours? April Fool's Day was months ago."

"April Fool's Day?" I asked. "How does a strange unofficial holiday relate to the predicament in which we find ourselves?"

She chuckled lightly. "I was saying that this seems like a very bad idea for a joke, Samuel."

I nodded. "It is indeed. But the only possible explanation is somewhat disturbing, and—oh good. Mother!"

Indeed, my mother was walking toward the holding cell, which was not far from the main reception area of the Edison police headquarters. "Samuel, I never thought I'd be putting up bail for—Janet!" Mother clucked her tongue. "How did he get you involved in this? I thought you'd decided to be sensible."

"I had, Vivian. But the prospect of working with your son was just too enticing."

"Don't joke, dear. You're in jail."

"Mother," I said, "does your arrival indicate that I am free to go? It's imperative that I get out of this cell immediately!"

Mother looked around the cell. "Why immediately? Is there a spider in there?" Mother knows I have arachnophobia, although she believes it to be more severe than it really is.

"No." There was no time to argue the point about spiders. "We have to get back to Questions Answered as soon as possible!"

"Oh my." Mother produced a yellow form from her purse. "This is the paper. It says you've posted bail." She beckoned to the officer at the desk beyond us. "Officer? My son has to leave." He nodded and waved a hand, in a gesture I believe was to mean that he would be there after a short wait.

"Officer!" I shouted. "This is an emergency!" He repeated the gesture, slightly more emphatically.

"I don't get it, Samuel," Ms. Washburn said. "I mean, I want to get out of here at least as much as you do, but you seem almost frantic."

"I *am* frantic! Don't you see? How could you not see?" My mind was racing. I knew that Ms. Washburn and Mother hadn't reached the same realization as I had, but I was not in a mood to try to understand others' feelings right now; there was something far more important to attend to, and it might already be too late to do any good.

"See what?" Mother asked, her tone reminding me to breathe.

I closed my eyes for a moment and reflected, as Dr. Mancuso has often instructed me to do. I did not take deep breaths, but I concentrated on respiration for ten seconds. It had the desired effect, the one that would get me out of my cell most quickly.

"Ms. McInerney went out of her way to lure me to her apartment, and then she deliberately implicated Ms. Washburn and me in crimes that had never taken place so that we would be brought and detained here. The only logical motivation to do those two things, in that order, was that she wanted us—specifically me, since she did not know Ms. Washburn was coming—to be away from Questions Answered for a period of hours. That means something has happened at our office that she did not want me to see. And if it is what I believe it to be, the result could be very serious indeed."

Ms. Washburn had heard this tone in my voice before, and she tensed in her shoulders and around her mouth. "Are you saying what I think you're saying?" she asked.

"I make no assumptions. It is possible that the offices have been searched for some artifact or piece of information the intruders believe they need, although I cannot imagine what that might be." Feeling the emotion welling up in me again, I struggled to sound calm. "But it is also possible that when we arrive, we will find a dead body in the office."

Mother turned toward the desk. "Officer!" she shouted. "We need you *now!*"

TEN

"THIS WAS WHAT WE were afraid of," Mother said.

We stared down at the body of Oliver Lewis, his carotid artery slashed, on the floor of the Questions Answered office. The positioning of the body, like everything else I could observe in the room, indicated that he had been murdered elsewhere and deliberately brought to my place of business to be discovered.

The Piscataway police, because the Edison officers we'd spoken to on the way out of jail did not share my belief in the urgency of the situation, had already been called, and would be here shortly. Mother, a handkerchief in her hand and covering her mouth, was standing in the far corner, by the pizza oven, to avoid being near Lewis's corpse. I stood over the body, but was now scanning the room for additional data to process. Ms. Washburn, looking more angry than upset (if I were reading her expression correctly), was in the client chair, notepad in hand, watching me and taking notes. Ms. Washburn does not trust portable voice recorders.

Mother had posted bail for Ms. Washburn once it had become obvious we were heading toward a very difficult situation. "I can't just leave her sitting here, and I really don't think she's going to skip town and I'll be stuck for it," she'd told me. "Besides, bail for this crime wasn't very much money at all." Ms. Washburn's brother, who had not yet left his home in Upper Montclair, sounded "relieved" not to have to make the trip, she'd told me after calling him, and would reimburse Mother for the bail money the next day.

"Simon's certainly going to find out about this," Ms. Washburn said now.

"I imagine so," I told her. "The news crews should be arriving just after the police, if not before. They have scanners that broadcast the messages the dispatcher sends to patrol cars, so any mention of a homicide will undoubtedly result in a great deal of news coverage. Your husband will definitely be seeing reports of this on the Internet, probably before you arrive home today."

"You're not making me feel better," she said.

That hadn't occurred to me. "I was not attempting to make you feel better," I said.

"You succeeded."

Mother's arms flapped a bit at her sides as mine used to do when I was less in control. "When are they getting here?" she said. "Shouldn't someone do something about that poor man? Cover him up or something?"

"We must leave the crime scene as untouched as we can," I told her. "Covering the body could contaminate the investigation for the Piscataway detectives."

Ms. Washburn's glance told me I was missing a "human element," as she would put it later. "Do you want to wait outside, Vivian?" she asked gently. "They'll want to talk to you, but it doesn't have to be in here." Apparently she felt the location of the interrogation would make the situation less upsetting for Mother.

Mother sniffed once and then stood her ground. "I'll stay here, but thank you, Janet."

It became a moot point because we saw Piscataway police cars arriving in the strip mall parking lot, one cruiser and one clearly a pool car for detectives. The police tend to buy the same models across departments, and they are more conservative than most passenger cars bought by consumers in an effort to "blend in."

There were four of them. Two uniformed officers got out of the cruiser and immediately walked to the unmarked vehicle, where a man and woman in business dress were standing and stretching as if after a long drive. It would have taken five minutes to drive from the Piscataway police headquarters, which would coincide with the time Ms. Washburn had called the police. The detectives waited for the uniformed officers to arrive at their vehicle. They appeared to issue orders to the uniforms for thirty-two seconds, then pointed toward the Questions Answered storefront. The two officers walked to my door looking determined. They entered without knocking, which made perfect sense.

"Piscataway police," the taller officer announced upon entering. His gaze was fixed on the three living people in the room and not the dead man who was at a much lower angle. He did not look down. "What seems to be the trouble?"

"It's the dead body, Ed," his partner told him, walking quickly toward Oliver Lewis's corpse. "What happened?"

"Clearly, he was either garroted or slashed across the throat with a very thin knife, severing the carotid artery," I answered. "He was murdered somewhere other than here—I would estimate at least a twenty-minute drive in the trunk of a car—and then deposited on the floor of my office, where we found him here six and one-half minutes ago."

"Samuel," Ms. Washburn said slowly, "the officer is asking what we saw."

The two officers were now staring rather openly at me, and the two detectives, standing just inside the doorway, studied the body more closely. They walked to the center of the room where Oliver Lewis lay.

"What happened?" the male detective echoed. I chose not to repeat my statement, a decision I reached mostly through reading Ms. Washburn's expression.

"We walked in and found that man there," Mother said. "Samuel thought we might, and then we did."

The detective looked at me. "You're Samuel?"

I held out my hand. "Allow me to introduce myself. I am Samuel Hoenig, and this is my business, Questions Answered."

The man didn't take my hand, but his partner did. "I'm Detective Maria Esteban, and the rude man who didn't introduce himself is Detective Andrew Dickinson," she said. "Why did you think you would find this man here, like this?"

Not wishing to be considered rude, I introduced Mother and Ms. Washburn, and then told Detective Esteban about the odd encounter between Ms. Washburn, myself, and Sheila McInerney earlier in the day. Before I had completed the story, I saw Detective Dickinson nod toward one of the uniformed officers, who began operating a tablet computer he carried, no doubt in an attempt to verify my account of the events, particularly our brief incarceration in Edison.

"I get all that," Esteban said. "But how does that lead to an expectation of finding a dead man in your office?"

"The only reason Ms. McInerney could possibly have to maneuver Ms. Washburn and myself into her apartment, and then into a holding cell in Edison, was to keep us away from here," I explained. "Given that she had manufactured an emergency that didn't exist at her apartment, and that it had allegedly involved violence to the point of bloodshed, the logical conclusion to reach is that she wanted us to testify to her 'husband's' tendency toward violence. So given those two facts, the idea that someone affected by violence, probably deceased because he would be unable to confirm or deny the account she wanted us to deliver, would be discovered here was not a difficult one to arrive at. I had hoped we'd find him before it was too late, but the plan that had been executed had succeeded."

Dickinson was now chewing on his lips as if they were itchy. The uniformed officer looked up from his tablet and nodded in Dickinson's direction, but I could not tell whether the detective had seen the gesture or not.

"That's a pretty big leap," Esteban said. "Just because you and your assistant—"

"Associate," I corrected.

"My apologies—you and your *associate* were held on what I'll admit were pretty flimsy charges, you concluded that Oliver Lewis was going to be murdered here and you'd find him?"

"I could not have accurately predicted the identify of the victim, but I knew there would be one, yes," I said. "But Mr. Lewis was not murdered here, that much is obvious. He was killed elsewhere and brought here to be discovered."

Esteban took a moment, but nodded. "You're right. There isn't enough blood on the floor for a guy whose throat has been cut like that. But how do we know you didn't clean it up? How do we know you didn't kill Oliver Lewis, if that's who this is?"

A small white van, no doubt carrying a crime scene investigation team summoned by the uniformed officers, appeared in the strip mall parking lot outside my window. I was relieved; the physical evidence in the room had been in danger of contamination until they could document everything. I had been careful not even to shift my feet since we had found Lewis's body, and my legs were weary from the effort.

"This is Oliver Lewis, or at least the man who identified himself as Lewis when he came to my office yesterday." I watched the four crime scene members walk in without introduction and begin to cordon off the crime scene, even as we stood inside it. "I can identify him positively as such. I am sure you will find identification somewhere on his person, because I can only assume the killer or killers want you to know exactly who he is. You will be able to prove that no one here is the murderer because you have logs of our departure time from the Edison police headquarters and these clinicians will surely establish the time of death as during the time we were being held. Whoever did do this killing is being very careful not to implicate myself, my mother, or Ms. Washburn in the crime, although I cannot begin to explain why they would want to avoid that."

"You could be covering for the killer," Dickinson suggested.

My mother looked positively insulted. "My son would never do that."

"What motivation would we have to mislead you about a body we found in my place of business?" I asked.

"You tell me," Dickinson said.

"It was an honest question. I really have no answer for it. I thought you might."

I often see people squint at me, as if I were an especially bright source of light, after I have said something that seems quite simple and reasonable to me. Both detectives were looking at me like that at this moment.

"Mr. Hoenig is not being sarcastic," Ms. Washburn told them. "He has a form of high-functioning autism."

As I expected, that brought exaggerated nods from the detectives, indicating that what Ms. Washburn had said explained quite a bit for them. I am never sure exactly how to react to such a gesture.

While the technicians began to videotape, photograph, and otherwise examine the area in which Lewis's body lay, Detective Esteban indicated we should move outside the cordoned-off area so the police could question each of us separately. My mother was assigned to one of the uniformed officers, Ms. Washburn to Esteban, and Detective Dickinson volunteered—not very enthusiastically, I felt—to interview me.

Mother must have asked to be taken outside, because the officer opened the door for her and I saw them walking toward a bench two doors down, at the craft store Sew It Up. Esteban ushered Ms. Washburn to the far corner of the office near the drink machine.

Dickinson, perhaps believing it would better coerce a confession out of me, sat backwards on the spare folding chair I keep for situations with more than one client. He was very near the yellow police tape surrounding Lewis's body. I sat in Mother's recliner, although I felt slightly uncomfortable usurping her traditional position.

"So tell me again how you know Oliver Lewis," he began. It is a standard tactic in interrogation to ask questions more than once. This helps to determine if the subject's responses are consistent, and it can sometimes serve to annoy the subject into saying something unguarded. Since I had no reason to guard my responses, Dickinson was using the incorrect strategy.

I felt it best not to mention that to him.

"I didn't know Mr. Lewis beyond having a professional interest," I said, explaining again about the question Ms. McInerney had originally asked me to answer for her.

"So she wanted to know if they were really married, or if he roofied her and then told her they were?" Dickinson said.

"That was the gist of it, yes," I told him.

"And what did you find out?" Again, a question that had already been answered, but not into the voice recorder Dickinson was holding toward me now.

"I have not adequately answered the question, although I am not sure that is still relevant. After being accused of breaking into her home, I am not certain that I will retain Ms. McInerney as a client."

"You think she'll fire you?"

"No. I am in the process of deciding whether or not I will continue to honor the contract."

Dickinson's mouth twisted in an unusual position. "You answer questions for a living?" he said with a tone that indicated some astonishment at the suggestion.

Resisting the temptation to point to the sign in my window, I answered, "That is what I do, yes."

"And people pay you for that?"

It was my turn to squint, I believe. The question he asked seemed to have already been answered, and there was in this case no point in asking it again; it was a yes/no question. "They do," I said after a moment.

"Why?"

Mother has repeatedly admonished me on what she calls my "really?" face, but I could tell I was making that expression now because the answer to Dickinson's question was so obvious. "Because they want the question to be answered, and I provide the service."

"What makes you so special?" he asked.

"What does this have to do with Mr. Lewis's murder?" My patience had been tested, and I confess it had been found wanting.

"Just answer the question, please. After all, that's what you *do*." I did not understand the emphasis Dickinson placed on the word *do*, but was fairly certain it was not meant to be complimentary.

"I am not special. I have a talent for observation and research. Most people have some talent. That happens to be mine."

"How many questions have you answered?" Dickinson asked. Once again I had to question the relevance of this line of questioning, but I could assume only that I would receive the same response if I noted that another time.

"In the six months since I have opened in this location, I have answered eighty-two questions," I told him.

"You don't have to look that up?"

"No, I don't."

Dickinson was holding a pencil, although he did not have any paper and therefore was not using it, relying on the voice recorder for his notes. Ms. Washburn could tell him that such devices are untrustworthy and that batteries tend to lose power at inopportune moments, but it was his choice. Now, he pushed the eraser into his forehead, resting his head on the end of the pencil.

"How many questions have you not answered?" he asked.

I did not understand, and told him so.

"How many times has someone asked you a question that you could not answer?" Dickinson said.

"Never," I reported.

"Never?"

"That is correct."

"You're saying that no one has ever walked in here with a question you couldn't answer," he said. The redundancy of the conversation was becoming an irritant.

"Yes," I said. I believe I did not betray my feelings through tonality.

"That's impossible," Dickinson said.

"It is possible, and it is the truth." I cannot guarantee my voice remained neutral that time.

Suddenly Dickinson's demeanor changed. His brows dropped, he leaned forward toward me, and his voice lowered considerably in volume.

Then he reached over and turned off the voice recorder.

"Do you think you could answer a question for me?" he whispered.

"Is that the question?"

"Shh!" Dickinson seemed panicked. "Quiet. No, that's not the question. The question is: Who killed Oliver Lewis?"

I considered that. "Are you asking me to consult with the Piscataway police department?" I asked.

Dickinson glanced briefly at Esteban, who was talking to Ms. Washburn and did not notice his look. I could not read the expression on his face, making me wish Ms. Washburn had been there to see it and explain it later.

"No. I'm asking just for myself. Can you answer the question?"

"I am able to, yes. The issue here is whether I will agree to do so."

Dickinson looked stumped. "What do you mean, whether you'll agree to?"

"Just that. I answer only those questions that interest me."

His eyebrows rose dramatically. "This murder doesn't interest you?"

"I did not say that. I said I have not yet determined whether I will answer the question. Are you willing to pay me my standard fee?"

To be honest, the question about my fee had two purposes, neither of which was entirely based in a desire for money. First, it was a way of determining how dedicated Dickinson was to the idea of hiring Questions Answered in lieu of doing the investigating on the crime himself. And just as importantly, asking about money gave me time to sift the situation in my mind.

I had promised Ms. Washburn there would be no danger if she returned to Questions Answered. So far, there had been the suggestion of a man with a knife (although no such person was ever spotted), we had been arrested on suspicion of burglary, and we had discovered a dead body in our office.

Now one of the detectives on the case was asking us to answer the central question for him, which seemed odd and ill advised. How could I keep the promise I'd made to Ms. Washburn and her husband under such circumstances?

That was not to mention the idea that if there were danger, I would prefer to be uninvolved in the question myself.

"How much do you charge?" Dickinson asked, which was exactly what I wanted, since it provided me with more time to consider.

I told him the amount of my usual fee. I am told that some businessmen, when they are not interested in taking a job, will overstate their fees, hoping that either the potential client will decide against hiring the firm, or that the extra money will make the proposed work more palatable.

Still, I found it difficult to inflate my fee in an effort to evade the question. If I didn't want to answer for Detective Dickinson, the money would make no difference—I could simply refuse based on my own lack of interest.

Dickinson nodded. "I can pay that," he said.

"Is it ethical to ask someone else to determine the culprit?" I asked. "Would you hire a private investigator to solve a crime for you?"

Mother walked back inside the building but saw that Dickinson was still talking to me. She must have assumed I was still being interrogated, and chose to stay at the other side of the office.

Dickinson's eyes flashed a moment of anger, then softened. "This is a special circumstance," he said, his voice even more subdued than before. I had to strain to hear him. "My close rate on cases has been ... a little down lately. We don't get a lot of murders in this town. I am interested in getting this case out of the way quickly, and making sure that I get the credit for it. Is that sufficient to interest you?"

Truthfully, it was not enough, and based on that incentive alone, I would have felt perfectly justified in refusing to answer Dickinson's question. In fact, I came very close to doing so at that moment.

But then it occurred to me that I had already been involved in the question against my will. Whoever had killed Oliver Lewis had done so with me as a central element in mind. He, she, or they had decided to remove me from my place of business, make sure I was detained against my will, and then place the body at the exact center—I hadn't measured, but I could tell—of my place of business.

A gauntlet had been thrown down in front of me. And my psyche demanded I find out who had thrown it, and why. If it was possible to earn my usual fee while satisfying my own curiosity, that was sufficient.

"I will answer your question, detective," I said to Dickinson.

ELEVEN

Detective Esteban, who was not soliciting Ms. Washburn to solve the crime on her behalf, took longer in interrogating her subject than Detective Dickinson had spent speaking to me. It was close to five p.m., then, when Mother, Ms. Washburn, and I were once again alone in the Questions Answered office.

Oliver Lewis's body had, naturally, been removed, but there was still yellow crime scene tape blocking off an area of the room. Not much belonging to the business—and by extension, to me—had been removed, since the perpetrators (I assumed it took more than one person to carry the cadaver into the room) had touched very little, and left a minimum of physical evidence aside from the victim himself.

"Detective Dickinson asked you to find out who killed Mr. Lewis, and you agreed?" Mother sounded surprised, or disappointed.

"I agreed because I realized I would have tried to answer the question simply for my own edification," I responded. "Since I was going to do so anyway, I saw no harm in collecting a fee for my efforts."

Ms. Washburn, hand rubbing her chin, paced around the cordoned-off area. "We can't let them get away with this," she said. It was unclear whether she had been following the conversation; she seemed lost in her own thoughts.

Mother looked stunned. "I beg your pardon?" she said.

Ms. Washburn turned toward her, perhaps startled. She took a moment and her eyes focused more clearly. "I said, we can't let them get away with this. Sheila McInerney and whoever is working with her have spent the past two days making a fool of Samuel and all of today making a fool of me. That is not okay. We have to—"

Her cellular phone rang, and she pulled it from her pocket and pushed a button. "I'll be home soon, Simon," she said. Then she listened for a moment. "Oh you saw that, huh? Yes, it was here, but— No. Simon, no. I wasn't in any trouble, nobody came after me. I don't care what you thought, it's— Can we talk about this later? Please? I promise, I'll be home in an hour. Chicken parm. Okay." She disconnected the call.

"I must apologize," I said to Ms. Washburn. "I made a vow to keep you away from any danger, and now your husband believes that vow has been broken."

She waved a hand in a gesture of dismissal. "Don't worry about Simon," she said. "He acts like he's more worried than he really is. I can handle it."

"Are you sure you want to?" Mother asked. "Your first day back, and there's a dead body on the floor."

Ms. Washburn's eyes narrowed to slits. "Yeah," she said. "That's what's making me sure I have to stay. They're not getting away with this while I'm on the job." She turned toward me before I had a chance to absorb her change of heart. "What's our first step?"

Knowing Ms. Washburn had promised her husband she would be home in an hour, and that her drive home to Cranford would take twenty-seven minutes in rush hour traffic, I condensed my answer. "Tomorrow, we will make a trip that I fear has already been rendered pointless, and once we confirm that, we will begin our search for the records that I believe will prove conclusively that Oliver Lewis and Sheila McInerney were indeed married, although much less recently than our client—that is, our previous client—had led us to believe."

Ms. Washburn did not say anything for a moment, looking at me. "Sounds like a date, then," she said. She picked up her tote bag and left the office.

Mother folded her arms. "You know she didn't mean a real date, don't you, Samuel?" she asked.

I nodded.

———

After checking via text message with Detective Dickinson, I spent a short while researching crime scene cleaning services on the Internet. Given there was only one in Middlesex County, I contracted with it to restore my office to its condition prior to the deposit of Oliver Lewis's body on my floor. Then Mother and I went home and had dinner. I watched the New York Yankees play a baseball game against the Toronto Blue Jays (which the Blue Jays won, seven runs to two) and, feeling unfulfilled, went to my room to sleep.

I found it difficult to fall asleep, however. I am not accustomed to being manipulated or outguessed, and I had been both those things on this day. While my ego was not especially bruised, as Ms. Washburn's appeared to be, I was taken by surprise. I thought for two hours and sixteen minutes about the events of the past two days and how I had failed to anticipate the turn of events that had taken place and led to Oliver Lewis's murder.

Finally, I got out of bed and walked downstairs to the kitchen. I was not especially hungry or thirsty, but I could not think of another room to visit. I decided I would take one of the sleeping aids Dr. Mancuso had prescribed, which I usually avoid. I am not fond of medication and resisted it the entire time I was in school, but I knew that the next day would be unusually taxing, that I would need to be sharper of mind, and that sleep would help produce that condition.

It was a mild surprise to find Mother already in the kitchen, preparing a cup of decaffeinated tea. "So you couldn't sleep either," she said when I walked in.

"Is something troubling you?" I asked as I sat at the table. The medication could wait, I decided.

"It's not easy to get that image out of my head," Mother answered, sitting down while she waited for the water to boil. "That poor man laid out on his stomach like that. Why would they arrange him that way? Why bring him to your office? It'll give me nightmares, for sure."

I patted her hand. The last thing I would want to do would be to disturb my mother. "We will answer all those questions when we answer the larger one," I said. "Who killed Oliver Lewis?"

Mother looked mildly surprised. "Isn't it obvious that his wife killed him?" she asked. "She went so out of her way to keep you from the office. She's the only one we know of who had a grudge against him, and she seemed to be afraid of him."

The water started to boil, and before Mother could stand, I did so, turning off the burner and pouring the water carefully over the tea bag in her mug. "I think we must operate under the assumption that everything Sheila McInerney told me was a lie," I said. "So we have no idea how she felt about Mr. Lewis, or if she truly had a reason to want him removed from her life permanently." I brought the mug to the table and set it down in front of Mother, who thanked me. "We need to gather a great deal more information before I can begin to formulate a theory."

Mother drank some of the tea, although from her expression I could tell the water was hot. "This is good," she said.

"It isn't. It's too hot," I told her. She smiled.

"You're too honest sometimes."

"It is not possible to be too honest. Although I have learned that it is possible to tell the truth too often."

"Why can't you sleep?" Mother asked. "Questions don't bother you this much. Not even that other time at the institute." She was referring to the other questions Ms. Washburn and I had answered involving a murder.

"I don't like being predictable. It worries me that Ms. McInerney, having met me just once, could rely on the idea that I'd do just what she wanted when she called the next day. It is troubling that I involved you and Ms. Washburn in an unfortunate incident simply by doing what was expected of me."

Mother blew on the tea and licked her lips. She took another sip and nodded. "You don't like being taken," she said. "Nobody does. But don't succumb to the danger."

"What danger is that?" I asked.

"Don't let it cloud your judgment. Don't stop making decisions based only on facts. Don't try to get even, Samuel."

The possibility had not occurred to me. "Have I ever done that before?" I asked.

Mother's mouth twisted into a half-smile. "You got kicked out of three nursery schools because you were exacting revenge on children who didn't play the games by the rules."

I had been told this story before, although I have no recollection of it. "So you said. What did 'exacting revenge' consist of when I was three?"

"You were a biter."

I stood. I kissed Mother on her forehead, which she knows is my least uncomfortable display of affection. "Don't worry," I said. "I have found more socially acceptable ways to act out my displeasure with rule breakers."

She looked up. "Really. How do you do it now?"

"I send them to jail." I turned and walked to the kitchen door, bidding Mother good night.

"Do you need a pill?" she asked behind me.

"I don't think so. My mind is clearer now."

I went back to my room in the attic and slept peacefully until seven the next morning.

———

Ms. Washburn picked me up at home at nine, as we had arranged the previous evening. There was no need for Mother to drive me to Questions Answered, and I got the impression that both women preferred not to return to the office just yet. Since I had another destination in mind anyway, it was of no significance, but there was no reason to think there would be another cadaver on the floor of the office. Why they were suddenly squeamish about a place where we had been a number of times before without incident was something of a puzzle to me.

I did not dwell on that when I sat in the passenger seat of Ms. Washburn's car. "Where are we going?" she asked. "You said the trip would be pointless, so I'm raring to go."

"Why would that—" I began.

"It's a joke, Samuel. Where to?"

"To Ms. McInerney's apartment."

Ms. Washburn started the car and began pulling out of our driveway. "That's pointless?"

"If I am correct, you will see."

The drive took fourteen minutes and was uneventful. Ms. Washburn knew I preferred not to turn on the radio while we were traveling, and she concentrated on the road. I asked, perhaps foolishly, if her husband had been upset with the events of the previous day. Ms. Washburn said, "It doesn't matter," and we did not talk again for a few minutes.

We approached the door to Sheila McInerney's apartment having waited for one of her neighbors to exit the building, thus leaving the downstairs door open. Ms. Washburn seemed to slow down as we walked down the hallway toward the apartment, so I arrived at the door first and waited for her to catch up.

She stopped approximately seven feet from the door and looked at me. "Are you going to knock?" she asked. Her tone communicated clearly, even to me, that asking why she was standing so far back would be an error.

"I don't think that is necessary," I said. "If the door is locked, I am mistaken."

Her eyebrows dropped in concern, but she said nothing. I reached for the doorknob and rotated it.

It turned, and the door swung open.

Ms. Washburn gasped a little and her voice dropped to a whisper. "Is there anyone or … anything … in there?" she asked.

"I sincerely doubt it." I walked through the door and did not look to see if Ms. Washburn followed. I knew her curiosity would compel her inside soon enough.

As I had anticipated, the apartment was completely empty. The scant furniture, the kitchen implements, the window treatments and even the area rugs were gone. I nodded to myself. Yes, this was what I'd known would be the case.

"It's as if no one had ever lived here." Ms. Washburn's voice came from just behind me and did not startle me. It seemed natural that she would be nearby. She'd seen me walk into the apartment, so she had known there would be nothing dangerous inside. I would have alerted her if it had been otherwise.

"In a sense," I said, "no one did."

TWELVE

"SHOULD WE CALL THE police?" Ms. Washburn was walking around the apartment slowly, as if expecting that in the other rooms, surely there would be some household accoutrements. But I knew for a fact there would be nothing, so I did not tour the living space. I was standing in the middle of what had been the main room, and I imagine I was wearing what Mother calls my "thinking face," which is ostensibly an unusually serious expression with pursed lips and downturned eyes. I know only that I was, indeed, thinking.

"To report what crime?" I asked. "Someone who leased an apartment has moved out. It happens thousands of times a day with no help from the authorities."

"That's not funny, Samuel."

"It was not intended to be."

She called from the bedroom. "Even the hangers in the closets are gone."

"I am not surprised. You might as well give up the search, Ms. Washburn; you'll find nothing here."

She walked into the living area, now a sea of unpolished wood, looking strangely puzzled. "How did you know there would be nothing here?" she asked.

"This apartment was meant to look like someone's home, but it was never really staged convincingly," I said. "There was no indication of daily life here. No clothing was out of place. No items were in the dish drainer or the dishwasher. The only disturbed areas were the ones Ms. McInerney and her compatriot or compatriots wanted us to see."

Ms. Washburn nodded. "The bloodstains and the open window," she said.

"I think the police will discover, if they took samples, that the 'bloodstains' were anything but blood. But even those have been cleaned up, and the window is once again closed, the screen down. This was not a living area. This was a stage set."

Ms. Washburn looked around the room and shook her head. "It's eerier empty than it was when we were supposed to think someone had jumped out the window. Why would someone go to all this trouble to convince us something was going on?"

"We were supposed to be witnesses, but when I began to find holes in the narrative they were creating, we became pawns. The longer they could keep us away from Questions Answered, the better."

"It feels a little personal, doesn't it?"

"It *is* personal, Ms. Washburn. Assuming Ms. McInerney was one of the architects of this charade—and I find myself hard-pressed to imagine a scenario in which she was not—this was targeted directly at me. She could have chosen anyone to act in the role she was preparing, and she decided upon me."

Her eyes searched my face for a moment. "Does that make you angry?" she asked.

"Any number of things make me angry, Ms. Washburn. This one offers both irritation and opportunity."

"Opportunity?"

"If I can understand the motivation behind it, the way this crime was planned can go a long way toward answering the question at hand. I believe it is time to confer with our client."

Ms. Washburn raised an eyebrow. "But we have no idea where Sheila might be now," she said.

"Our other client."

We used Ms. Washburn's cellular phone to call Detective Dickinson, and since I suggested (some might say *insisted*) we meet in person, he directed us to Henry's, a diner on the Livingston campus of Rutgers University in Piscataway. Dickinson said no other Piscataway police officers would be on campus, as the university has its own force and the town gets involved only when a serious crime is committed.

He was sitting in a booth at Henry's when we arrived, scanning the menu. He was seated facing the door—the better to avoid any surprise visitors—and nodded at me when Ms. Washburn and I walked in. We joined him in the booth.

"The food here isn't bad, but it's not like a real diner," Dickinson said. "I mean, the fries are made from sweet potatoes."

When a waiter—surely a student, judging by age and demeanor—arrived, Dickinson asked for a grilled cheese sandwich and a soda. It was not yet time for lunch, which I eat with Mother every day anyway, so I ordered nothing. Ms. Washburn requested a cup of coffee, and I believe she did so simply to be polite. She respects people at their work, and would think we were wasting the waiter's time if she did not pay for something.

I understand her respect for workers, but I was neither hungry nor thirsty. It would make no sense to waste food or drink.

"What was so urgent that we had to meet?" Dickinson asked once the waiter walked away. The diner was not doing very brisk business at this hour, but then college students who do not have early classes tend to sleep late. He was keeping his voice low although it was highly unlikely there was anyone within earshot who might have an interest in our business. "Have you solved the case?"

"Mr. Hoenig does not solve cases. He answers questions." Ms. Washburn said it before I could have.

Dickinson waved a hand to indicate her statement was irrelevant. "Whatever. Did you figure it out?"

"Not yet," I said. "I need more information, and that's why we are here."

"You need information from me? What am I paying you for?"

I heard Ms. Washburn make a noise deep in her throat, but she said nothing. I answered, "Presumably, you are paying me to take the information and interpret it correctly. If I am reading the situation properly, you do not trust yourself to do so." Dickinson's face, surprisingly, twisted into an angry expression while his right hand extended its index finger toward me, but I did not give him time to react verbally. "First, I need to know if you have discovered any evidence that Sheila McInerney and the murder victim Oliver Lewis were indeed married."

Dickinson seemed to drop whatever intention he had of arguing with me and put his hands flat on the table. "Of course we did. They were married in Stanford, Connecticut, just under seven months ago."

"Seven months?" Ms. Washburn said. "Sheila told Samuel they'd only been married a few weeks."

"She also said they were married in Darien, Connecticut," I reminded her. "I do not see a reason to assume anything Ms. McInerney told us was true."

"That's probably a decent bet," Dickinson noted. "Because her real name is not actually Sheila McInerney. It's Cynthia Maholm." (He pronounced the name "Mah-HOL-em," but I believed it to be

"Ma-HOME.") "Luckily, the records indicated she went by the name McInerney professionally once she was married."

"Was Oliver Lewis's real name McInerney?" Ms. Washburn asked.

Dickinson shook his head. "No, his name was in fact Oliver Lewis. But our pal Cynthia apparently wanted people to think she'd married a guy by the name of McInerney, so she used that one."

The sense of that decision eluded me. "Why would she want people to think her husband's name was McInerney?" I mused aloud. "Wouldn't everyone she knew before her marriage know her real name, particularly her first name, which normally wouldn't be changed?"

"More questions, and no answers yet," Dickinson said, looking directly at me. "I don't understand why I'm doing all the work, and you're the one getting paid."

Of course, Dickinson was drawing a salary from the Piscataway police department, and I had not yet been paid at all, but again, it felt like that information would not contribute to the conversation in a productive way.

"Have you contacted the Edison police?" I asked Dickinson. "Did they do any analysis on the supposed bloodstains found in Ms. Maholm's apartment?"

The waiter reappeared carrying Dickinson's food and Ms. Washburn's coffee. Dickinson told the young man that he had taken far too long to bring the order, and the waiter, who I felt had done nothing of the sort, apologized. I saw Ms. Washburn's eyes harden as Dickinson suggested the waiter not expect a very large gratuity. The young man said nothing. Obviously our professional discussion ceased until he once again left the table. Once Dickinson had taken a first (very large) bite of his grilled cheese sandwich, he sipped heavily on his soda, then sat back and considered my questions.

"After Oliver Lewis's body was discovered, of course we got in touch with the Edison department to ask about the scene with you two earlier in the day," he said, a slight twist in his mouth indicating he might be amused by what he was saying. "The stains were not blood at all. They were red nail polish."

"That was what Mr. Hoenig had expected," Ms. Washburn said. I noticed she had not yet sipped any of her coffee.

Dickinson's expression seemed less amused now. "Yeah, well. Edison wanted to talk to you about that too. You might be hearing from a Sergeant Polk. But I did remind them that all that happened on their turf was an alleged B and E with a very suspect accuser. My guess is they won't be calling unless they find something really unexpected."

He appeared to expect some kind of reward or acknowledgement, as if he had done Ms. Washburn and me a great favor. I saw no reason to interrupt, and Ms. Washburn also said nothing for nearly one minute.

"When she was posing as Sheila, this Cynthia Maholm mentioned three names of friends. She said her friend Jenny LeBlanc threw the party where she met Oliver Lewis." Ms. Washburn was not referring to notes, and even though she had not been present at the conversation in question, she was accurate in all her facts. "She said that Lewis showed up with someone named Terry Lambroux, but that she had never met Terry and didn't know which gender Terry was. And she said that someone named Roger Siplowitz had been there when she and Lewis got married. Do we have any idea whether any of those people are real?"

Suddenly Dickinson seemed quite engrossed in his food. He did not look up to make eye contact with either of us. "I haven't had time to look into that yet," he said.

Ms. Washburn and I exchanged a glance. It was possible that Detective Dickinson was not the most energetic member of the Piscataway police department.

"Why don't you leave that to me?" I suggested, on the assumption that the task would be completed much more quickly and efficiently in hands other than those of Detective Dickinson. "I will report back to you very soon."

Dickinson nodded. Then, as if struck by a thought, he looked up from his plate and into my eyes. "You didn't seem surprised by anything I told you," he said.

"I was not surprised," I assured him. That information, I believed, would give him confidence that he had contracted intelligently.

"Why not?" Dickinson appeared almost oppositional, his hands balling into fists.

"Because it makes sense, except for Ms. Maholm changing her name," I answered. "That did not surprise me so much as it instilled in me a desire to do more research. Ms. Washburn?" I gestured to my associate, who stood up so we could make our exit.

On our way out, I noticed Ms. Washburn laying a five-dollar bill on the table and anchoring it under her untouched coffee cup.

THIRTEEN

"ARE YOU UNCOMFORTABLE GOING back to Questions Answered?" I asked Ms. Washburn.

She was driving us to the office where we could begin our research into the questions posed by Detective Dickinson and the predictable, if still irritating, disappearance of our purported client Sheila McInerney, aka Cynthia Maholm.

"I told you," my associate said, not diverting her gaze from the road, "I've made my decision, and what my husband thinks is between him and me. You don't have to worry, Samuel."

"I was asking whether it was difficult for you to return to the office after our discovery of the corpse there yesterday," I explained. "When you asked where we were going and I told you, your face blanched a bit."

She drew a quick breath and let it out. "Oh. Well, it does dredge up some unpleasant images, don't you think?"

"I did not know Oliver Lewis well enough to mourn him," I told her. "The fact that his body was in our office makes me angry, not sad. I am much more concerned with finding the people who chose to deposit it there and see to it that they are punished for their crimes. Since our professional center is in that office, I see no reason not to return there."

Ms. Washburn made a left turn. We were less than one half-mile from the office, and she was not procrastinating by slowing down or diverting our path. "I get that," she said. "But some of us associate places with memories we wish we didn't have, and that makes it difficult emotionally to go back to that place. Don't worry about me; I'll be fine when we're there."

We arrived at the strip mall and saw the van for Extra Safe Cleaning parked outside. I had almost forgotten I'd contracted with a crime scene cleaning service, and hoped the bulk of the work inside had been done. I said nothing to my associate as we exited the car and entered the storefront. Ms. Washburn's eyes darted around the room once we were inside, but she did seem to relax once she saw that it had indeed been subject to a very thorough cleaning.

Two figures in matching blue suits not dissimilar to hazmat clothing were completing the task as we entered. With respirator masks on the lower halves of their faces and the shapeless uniforms covering them from head to toe, it was difficult at first to discern that one was a man and the other a woman. The latter approached Ms. Washburn and me once we were inside.

"Sorry," she said, "this building is being cleaned. The business is not open right now." Through the mask, her voice sounded slightly husky for a woman, but it was unquestionably female.

"We are aware of that," I said. "Allow me to introduce myself. I am Samuel Hoenig, the proprietor of Questions Answered, and this is my associate, Ms. Washburn." I did not extend my hand as I usually do when meeting a person new to me because the gloves both were wearing seemed to preclude touching.

"I'm Hazel Montrose," the woman answered, "and this is my partner Jonah Wainwright. Sorry we didn't recognize you, Mr. Hoenig."

"Not a problem," Ms. Washburn told her. "Samuel is not offended and neither am I. I'm Janet." She did extend a hand, but Hazel Montrose did not accept it.

"Sorry," she repeated. "We're kind of gross, and it's against policy."

Ms. Washburn waved a hand to indicate she was not insulted. Meanwhile, Jonah Wainwright was completing his task, which appeared to be the removal of a very large wet/dry vacuum device from the room. He paid no attention to Hazel Montrose, Ms. Washburn, or myself as he rolled it out the door. I could see him loading it into the Extra Safe van in the parking lot.

"Was it a…difficult job?" Ms. Washburn asked. She seemed to be struggling to avoid looking at the spot where Oliver Lewis had lain.

"Actually, no," Hazel Montrose responded. "I've seen a lot worse, believe me."

It occurred to me that talking to someone with Hazel's experience might provide some direction in answering the question at hand. "Do you have to leave immediately?" I asked. "I have a few questions, if that is all right."

I could not read Hazel's expression through the respirator mask, the clear shield covering her eyes, and the blue repellent hood over her head, so when it took her a moment to answer, I wondered if I had said something that could have been misconstrued. It would not be unusual for me to do so, although it is rarely my intention.

"Do you see an area we might have missed?" Hazel asked.

Ms. Washburn, as she often does, reacted to the situation more quickly than I did. "No, Samuel isn't saying that. Our business is to answer questions, and since the question we're currently researching involves the…job you just did, he believes you might be helpful if you can spare the time." I could not have articulated nearly as well.

Again there was a pause as Hazel considered the proposal. "Do you need both of us?" she asked.

This time Ms. Washburn deferred to me. "It is better to hear more than one perspective when possible, but if one of you is inconvenienced by the suggestion, the other will certainly suffice," I told Hazel.

"Jonah has a one-man job next, and he was going to drop me off," she replied. "Can you give me a lift when we're done?"

I looked to Ms. Washburn, who supplies the transportation for Questions Answered. "Of course we can," she said.

"Let me go change and I'll be right back," Hazel suggested, and she did not wait for a reply before walking out to the company van. She climbed into the back of the vehicle, out of my line of sight.

Ms. Washburn sat in her traditional spot, in the chair near Mother's recliner and next to my desk. It occurred to me that since she would now be working here on a more permanent basis, it would make sense to procure a second desk for her. One advantage would be that she could answer the company telephone, something that has always been a source of some anxiety for me.

"They did a nice job," she said, surveying the room. "I'd never know anything had happened here, and besides, a lot of the dust is gone."

"I examined the area before they arrived this morning," I said, "so any information I could have seen on first glance was not removed before I could make note of it."

I sat behind my desk and turned on the Mac Pro, which was notably free of dust for the first time in recent memory. Still, the idea that someone other than me had been handling the items on my desk was somewhat disturbing; I did my best to focus on the task at hand.

By the time I had run a simple Google search on the name Terry Lambroux, Hazel Montrose had walked back into the Questions Answered office. She was no longer wearing the protective clothing or mask, and was now in a pair of casual trousers and a blue polo shirt which bore the logo for Extra Safe Cleaning.

Her face was now much more visible, and it was clear-eyed and open, to the extent that I could interpret it. I could not speak for most other people, but when conforming to the standards set by society, Hazel was an attractive woman in her early thirties, about my age. That was, however, clearly outside the scope of the question I needed to answer, and so therefore irrelevant.

"How can I help you, Mr. Hoenig?" she asked as she settled, with the prompting of Ms. Washburn's gesture, into the client chair in front of my desk.

"First, allow me to compliment you on the quality of your work," I said. "The office is completely free of any reminder that something unusual occurred here." I glanced at Ms. Washburn in an attempt to elicit her reaction because she had been concerned about, as she had put it, "unpleasant images" our office might now harbor. But she was looking at Hazel, and not at me.

"Thank you," Hazel said. "It's difficult work, but very satisfying when it's done. Jonah does the really hard stuff." She did not elaborate.

"Did you notice anything unusual about this scene?" I was attempting to ask without prejudicing the answer. There were specifics I could have asked about—like blood spatter and bone fragments—but there was no point in asking for information I had observed on my own, and leaving the question more open-ended allowed Hazel to provide anything she had seen. Too often one asks about a specific detail and misses out on more useful data because the topic was never raised.

"Well, it was a pretty easy cleanup, and that seemed odd," she answered after a moment. I noticed Ms. Washburn's notepad and pen were out of her bag and in her hands. I had not needed to prompt her.

"Why is that odd?" Ms. Washburn asked. "What should have made it harder?"

"Don't get me wrong—I'm not sorry there wasn't more to do. What I meant was, you expect there to be more work in a room that clearly had a dead body, and not one who died of natural causes."

"You could tell that from the outline on the floor," I suggested.

"Yes, and from the bloodstain. But that's what I meant. Someone dies of an injury, one that seemed to have been from the area of his throat, and you don't see much blood. That's strange." Hazel did not flinch at the mention of blood; this was her line of work. Just another day at the office, Mother would say.

"We assume then that the victim was killed somewhere else and brought here to be discovered," I said.

"Probably right. And we found no blood trail coming into the room. That might mean that the body was somehow contained, in a bag or something, before being dumped in the middle of the floor," Hazel suggested.

I had considered that, but I complimented Hazel on her observational skills anyway. "Was there anything out of the ordinary anywhere else in the room?" I asked. "I assume you had to consider the entire space."

Hazel nodded. "Yes, including the bathrooms and the—I guess it used to be a kitchen, where they made pizza. There are two ovens."

"Was there anything related to the crime in either of those areas?"

"No. But there were also no scratches in the floor or the door. There was no broken glass anywhere. There was no smell of burned wiring. Aside from the area where the dead guy was lying, this was a perfectly innocent office." Hazel's gaze was almost competitive; it was as if she and I were trying to see how much the other had been able to observe and what each of us could deduce from the observations.

"So there was no sign of forced entry. Whoever deposited Oliver Lewis's corpse at Questions Answered had a key or the combination to—" I stopped when I saw the look on Hazel Montrose's face.

Her eyes were wide and her mouth was open and breathing with a shallow sound, as if she'd just come out of the water after an easy swim but was regulating her breath to normalize it. She swallowed, hard. "Did you say Oliver Lewis?" she asked.

"Yes," Ms. Washburn said without looking up from her notes. She had not seen Hazel's reaction and was sitting too far from her to hear the slight change in her breathing. "Oliver Lewis was the name of the man who was killed yesterday."

There was only one explanation that fit the facts, but it was extremely unlikely. "Did you know him?" I asked Hazel, and Ms. Washburn looked up and reacted, startled, to Hazel's shocked look.

"No. I mean, it's such a common name," Hazel said. "I'm sure it's someone else."

"Describe the Oliver Lewis you know," I suggested.

"It's silly."

"Please. It would be a great help." In truth, the probability was that her information would not contribute to answering the question at all, but even with my difficulties reading faces, there was no mistaking Hazel's expression—she thought the Oliver Lewis she knew *was* the one who had ended up on my office floor. And while she was shocked, she was not surprised.

Hazel looked at me, then at Ms. Washburn, who appeared concerned but whose pen was poised over her notepad, then back at me. She waited a moment that seemed long but lasted only four seconds.

"All right," she said. "He's big, about six-two, but he's solid, you know? Not like six pack abs or anything, but not heavy. Big eyes, brown. Tends to dress up a little. Wears his hair slicked back straight, thinks it makes him look like a Wall Street sharpie or something."

"And what did you observe about the body in this room when you were cleaning up?" I asked.

"Samuel," Ms. Washburn said. Her voice seemed to have some rapprochement in it, but I could not understand why it would.

"Well, the body was gone when we were working," Hazel pointed out.

"But you could determine the man's height and approximate proportions," I suggested.

"Samuel," Ms. Washburn said more forcefully.

Hazel sat back in the chair and gasped. "It was him, wasn't it? It was Ollie who got killed." She did not cry, but I believe she might have wanted to do so.

"I'm afraid so," Ms. Washburn said before I could speak. "I'm so sorry. How did you know him?"

Hazel looked stunned, and stared straight ahead. "Until a little more than two years ago, he was my husband," she said.

FOURTEEN

I TRIED TO GATHER my thoughts quickly, but realized it was best to forego speed and concentrate on logic and accuracy. The idea that Hazel Montrose had been Oliver Lewis's wife before he married Sheila McInerney (Cynthia Maholm) was disruptive to every train of thought I'd had on the question at hand, and on the one Cynthia herself had posed only two days earlier.

"You were married to Oliver Lewis?" Ms. Washburn said, her voice suddenly hoarse.

Hazel, eyes moist, nodded. "What happened?" she asked.

"His carotid artery had been severed," I told her. "We are attempting to answer the question of who did that. Part of the answer will be to understand why it was done."

Ms. Washburn gave me what I have known to be a stern look. I suddenly understood that I had seemed insensitive to Hazel's pain, assuming she was upset by the death of her ex-husband.

"My apologies," I said. "I am sorry for your loss."

Hazel held up both hands, palms out, and shook them. "It's not your fault," she said. "It's just that it came so out of left field."

I am something of a baseball aficionado, and understand that "out of left field" is an expression that indicates a concept is unexpected or hard to understand. But why such a thing comes from left field and not center field or right field baffles me. I chose not to express that feeling to either Hazel or Ms. Washburn at the moment. The fact that the message had been received and understood was enough.

"Of course," I responded. "You had merely done your job cleaning up. You were unaware that you were removing traces of your ex-husband."

Ms. Washburn's eyes rolled a bit, but she remained silent. I would have to ask her later why what I'd said was inappropriate when it was accurate and, I thought, empathetic.

Hazel dabbed at her eye and sniffed briefly, then seemed to rally her thoughts. She sat up straighter in the chair, looked me in the eye and asked, "How can I help?"

"Tell me how you met Oliver Lewis and married him," I suggested.

"I met him through a friend we both knew," she said. "About three years ago, in the spring. We started dating and got married only two months later. We were married for a year but lived apart after only about six months. It took a while for the divorce to be finalized."

"What is the friend's name?"

"Roger Siplowitz. I went to college with him, and Ollie ... I honestly don't know how Ollie knew Roger."

Ms. Washburn, pad back in hand, leaned toward Hazel. "Do you have current contact information for Roger?" she asked. Ms. Washburn is very efficient, and knew I would be asking that very question next.

"No, I lost touch with him after the divorce," Hazel answered. "You know how the wife gets some of the friends and the husband gets the others? Ollie got Roger."

The thought continued to nag at me. Life does contain coincidences, but the idea that Oliver Lewis's first wife had simply chanced to be the crime scene cleaner I had contracted to remove the traces of his murder was too unlikely to ignore. There had to be a connection somewhere.

"When is the last time you saw Oliver Lewis?" I asked Hazel.

"When we signed the divorce papers in his lawyer's office, about two and a half years ago. We had no reason to get in touch after that. We didn't have any kids. We didn't even have a dog."

I closed my eyes, which sometimes helps divert me from the visual stimulus in front of me—in this case, Hazel—and focus on the deeper problem at hand. Oliver Lewis had been married twice. His first wife had divorced him, and the second one (assuming Dickinson's information was correct and Cynthia Maholm really had been married to Lewis) had hired me ostensibly to discover who her husband was and whether the marriage he claimed to have with her was legal.

Opening my eyes, I asked Hazel, "Were you aware your ex-husband had remarried?"

For a moment it looked like Hazel was trying to translate the strange language I was speaking to her into something more recognizable. "No," she said simply. "Who was he married to?"

Ms. Washburn caught my eye with a glance, drew in her lips and spread her hands a bit, a gesture I have learned indicates one should speak carefully. "His current wife"—I eschewed the term *widow*— "is a woman named Cynthia Maholm, who sometimes goes by the name Sheila McInerney. Do you know her?"

Hazel's brow furrowed, but she shook her head to indicate a negative response.

"Was…" Ms. Washburn seemed to hesitate, as if wondering whether she would cause Hazel some sadness by continuing, but the question was begun. "Was Oliver ever married before you met?" she asked.

The thought had not occurred to me that there might be more ex-wives in Oliver Lewis's past. Should any of them be women I had met before, I would have to seriously reconsider my notion about the plausibility of coincidence in daily life.

"No," Hazel answered. "I was Ollie's first wife." That simplified matters and I was grateful for it. More ex-wives would have increased the number of uncomfortable interviews I would have to conduct in answering the question.

"What was it about him that made you want to marry him?" I asked. I cannot say for certain that the question was directly related to my work; the subject has always puzzled me. I do not understand how a person can feel so strongly about another, be so certain, that he or she would commit every remaining moment of life to the other. It is irrational and improbable, which is likely why so many marriages end in divorce. Or in this case, murder.

Hazel smiled, but I was sure Mother would say it was a sad smile. Her lips did not curl upward symmetrically and her eyes looked down a little.

"The cliché is supposed to be that he made me laugh, right?" she said, but neither Ms. Washburn nor myself answered her. "Well, Ollie didn't make me laugh. He was never a very happy guy."

Ms. Washburn, perhaps against her better judgment, asked, "Then what was it?"

Hazel's attention seemed to focus. But she looked at me, not at Ms. Washburn, when she said, "I think he made me feel like I was the center of his world. Until I wasn't anymore."

"There were other women?" I said. I did not look to Ms. Washburn for a reaction.

Hazel tilted her head to one side and nodded slightly, flattening her mouth. "Probably," she said. "All I know is that after we were married and he'd gotten what he wanted, I wasn't a priority anymore. I think for Ollie, the pursuit was more important than the possession, if you know what I mean."

I did not, but I trusted that Ms. Washburn did.

Hazel had little to say after that, and Ms. Washburn offered to drive her home. Hazel accepted the ride. I opted to stay in the office for several reasons: I was behind on my exercise, which was a concern; Mother would be arriving to drive me home for lunch in forty-seven minutes (or forty-eight—Mother is not always precise); and I presumed that if Hazel had more information to add to our ongoing work, she might be more likely to tell it to another woman without a man present. I am not certain about the motivation, but people of both genders tend to be less circumspect when among members of their own sex.

They left after Hazel bid me farewell, and Ms. Washburn said she would return within the hour. I mentioned that Mother would probably pick me up for lunch shortly and Ms. Washburn said she would meet me at the house I share with my mother. I nodded. It occurred to me after she left that Mother would have wanted me to invite Ms. Washburn to lunch with us. I felt it would be unwise to call her cellular phone while she was driving, however, so I left it unsaid.

The time alone gave me an opportunity to research a few of the multitude of loose ends hanging from this question. (I try to use metaphors occasionally in an effort to incorporate them into my natural speech pattern.) I began where I had been interrupted when Hazel had returned from the van, investigating the name Terry Lambroux.

Google is not the best way to search for something, but it is the simplest, and to begin an inquiry, simplicity can be a gateway to more substantial information. So I started with a straight search of the name as an attempt to find a direction.

There were no entries.

It is extremely unusual for a name to have generated absolutely no hits in a search on the most wide-ranging search engine in the world. I should have expected to find at least some erroneous links, to dishes made with lamb or other people named Terry. To get no results was in some ways unsettling; it had never happened to me before.

I tried the names "Terrence Lambroux," "Teresa Lambroux," various alternate spellings of both names, and then "T. Lambroux."

Nothing appeared. The same was true when searching Google Images, which at that point was no longer a surprise at all.

I will admit to sitting behind my desk staring at the Mac Pro for at least thirty seconds in wonder. Then I used various other search engines and a few specialized sites I know of to search for missing people, and each time was rewarded with the same lack of data.

It seemed, at least as far as the Internet was concerned, there was no such person as Terry Lambroux.

———

"Well, that's certainly odd," Mother said.

We were removing plates and utensils from the kitchen table and I was placing them in the dishwasher. Had Mother been clearing the table, she would have put everything into the sink and washed it all by hand, arguing that it was just the two of us and the dishwasher wasn't necessary. I worry about her health more than she does, or at least more than she will admit to, and I try to keep Mother from doing anything she doesn't have to do. She has had cardiac issues in the past.

To distract her from my dishwasher use, I was informing her about my most recent efforts involving Detective Dickinson's question. "At least I did find some mentions of Roger Siplowitz," I answered. "He apparently is an attorney specializing in family law in New Brunswick, but as far as I can discern, he did not participate in Oliver Lewis's divorce from Hazel Montrose."

"How do you know that?" Mother was putting mustard and mayonnaise back into the refrigerator, knowing well of my disgust for such substances.

"There are court records when such an action is filed," I said. "They are a matter of public record, and can often be found online."

The doorbell rang, which interrupted our cleanup activities. Mother always answers the door when she is downstairs because she knows I am not fond of surprises. But in this case, I expected Ms. Washburn to be in the doorway, and so she was.

Mother immediately asked if she'd like some lunch, but Ms. Washburn said she had eaten a small salad with Hazel Montrose, which surprised me. "I believed you were simply driving Hazel to her home," I said.

"She wanted to stop," Ms. Washburn said, sitting at the kitchen table. Mother and I, having completed the cleanup process, joined her there. "She was pretty upset about what happened to her ex-husband, and she asked me to stop at a coffee shop so she could compose herself."

This led me to conclude that Hazel must be living with another person or more, since she seemed to have issues about being visibly emotional when she arrived at her home. But I did not voice that opinion (and it was just that) because I wanted Ms. Washburn to continue. Clearly, Hazel must have said something of significance for Ms. Washburn to mention the conversation so soon after arriving.

But Ms. Washburn studied my face a moment, intent. "You've decided Hazel's living with a guy, and it's bothering you," she said.

"Amazing," Mother chimed in. "I was thinking the same thing."

That was, to say the least, odd. While I had been speculating about Hazel's motivation for delaying her return home, it was not troubling me in any way. "I don't understand," I said.

"Come on, Samuel." Ms. Washburn folded her arms, a posture which I have learned can be a signal of resistance or of a person who is defending an unpopular position. This confused me further, as it seemed the scenario would cast me in that role. "You have a little crush on Hazel Montrose, and you don't want her to be married or living with someone. It makes sense."

"A crush?" It was a ridiculous statement, but I was sure it would be considered rude for me to say so. "I have no such feelings."

Mother laughed.

"You were flirting with her all through the interview, Samuel," Ms. Washburn said. I was unfamiliar with the smile she was adopting. "And I have news for you: she was flirting back."

"I believe you are mistaken, Ms. Washburn. Hazel was simply someone who had information I required, and I was acting as anyone would to ingratiate myself with her and extract the data."

Ms. Washburn's smile got wider and more difficult to read. "Really. Samuel. I've known you for months. We've answered questions together. We've almost died together. But you continue to call me 'Ms. Washburn'. You knew Hazel for maybe a minute and a half and you were addressing her by her first name."

Mother nodded. "It's nothing to be embarrassed about; it happens to people all the time."

I shook my head at the absurdity of the conversation. "I am not the least bit embarrassed. I have no 'crush,' as you put it, Ms. Washburn. I believe you misread the body language during my interview with … with Ms. Montrose."

Ms. Washburn exchanged a look with Mother, who shrugged.

"Okay," my associate said. "Do you want to hear what *Hazel* said at the coffee shop?"

I ignored her emphasis on our acquaintance's name and said, "Of course, if it is of interest to our work."

Ms. Washburn seemed to become suddenly interested in the salt-shaker on our kitchen table. She picked it up and examined it, although

I have never considered it to be especially interesting in design. "She said she wasn't surprised someone had killed Oliver Lewis." I caught a slight flicker of her eyelashes as she looked quickly at me to gauge my reaction.

"There are many people who would say such things about their ex-spouses," I noted. "Did she mention a reason she was not surprised?"

Ms. Washburn looked a little disappointed that I had not been startled by her revelation. "She said he had a pattern of pursuing people, mostly women, and then abandoning them when he had won them over."

I reminded her that Hazel had said virtually the same thing when I was questioning her.

"But she said he'd done that with someone he shouldn't," Ms. Washburn went on. "Apparently some woman he'd led on was suing him."

"Do we have a name?" I asked.

Ms. Washburn looked away. The lack of eye contact signaled some degree of disappointment with herself, I believed. "She wouldn't tell me," she said. "She said Ollie would tell her about this other woman when they were married, just to upset her. But she wouldn't give out the name."

I put up my hands to show that it was not important. "The strongest probability is that Oliver Lewis was lying in an attempt to hurt his wife," I said. "Keep in mind that we have a very strong suspect in Ms. Maholm, who went to such elaborate lengths to distract and implicate us. I believe our first order or business should be locating her."

Ms. Washburn nodded. "Back to Questions Answered, then?" She stood up, as did I. Mother stayed seated, as it was clear she was not about to come with us.

"No," I told Ms. Washburn. "Not yet. Instead, please drive me to Darien, Connecticut."

FIFTEEN

"THIS IS GOING TO be at least an hour and a half drive," Ms. Washburn said.

"Yes, that is an accurate approximation," I answered, and immediately wondered whether an approximation can be considered accurate.

"With traffic, it could be as much as three hours."

"That is true, although unlikely."

"You don't know the Connecticut Turnpike. What is it we're going for that can't be scanned, emailed, faxed, or iPhoned?" Ms. Washburn asked.

I wanted to correct Ms. Washburn's use of the noun *iPhone* as a verb, but I knew that people do not appreciate such statements. I could surmise her meaning and so replied, "We are attempting to persuade a justice of the peace to relinquish records of the wedding we know took place between Oliver Lewis and Cynthia Maholm," I said.

"And that can't happen electronically because ... ?"

"Because it is not the delivery of the records that is the difficult part. It is the *surrender* of the records. It will take some persuasion, and that is best accomplished in person. You know I am not especially effective on the telephone."

"But I am," Ms. Washburn protested.

"There is also the matter of the photographs," I said.

She drove silently for some moments. "What photographs, Samuel?"

"Every justice of the peace presiding over a wedding would have someone nearby taking photographs, which would no doubt be sold to the happy couple," I explained. "Was your wedding performed by a justice of the peace?"

"No."

I waited, but she said nothing else. "The photographs can tell us who else was present at the wedding, and might give you especially some insight into the mood of Cynthia and Oliver when they were married."

"Because I'm more likely to read their facial expressions in the pictures," Ms. Washburn said, nodding slightly.

"Yes."

"It's a long drive for something that skimpy," she said. "Is this our best lead so far?"

"Our best lead, as you put it, is to find Ms. Maholm, but we do not have a clear path to follow for that," I reminded her. "If you have an idea as to how to locate her, I would be happy to turn back toward Middlesex County immediately."

Ms. Washburn was silent for 7.4 miles. Then she pursed her lips. "How badly do you want those photographs?" she asked.

I sensed there was an underlying message to the question, but I was at a loss to identify it. "They are the most likely source of new information we have at the moment," I reiterated. "Why do you ask?"

"I have an idea," Ms. Washburn said. "Do you trust me?"

"I think you know the answer to that question."

"Fine." She changed lanes to the right, not impulsively or dangerously, but certainly more quickly than normal. I believe I was successful in cloaking my sharp intake of breath. Ms. Washburn signaled a right turn, and took the next jug handle marked U and Left Turns.

"Where are we going?" I asked, fighting the impulse to bite my lips. I am not the most sedate passenger in a moving vehicle, given the statistics of automobile accidents occurring each year.

"To New Brunswick. To Roger Siplowitz's office. Remember? You said Cynthia told you he took pictures at their wedding."

"So she did. But should we believe anything she said?"

Ms. Washburn was able to shrug her shoulders without affecting her efficiency as a driver. "I don't know, but I'm sure of one thing."

"What is that?" I asked.

"New Brunswick is closer than Darien, Connecticut."

———

We had not found a home address for Roger Siplowitz, but it took only a quick Google search to determine the location of his office, which I programmed into Ms. Washburn's global positioning device while she drove. It was not difficult to get to New Brunswick, she said. Finding the office was the tricky part.

But in practice, there was no trouble finding the law offices of Jennings, Masterson & Siplowitz. Many attorneys have offices near the Middlesex County Courthouse on Bayard Street, and Siplowitz's firm was no exception, located on Paterson Street, only one block to the north. Because it was three in the afternoon it was not difficult to find an available parking space only thirty yards from the front door to the office, which had a door painted bright red. It was a relatively small building, a converted townhouse with two concrete steps leading up to the door, which required a visitor to be buzzed in to enter.

Inside, the décor was somewhat more lush. Thick carpeting on the floor of the reception area was complimented by real plaster-work on the walls, two of which held original oil paintings by an artist named Friedman, according to the signature in each lower right corner. The receptionist sat behind a small oak desk with a telephone console and a banker's lamp with a green hood. The lighting in the room was incandescent, not fluorescent like at Questions Answered, as I had "inherited" the lighting from San Remo's.

The receptionist herself was a very elegant African-American woman, roughly thirty-three years old, dressed conservatively. She was not on the phone when we entered, but having buzzed us in, knew we would be entering. She smiled professionally and looked attentive when we asked for Roger Siplowitz.

"Does Mr. Siplowitz expect you?" she asked, although she certainly was aware we were not on his calendar for this time.

"No, he doesn't," Ms. Washburn said, "but it's a pretty urgent matter."

"I'm sure it is," the receptionist answered in a very smooth voice. "However, Mr. Siplowitz is all booked up for the afternoon, and he just doesn't have the time."

"Please mention the name Cynthia Maholm," I interjected. "If you say we've come about her, I'm sure he'll want to see us."

The receptionist's eyes narrowed. When some people do that, their faces take on a look of anger bordering on intended violence. With this woman, my impression was more that she was trying to understand as fully as she could. The eye adjustment was undoubtedly involuntary.

She picked up the phone and pushed a button, her gaze never leaving mine. It was an effort, and not a small one, for me to maintain the contact. My instinct is to look away from someone gazing in my direction. The attention is disquieting and the other person's eyes always seem disapproving if I don't focus hard and try to remember the sample expressions I have been shown. It took years of effort to recognize and process emotional expressions. It still does not come naturally, or comfortably.

After a moment, the receptionist said into the phone, "Maggie, is he there? Tell him there's a Mr. Hoenig and a Ms. Washburn and they said to mention the name Cynthia Maholm." She remembered each name and pronounced each one flawlessly without having written anything down to use as a reference. This was, clearly, a very highly skilled receptionist.

For thirty-four seconds all of us waited for a reply. I took the opportunity to avert my glance and focus on the painting to my left, which was of an open field on a spring day. The technique was excellent, although I was not affected emotionally by what I saw. I do some painting myself, but my goal is always to accurately portray my subject and not to evoke some emotional response from the viewer.

The receptionist suddenly became more animated as the person she had called must have spoken again, but we could not see any change in her demeanor overall. "Okay," she said, and disconnected the call. She looked at Ms. Washburn. "Mr. Siplowitz will see you in a moment."

Ms. Washburn looked surprised, although I could not determine why she should be; the real name of his deceased friend's wife would surely get us an audience with him if he had known it at all, and there was no reason to think he had not.

The receptionist pointed behind her toward a corridor. "There's an elevator there," she said. "Third floor. His assistant, Maggie, will meet you." She handed Ms. Washburn a visitor's pass, which was somewhat unusual but not unheard of, and Ms. Washburn thanked her for the help. We walked to the elevator.

Once there, Ms. Washburn pushed the button and the doors opened. We stepped inside, for the first time out of earshot of the receptionist, and Ms. Washburn asked me, "Why do you think he decided to see us if he's that busy?"

The doors closed and we could feel the lift of the elevator begin. "He was not as tightly scheduled as he would like us to believe," I said. "Most such people are not. The receptionist and Mr. Siplowitz's assistant are gatekeepers intended to keep unwanted visitors from gaining access."

"I'm aware of that," Ms. Washburn said. "I'm wondering why he's agreeing to the meeting."

"We've indicated we know something about Cynthia Maholm, which most people could not claim," I said. "Mr. Siplowitz is curious."

It was not a long elevator ride. The doors opened, and a very fashionably dressed woman in her thirties was beyond them. "Hi! I'm Maggie," she said, extending a hand, which Ms. Washburn was quick to accept on my behalf. "I'm Roger's executive assistant. Please come this way."

It would have been interesting to ask Maggie her favorite Beatles song, since there is one called "Maggie Mae "(not to be confused with the song "Maggie May" by Rod Stewart), but there was no time. She led us to a door only fifteen feet from the elevator. It bore a heavy gold-colored placard embossed *Roger Siplowitz*, and Maggie opened it and led us inside.

There was a waiting area within where Maggie's small but neat desk stood (exhibiting a name plate reading *Margaret Caruso*), but she walked directly to an unmarked inner office door and knocked.

"Come," said a male voice inside.

Maggie opened the door but did not walk inside the office. She indicated that we should.

As we did, I heard Ms. Washburn very quietly observe, "The great and powerful Oz."

Roger Siplowitz was a hale-looking man in his mid-thirties. He had not yet begun to lose his hair, although judging by the oil portrait hanging behind his desk of a man whose close resemblance to Roger indicated he was a relative, he would do so fairly soon. He was tanned and appeared fit, and he too extended a hand, which Ms. Washburn intercepted.

"Roger Siplowitz," he said. After some explanation and training, I have accepted that many people introduce themselves in this fashion, although it seems an odd thing to say to a person as you shake her hand. The logical assumption would be that the speaker was naming the person he is meeting, which is not the case.

"Nice to meet you," Ms. Washburn said. "I'm Janet Washburn, and this is Samuel Hoenig."

Siplowitz, assuming merely that Ms. Washburn was the first to want to come into physical contact with him, broke the handshake and pushed his arm in my direction. Ms. Washburn flashed me a concerned look, but I understood the process and that it is not always avoidable. I concentrated on not noticing the perspiration on Siplowitz's palm except for its possible indication that he was nervous.

"Allow me to introduce myself," I said. "I am Samuel Hoenig."

"Nice to meet you, Sam." Siplowitz gestured toward a leather sofa on the wall opposite his desk, but Ms. Washburn took a seat on a matching leather chair in front of Siplowitz's work space and indicated I should do the same. I complied, wondering if this was somehow symbolic. I would have to ask Ms. Washburn later.

Neither Ms. Washburn nor I corrected Siplowitz on my name, however. I wanted to, but was concerned I might be perceived as impolite.

"How can I help you two?" he asked, settling in behind his desk in a grander version of the chairs Ms. Washburn and I were utilizing. His had wheels. I did not correct him on his grammar, either. The error made replacing *may* with *can* is too common. If one were to point it out every time, it could take up too much of a day.

"We are attempting to answer a question about the death of Oliver Lewis," I told him. "I understand you were a friend of his."

Siplowitz shook his head. "You understand wrong. I knew Lewis, but we weren't friends. I met him at a Bar Association function a couple of years ago. He wasn't all that interesting, frankly, but women liked him and at the time that made him a good person for me to be around." He leaned over in a "conspiratorial" pose toward Ms. Washburn. "Don't tell my wife I said that, okay?"

Another thing I would later have to ask Ms. Washburn to explain.

"So you were not friends, but you did socialize; is that correct?" I asked.

"Yes. For a while. Then I met Corrine and suddenly it wasn't that important to be around a guy who could attract women."

"Tell us about Cynthia Maholm," I said. I did not want to lead his answer with anything more than that—it was important to see what Siplowitz would volunteer.

"I didn't know a Cynthia Maholm," he said.

I gave him seven seconds, but there was no additional information offered. It made no sense that Siplowitz had never heard of Cynthia Maholm. Ms. Washburn looked less puzzled, but more suspicious.

"If you didn't know her, why did the mention of her name get us into your private office?" she asked.

"Because the woman I know is named Sheila McInerney," Siplowitz responded. I believe there might have been the hint of a smug smile as he spoke, but it might also have been that he needed to burp and felt he could not do so in our company. Either explanation was possible.

"No matter her name, you did attend the woman's wedding to Oliver Lewis, didn't you?" I asked after a proper interval of three seconds, during which I had determined that Siplowitz's office also housed a Phi Beta Kappa key preserved under glass in a corner next to a plaque reading, *Howard J. Siplowitz, 1962.*

"Yes, I was there. I was at the party where Ollie met Sheila, so they invited me to the wedding. I talked to my wife about it, and we couldn't come up with a believable excuse to avoid going, so we went. I like Connecticut well enough, anyway. We spent the night in a very cozy bed and breakfast in Norwalk. They had crepes for brunch on Sunday."

Before I could ask what was foremost in my mind, Ms. Washburn said to Siplowitz, "But you took pictures at the wedding, didn't you? We were told you were sort of the unofficial photographer."

He waved a hand casually, indicating that what she had said was silly. "Who told you that—did Sheila? Haven't you realized by now that you can't trust a thing that woman says?"

Again I was about to pose the question I'd been formulating, but Ms. Washburn, to her credit, was not about to let Siplowitz dismiss her. "Did you take pictures, and if so, may we see them?"

This was now becoming an interesting and useful discussion. The question itself was fairly straightforward, naturally. But the effect it had on our subject was quite revealing: Siplowitz dropped his eyebrows to a very low position, leaned forward in his chair, and tightened the muscles around his mouth. His expression was exactly like one I remembered from social skills training over the word *cross*.

"People don't come here and talk to me like that," he said in a low tone.

I am certainly no expert on social intercourse, but it seemed to me that the lawyer's reaction far exceeded its impetus. Ms. Washburn had merely asked about any potential photographs from the wedding of Oliver Lewis and Cynthia Maholm, and refused to let Siplowitz treat her as a triviality and evade the question. He was responding as if she had accused him of some minor illegality or said that he had been exceedingly rude.

Ms. Washburn did not flinch. "I'm simply asking if there are pictures," she said. "I don't think what I said—"

"I don't have to sit here and listen to this," the attorney went on. "I was nice enough to interrupt my day for you when you arrived without an appointment, and now I'm accused of lying in my own office!"

"Nobody said you were lying," I pointed out. "As far as I can tell, no one even implied it. You, sir, appear to be overreacting."

Siplowitz stood up abruptly and slapped his hands flat on the desk in front of him. Because there was no blotter but a mouse pad, one hand hit wood and the other fabric. The sound Siplowitz had probably intended came out as part sharp report and part splat.

"That's it," he announced. "You have crossed the line. Please leave my office immediately or I'll call building security and have you removed."

Ms. Washburn's expression indicated that we were trapped in a room with a dangerous lunatic. She stood.

I did not. "This building probably has only one security guard, and I doubt he or she is armed," I said. "That would not be a very credible threat, even if we were violent or in some way dangerous, which we are not. We are merely asking about photographs. Do you have them?"

"Out!" he shouted. "Maggie!"

Perhaps he thought his secretary was the security detail he'd mentioned. "Ms. Caruso is your assistant," I reminded him.

This seemed to baffle Siplowitz; he stopped, his expression changing from furious to incredulous. "I *know*," he said.

Maggie appeared in the doorway looking alarmed. "Is something wrong?" she asked.

Siplowitz made a clear decision to return to his apoplectic state. "These people are threatening me!" he exclaimed. "Have security remove them!"

I saw no point in continuing this discussion. "We are doing nothing of the kind," I said for the benefit of Maggie and her employer.

"But if you are this disturbed by our presence, we will certainly leave now. I have just one last question for you, Mr. Siplowitz."

The attorney's voice dropped to a growl. "What is it?"

"What did the bed and breakfast serve on the crépes?"

"Blackberries," Siplowitz said. "And they were delicious."

We left.

SIXTEEN

It was now too late to set out for Darien, Connecticut, so Ms. Washburn apologized for suggesting the time-consuming detour to New Brunswick. But I told her on the drive to Questions Answered that our decision to meet Roger Siplowitz had probably provided more information about the question than the photographs of Oliver Lewis's wedding could have.

"Really? I didn't see how we got any information out of that stuffed shirt." I did not comment on the expression she'd used, but it has always been a source of some amusement to me. I tend to picture a shirt overflowing with the kind of stuffing served with roast turkey at Thanksgiving dinner when Mother invites our small coterie of family and one or two friends of hers.

Perhaps this year I would invite Ms. Washburn and her husband. But it was possible Simon Taylor would not be amenable to visiting with me, as he believed she should not work for Questions Answered. Or perhaps they had some family obligation of their own for the holiday. It would be difficult to know whether such an invitation would cause Ms. Washburn more difficulty than pleasure. Social interactions are difficult.

"Samuel," I heard her say. "You're drifting."

I refocused my attention on the matter at hand. "My apologies," I told Ms. Washburn. "Sometimes my thoughts do wander." She nodded. "We must concentrate on finding Cynthia Maholm."

"I asked how we'd gotten more information out of Siplowitz than we could have from the wedding pictures," she reminded me.

"So you did. The fact is, Mr. Siplowitz, with his abrupt dismissal of us after we dared to ask about the wedding photographs, specifically *his* wedding photographs, indicates that there is indeed something being hidden, and that something might be visible in the official images taken by the justice of the peace. He would know we could go to Darien and get those. He was more concerned that we not see the photographs he took himself."

Ms. Washburn's mouth twitched, not involuntarily. She was considering. "So how do we get to see them?"

"That is a question we will have to tackle at a later time, although I have some ideas. First, there is finding Cynthia Maholm."

We arrived at Questions Answered three minutes later. Unlocking the door is something I do quite carefully during a normal week, but after having had a cadaver deposited on my floor, I was even more diligent about seeing that the office was secure. I saw Ms. Washburn fall back a bit, waiting for me to admit us, but also being more reticent about coming inside until I had turned on the light and determined nothing had been tampered with.

"It's quite safe," I said as we entered.

"I know."

I had decided, since Ms. Washburn had returned to Questions Answered, that her natural talents were plentiful, but she could be aided by understanding and applying my own methods of answering questions. She was already quite a useful member of the team, but with training, she could do much more than simply drive me from location to location and smooth out some of the more difficult moments my Asperger's Syndrome engenders.

As I turned on my Mac Pro, I asked her, "What do you think the best method would be to find Ms. Maholm?"

Ms. Washburn did not engage in a pointless conversation about the reasons I would ask her a procedural question when I clearly had a plan in place already. She immediately answered, "There's no point to going back to the apartment; she had clearly moved out. And there's no sense in seeing if she left a forwarding address with the landlord. She's probably paid up through the end of the month and hasn't informed the owner she's left."

I nodded. "Very good. So?"

"If it were me, I'd see if I could find a friend or relative, someone who knew her well before the marriage to Oliver Lewis, and see where she'd go. She either has enough money to stay hidden in hotels indefinitely, which would require lots of fake IDs, or she has someone who's willing to put her up."

I applauded. "Excellent, Ms. Washburn. Truly. Very insightful."

"So how'd I screw it up?"

Her suspicion baffled me. "Why do you think you've made an error? Have I given you the impression you were not competent at what you do?" I asked.

Ms. Washburn shook her head. "Never. But you're always smarter than me."

"I am not, necessarily. But even if I am, you are certainly capable of analyzing a situation and finding the aspects of it that I will miss." The Mac Pro had booted up, so I began my search.

"Did I do that just now?" Ms. Washburn asked.

"No."

Ms. Washburn sat down with a look on her face that I could not interpret. She pulled her cellular phone from her pocket and pushed buttons on it.

While Ms. Washburn had indeed hit several relevant points in her analysis and come to a few conclusions I had reached myself when we were standing in the empty apartment of Cynthia Maholm, she had not completely focused on the solution I felt was most promising in our current difficulty.

"I am attempting—" I began.

Ms. Washburn put a finger to her lips. "Shhh."

"Ms. Washburn, I wanted to explain."

She repeated the gesture and the sound. I determined this was something I would not comprehend intuitively, and therefore could not currently analyze. So I returned to my Internet research.

Ms. Washburn had been correct: No matter what Cynthia Maholm's plan had been, whether she was involved in the death of Oliver Lewis or not, she had vacated the apartment that had been her home for at least six months and was now in need of at least temporary accommodations.

It was possible that whatever activity had produced this condition might have involved a large sum of money, although there was no evidence of that yet. But people rarely created such hectic and disruptive conditions in their own lives without a motivation of either a romantic nature or a financial one, the latter being more likely in most cases.

So if Cynthia was indeed now out of her home, with some extra funding or not, she needed a place to stay. And it was most likely that a woman her age, if she were not immediately involved with a man to follow her deceased husband, would rely on family for her housing.

If it were me, which it would never be, I knew where I would go. So I was searching for some information about Cynthia Maholm's parents.

There was little on the most common search engines about Cynthia. But she had graduated from Teaneck High School, according to her Facebook profile, and that would indicate that her family had resided in that town for a while at least.

A look into online telephone directories—there are some that require no payment, but most do; you have to know where to look—indicated there were three listings for people named Maholm in Teaneck at this moment. Marcus Maholm was, I discovered with some research, a ninety-three-year-old retired college professor, unlikely to be the father of a woman in her thirties. It was true that he could be Cynthia's grandfather, but that was a secondary possibility to be explored only if a primary candidate—a possible parent—could not be located.

I concentrated my research, then, on the other two listings under the name. It took very little time to eliminate the first, which was Maholm Auto Repair. Even if one of Cynthia's parents was the proprietor, it was extremely unlikely that she would be living on the premises.

The next, however, held some promise, although it was hardly a certainty. The listing was for L. Maholm on Edgemont Terrace. I glanced up at Ms. Washburn, who was still manipulating the screen on her cellular phone, wondered just for a moment about that, and then continued searching for an L. Maholm at the address in Teaneck.

Certainly it would have been possible to simply call the number listed next to that name on the directory, but the telephone presents a plethora of uncomfortable possibilities for someone with Asperger's Syndrome, at least in my case. Even considering my challenges with reading facial expressions, it is more difficult to read tone of voice without the help of a visual cue that might help determine meaning. Calling someone I had never met to ask if he or she was Cynthia Maholm's parent was not a scenario I relished.

Perhaps I could ask Ms. Washburn to make the call, but she seemed quite engrossed in the activity on her cellular phone. So I began searching a number of reliable websites that offer information about people given the amount of information one has at one's disposal. There are some issues with privacy, but not many, as I was not attempting to discover L. Maholm's buying habits or browsing history (although that certainly could be made possible—the Internet is not at all a secure instrument for those who have information they'd care not to divulge involuntarily).

It took another twenty minutes, but I believed I was closing in on the mysterious L. Maholm. I had narrowed down the possibilities regarding the person's first name to Landon Maholm, who it did not appear had lived in Teaneck but had resided at one time in neighboring Leonia. The other, more likely candidate was…

"Louise Maholm," Ms. Washburn said, still staring at the screen of her cellular phone. "She is fifty-two years old, divorced, working at a branch of Valley National Bank as a bookkeeper. And she has a daughter whose name begins with a C."

I nodded at my associate. "Very good, Ms. Washburn. Is the daughter Cynthia Maholm?"

Ms. Washburn contorted her face on the right side to indicate she couldn't be sure. "She's referred to as Cyndee, so I'm guessing it is, but you never know."

"Excellent work. How did you find her?"

"Through a site called alums.com," she answered. "They help people organize class reunions, and Louise attended her thirty-fifth late last year."

I checked the time on my Mac Pro; it was after five p.m. "It is probably too late to begin a fact-finding trip to Teaneck now," I said.

"You bet. I told Simon I'd be home by six, and I intend to be. After spending part of yesterday in jail and then having to answer questions about a dead body, I'm making sure I'm home on time for dinner."

It was all reasonable from Ms. Washburn's point of view, but to me the question we were asked to answer was all I could consider. "Do you have time to make one telephone call?" I asked.

Ms. Washburn's eyes narrowed. "Louise Maholm?"

"Precisely."

"I can do that," she said. "But is it wise to warn her that we might suspect her daughter is staying with her, but we can't come to find out until tomorrow?"

It was a very logical thought process, but I found myself feeling frustrated and impatient. "I would not call that wise, no," I said through unintentionally clenched teeth.

"All right then, Samuel," she said with a cheerful lilt in her voice. "Let's drive you home so I can go home."

I let out my breath. "You go ahead," I said. "I will email my friend Mike the taxi driver, and he will take me home at six forty, when I normally leave."

Ms. Washburn paused a moment, nodded and stood up. "Okay, then. Good night, Samuel." She left with an expression on her face I did not recognize. I wondered if I looked into a mirror whether I would recognize the one on mine.

I spent the next eighty minutes attempting to find Jenny LeB-lanc, the friend the ersatz Ms. McInerney had mentioned as the hostess of the party at which she claimed to have met Oliver Lewis—an assertion we now knew was a lie. While easier to locate than Louise Maholm, Jenny's contact information was not a simple search, as she appeared to have moved several times in the past two years. She was, if the information I had unearthed could be trusted, now living in Fords, New Jersey, not far from where I was sitting at the moment.

I contacted Mike the taxi driver, who said he would be by shortly to pick me up for the ride home. I emailed him on his cellular phone that I would appreciate the ride, but that I was not quite ready to go home. "If you don't mind, I'd like to go to Fords," I typed.

In thirty-eight seconds the reply came back: "Wherever you want, Samuel."

I called Mother and told her I would be a little late for dinner.

SEVENTEEN

"This does not look like a criminal mastermind's house," Mike said.

Mike is a large man who began driving a taxicab after returning home from military service in Afghanistan, he told me. "I'm not comfortable staying in one place all day," he had said the day we met. Mike's favorite Beatles song is "Two Of Us," whose lyrics are about being on a long road and having the pleasure of another person's company, something I have always strained to understand. I found it especially interesting, since one would expect that a taxicab driver's favorite would be "Drive My Car."

I had met Mike two years earlier at Newark Liberty International Airport, after having dropped Mother off for a flight to Colorado Springs where she was going to visit her sister Aunt Jane. She had insisted on my seeing her off, despite the security measures that would not allow me past the outermost areas of the airport. I had suggested she merely call me when she arrived in Colorado Springs, but Mother can sometimes be unreasonable about such things.

She had handed me one hundred dollars in cash—this was two years ago, before I began to earn a living at Questions Answered—and suggested I take a taxi home to Piscataway. (We had parked Mother's car in what I had determined was the most economical long-term lot at the airport.) It was not my favorite idea; I do not care for taxicabs, or at least did not until I met Mike. The thought of all the people who had sat in the back of the car where I was seated made me feel ill.

I stood in the line for cabs at the designated spot outside the terminal and allowed six parties to pass me and get into a car. Each one had looked so unspeakably *used* that I had not been physically able to open the door.

Finally, a yellow Prius emblazoned with the insignia *Military Transport* drove up. The car was clearly new; it gleamed on the outside and my inspection of the inside found it to be spotless. It was against my better nature, but I got inside and closed the door.

I gave the driver my address and he turned to look at me. His large, expressive face (so much so that I have never had trouble interpreting Mike's signals) seemed concerned. "That's not a cheap fare," he said. "That's about sixty dollars."

"I have one hundred," I volunteered, and showed him the five twenty-dollar bills to prove my honesty.

The driver laughed. "Put those away, man," he said. "Don't go showing your money to everyone you meet."

"I didn't. I showed it only to you. Can you take me to Piscataway?"

"Yes, I can. I'm Mike."

"Allow me to introduce myself. I am Samuel Hoenig."

He laughed again. I was not aware I'd said something humorous. "Nice to meet you, Samuel. Buckle up and enjoy the ride."

I thought it unlikely I would enjoy the experience, but knew it was best not to mention that. While driving, Mike told me I was his first passenger, which explained why the cab was so neat. And he went on to tell me of his military experiences. Normally I find such stories—those that people volunteer about themselves—less than

131

interesting, but Mike has a very easy manner. I have, since that day, called him whenever I needed a ride and Mother or Ms. Washburn could not provide one. He has always come from his base in New Brunswick to help me.

Now he was looking concerned again. "You sure you want to just bust into someone's house like this?"

The house in question, belonging (according to the records I had found online) to a Ms. Jennifer E. LeBlanc, did not look especially imposing. It was a Cape Cod style with expanded dormers on the second floor, blue, with a brick facing on the lower half of the exterior.

"I am not going to break into the house," I assured him. "I am going to ring the doorbell."

"Yeah, but you didn't call and tell them you were coming," Mike reminded me, which was unnecessary.

"I did not want Ms. LeBlanc to panic and flee if she is indeed harboring her friend Cynthia Maholm." I had told Mike about the question I was considering as he drove me here.

"Still seems rude." That worried me, because I often am not aware when I am doing something considered impolite. I spend a great deal of time pondering this issue.

There was nothing else to do, though. Mike parked the car across the street from Ms. LeBlanc's residence and I got out of the back seat, which he kept very nearly as spotless as the first time I'd sat in it. Mike is a very professional taxicab driver.

"You want me to have your back?" he asked through his window as I checked for traffic and began across the street.

"My back?"

"Do you need me to back you up?" Mike attempted.

"Shouldn't I be going forward?" I asked.

"Forget I said anything." Mike shook his head just a bit.

I thought it unlikely I would forget, but continued across the street. I climbed the three steps to the front door and rang the doorbell, as I had told Mike I planned to do. I turned and could see him watching me from the driver's seat of the taxicab.

He looked concerned.

After six seconds, the porch light came on and I heard the dead bolt in the front door open. A tall woman with red hair, wearing jeans, a short-sleeved shirt, and a knitted shawl around her shoulders, opened the door and looked at me. "Aren't you kind of old for NJ PIRG?" she asked, referring to the New Jersey Public Interest Research Group, which often employs college students to canvass neighborhoods during the summer.

I introduced myself and asked if she was indeed Ms. LeBlanc. "Who wants to know?" she asked.

This was confusing, as I had just introduced myself. I decided she must mean that I should explain why I was asking the question. "I am researching a question that involves a Ms. Cynthia Maholm, and I have some evidence that she is a friend of yours," I said.

The woman's face hardened at the mention of my former client's real name. "You a cop?" she asked.

I reiterated that I was the proprietor of Questions Answered and not a member of any police force. "I am here because Ms. Maholm appears to have left her apartment abruptly, and I still have a report to make to her."

"And you thought she might be here?" The woman, who I decided was indeed Ms. LeBlanc, looked suspicious.

"Yes," I told her.

"Well, she's not."

That was not a very detailed denial, nor a particularly convincing one. "If she is not, are you able to give me some indication of where she might have gone?"

Although I was not directing my attention toward him, I saw Mike watching me from what Mother calls "the corner of my eye." Eyes, being round objects, do not have corners. Mike was, however, almost at the limit of my peripheral vision, so I had to focus to see what he was doing. He was pointing to my right, and to the right of the doorway in which Ms. LeBlanc and I were standing.

I tried not to be obvious about my glance in that direction. Working very carefully not to turn my head abruptly, I broke eye contact with Ms. LeBlanc, which was not at all difficult for me, as she said, "No. I have no idea where she is. Sorry."

Turning my head down, as if dejected, gave me the opportunity to turn it in the direction Mike had indicated. There, through the window one room removed from the doorway, was the figure of a woman on the curtains.

"But you *are* Jennifer LeBlanc, are you not?" I asked, simply because I did not want my hostess to terminate the conversation.

There was a pause. The woman behind the far curtain moved away from the window. I could not get a clear view of her, but I was almost certain she was not Cynthia Maholm.

"Look, pal," the woman in the doorway said. "You come barging into my house in the middle of the night asking questions, I'm not telling you anything. Get it through your head, okay?"

So many thoughts were flooding my brain I did not know which one should be addressed first. I had not barged into her home; the fact was, I was still outside and it was getting slightly chilly on the porch. Second, it was odd that Mike had used very similar language before we had arrived, suggesting that I meant to "bust into" Ms. LeBlanc's home when I had no such intention. Third, it was hardly the middle of the night. Before seven p.m. could barely be considered even late evening. And there was the image of getting something through my head, which is in common usage, but always sounds like it would be painful.

But mostly, I was concerned about the other woman in the house with Ms. LeBlanc. Who was she, and what was it the woman in the doorway was trying to hide?

Diplomacy, of course, is not my strongest talent, but I had to make an attempt to keep the lines of communication open. "My apologies, Ms. LeBlanc," I said, and waited for two seconds to allow her time to correct me. She did not. "It was not my intention to upset you in any way. I have a neurological disorder that makes it difficult for me to terminate a contract or an obligation before it is fulfilled. Ms. Maholm contracted with me to answer her question, and until I am able to do so to her satisfaction, I will be forced to keep searching for her to the exclusion of sleep or nourishment." Most people with little knowledge of Asperger's Syndrome—which I had not named aloud—do not understand its "symptoms," which I consider personality traits. Sometimes, invoking the existence of such a "condition" makes people less suspicious of my motives, I had observed.

Indeed, that appeared to be the case now. Ms. LeBlanc, mouth slightly agape, took a step back. "I'm sorry," she said. "I had no idea."

I did not point out that there was no reason she should have had any idea, particularly about something I had grossly exaggerated. I did my best not to smile at the positive effect my ploy had created.

"It's all right," I insisted. "May I come in for just a minute, please? It is getting a little cold out here."

She pulled the shawl a little more tightly around her shoulders. This was also a good sign. But her look over her own left shoulder, an indication she was worried about the other woman in her house, was not.

"This really isn't a very good time," she said.

"I don't mean to trouble you. But it would be a great help if I could use your restroom." I had no intention of using a bathroom in a strange house, but I could certainly pretend to do so convincingly if it would get me inside the house.

Ms. LeBlanc's mouth twitched a little. "I suppose you can come in," she said, her voice louder, no doubt a signal to the clandestine guest. "Go ahead. It's the second door on the left." She took a step back, allowing me in but blocking access to the room in which I had seen the woman in the window.

"Thank you," I said as I stepped inside. I did not attempt to push past her and reveal her comrade, who must have gotten the message and moved away from the entrance hall. She was not visible in the room, clearly a dining room, where I'd seen her before. "I'll just be a moment."

I walked to the door she had indicated and went inside the bath-room, really a powder room in real estate parlance. I glanced at Ms. LeBlanc as I closed the door, and she was looking away from me, toward the dining room. Her other guest was obviously still there, out of sight.

Luckily, the powder room was equipped with an exhaust fan. I took the handkerchief out of my pocket and flipped the switch to ac-tivate it, creating some mechanical noise to cover anything I might do while formulating a plan. Then I opened the medicine cabinet, but it contained no prescription medications on which I might find a name I might have known or one I had not. This room was not meant to be the main bathroom. I had no idea if Ms. LeBlanc lived alone.

I considered asking for a glass of water when I left the room, but there was a plastic cup on the sink in the powder room. More daunt-ing, if my hostess was feeling contrite and decided to give me some water in one of her glasses, I would be required to drink it, and I did not know Ms. LeBlanc well enough to do that.

Another plan of action was clearly needed. The only reasonable thing was to be dogged and refuse to leave until Ms. LeBlanc identi-fied the other woman, who must have some connection to Cynthia

Maholm, and explain what she knew and where I might find the woman who had hired, then deceived, then betrayed me. The aggressive approach, no matter how unnatural it was to my nature, was the best chance for progress under these circumstances.

I used my handkerchief, which would have to be laundered after tonight, to activate the flush lever on the toilet, feeling somewhat guilty about wasting the water, then actually did wash my hands and dry them, reluctantly, on a small hand towel left on the vanity. I repeated the action on the switches for the light and the exhaust fan, opening the bathroom door armed with my new aggressive approach.

That was somewhat dampened by the sight I took in upon exiting the bathroom: Less than eight feet away, standing in the corridor I'd walked from the main entrance, was the woman I assumed was Jennifer LeBlanc.

I did not employ the aggressive approach with her because she had a handgun trained on me.

My first thought was, "I'm certainly glad Ms. Washburn is not here."

EIGHTEEN

"Now tell me who you really are." Jennifer LeBlanc held the handgun very steadily in her left hand. There was no trace of emotion in her voice and no sign of the other woman I'd seen in the hallway behind her.

"I am who I said I am," I responded. "I am Samuel Hoenig of Questions Answered, and I am looking for your friend Cynthia Maholm."

"No, you're not." She took a step closer, but I did not raise my hands in the air as people do on television or in films. I had not been instructed to do so, and knew I had no weapon concealed on my person. "You're a cop or a detective or something and you think you can use Cindy's name to get in here. Now think really hard because this is the last time I'll ask you: Who are you?"

"I am Samuel Hoenig." There was no alternate answer because I *am* Samuel Hoenig. "I don't understand why you are threatening me."

From behind Ms. LeBlanc came a smaller, lighter voice. "I believe him, Jen."

The woman with the gun flinched, then seemed to remember she was supposed to be the aggressor and snapped back into her stance, aiming directly at my midsection. "Just stay there," she said slowly.

Louder, to her companion, she added, "Don't come in. I don't want him to see you."

"I have already seen her," I pointed out. "Through the window." I realized shortly after that this might not have been the best strategy. If Ms. LeBlanc did not want me to see her guest and was holding a gun on me, reporting that I'd done so could cause her to become angry. I don't always anticipate the reactions of others in a reliable fashion.

She did not react with fury, however. She simply looked me in the eye, something I worked at maintaining because I have been told it is more difficult to hurt a person when maintaining eye contact (although I don't know why that would make a difference) and said, "So you were looking for her."

"No, I was looking for Cynthia Maholm. If that is not Cynthia, then I am not looking for your friend."

"So it's okay then." The woman from the other room stepped into the hallway behind Ms. LeBlanc. She was younger, perhaps in her late twenties, and smaller, wearing a sundress and speaking in a tone that suggested innocence. "He's not looking for me."

Again, Ms. LeBlanc seemed unnerved by her companion's refusal to treat me like a dangerous invader. She started to turn toward the other woman while holding the gun straight at me. "Don't do that!" she shouted. "You're jeopardizing everything!" She turned her attention back to me.

I decided that if Ms. LeBlanc were going to shoot me, she would have done so by now. I did not move toward her, which could have been seen as threatening, but I let out my breath. "Ms. LeBlanc, you have no reason to disbelieve me. Obviously there is some situation between you and your friend that you wish to keep from the authorities. I am not affiliated with any governmental or criminal justice organization, and I am not looking for anyone but my client,

Cynthia Maholm. So may we please discard the charade that you're about to kill me?"

Perhaps that was the wrong tactic. Ms. LeBlanc's mouth curled into a snarl and her eyes seemed to be searching my body for the right place to aim. "I can't take the chance," she said.

And she pulled back the hammer on the gun.

"Yes, you can," came a voice from behind them. As the two women turned, Mike stepped into the hallway at its connection to the foyer. He was carrying a pump-action shotgun he keeps in his taxicab "in case there's trouble." "If Samuel says he's not a threat to you, he's not," he continued.

Ms. LeBlanc moved just a bit toward him.

"You're going to want to put that down," Mike said. "I have had practice with this thing, and before that I was a marksman for the Army. So you don't want to go up against me with a gun."

"I can't take a chance," Ms. LeBlanc reiterated.

Before she could turn more into Mike's line of fire, I stepped forward and positioned myself between the two, effectively blocking either person with a firearm from using it on the other without hitting me.

"Samuel," Mike said. Clearly, he was the one who would be more reluctant to fire in my direction.

"I believe I can defuse the situation with no one being hurt," I said, although an idea was only now forming in my mind. I turned toward the younger woman and asked, "Is there something I can do to help you?"

"I'm hiding here from my ex-husband," she said. "I need to keep him away from me until my baby is born."

"Amy!" Ms. LeBlanc shouted. "What are you doing?"

"She is telling me her problem," I answered before the young woman, who looked a little confused by Ms. LeBlanc's livid response, could do so. "If I know more, I might be able to help."

"You're not doing *anything*," Ms. LeBlanc insisted. "You're working for him, aren't you?"

"I am working for Cynthia Maholm," I said, which was technically true, in that Ms. Maholm had not terminated our contract. I felt it best not to mention Detective Dickinson on the very slim chance that he was the ex-husband Amy had mentioned. If I were working for him, it would be best now to have what is called "plausible deniability." I added, "But I can certainly help the two of you in this situation if everyone is willing to discuss it calmly."

"Samuel, I want you to duck down right now," said Mike, who was still aiming his shotgun over my shoulder in Ms. LeBlanc's direction. "I don't want to hurt her, but I'm not going back to your mother and tell her I let you get shot."

"Aww..." Amy said. "He has a mother."

She did not seem to be speaking ironically, but the fact is that everyone, at least when starting life, has a mother. The fact that mine was extant, which appeared to be her point, seemed irrelevant.

"I'm not going to duck down," I told Mike. "Because Ms. LeBlanc is not going to shoot me. Are you, Ms. LeBlanc?"

Jennifer LeBlanc was looking at Amy, not at me. She turned at the mention of her name and her face seemed almost surprised by the interruption of her thought. "No," she said, with a tinge to her voice that I believe might have actually been sadness, as if she had been looking forward to shooting me and was now unable to do so. She lowered the gun. "Go ahead. Do what you're gonna do."

I nodded to Mike. "Thank you for the help. Now the ladies and I are going to sit and talk for a bit. Would you prefer to stay or go back to the cab?"

Mike lowered his shotgun but held onto it. "I think I'll stay and hear what everybody has to say," he said. "I'm off the meter."

We went to the kitchen, where Ms. LeBlanc said she and Amy had been before I had arrived. There were indeed two glasses of what appeared to be red wine poured and sitting on the table in the medium-sized room that featured a small table to one side opposite the fairly new appliances. It was not a state-of-the-art facility, but it was definitely serviceable.

"Do you want some wine?" Amy asked. "Mine's just grape juice because I'm pregnant, but you can have the real thing."

Jennifer LeBlanc looked at her companion with an expression that appeared to merge affection with exasperation. "They're here to kill us, Amy," she said in a hoarse voice. "You don't have to give them a drink first."

"We are not here to kill anyone," I said, trying to make my tone sound authoritative, a pursuit in which I believe I was not successful. "We are here to try to make sense of the situation, and then Mike and I are going to leave and you two ladies will go on with your evening. There was never any violent intent on our part until you produced a gun."

"I told you," Amy scolded Ms. LeBlanc.

Her hostess sat down heavily in her chair and took a drink from her glass, which must not have been filled with grape juice. "What do you want?" she asked wearily.

Mike leaned against the counter to the left of the stove, his hand on the shotgun, which he rested on the countertop. He did not grip it, but maintained contact in the event he might need the weapon. He is a very good listener in addition to being an extroverted taxicab driver, so I could rely on him to remember any nuance I might miss.

"As I said, I am here to try to ascertain the whereabouts of Cynthia Maholm," I said. "But I meant it when I said that I would help with any situation you and Amy might be involved with if I can. Do you know where Cynthia is?"

Both women shook their heads. "I haven't heard from Cindy in at least two months," Ms. LeBlanc said. "We're not really close or anything. We just keep tabs on each other when there's a major change in our lives. When I met Amy, *that* was a big change. So after a few weeks I got in touch with Cindy. But like I said, that was a couple of months ago."

Amy, who seemed content to be a spectator, merely nodded in agreement.

"Have you known Cynthia for a long time?" I asked. Perhaps Ms. LeBlanc would have contact information for other old friends who might be more in touch with my erstwhile client than she.

"No, less than a year," she answered. "I didn't meet Cindy until she was already getting married. But I was too late to change her mind."

That must have piqued Mike's interest, because he stood a little straighter and asked, "You tried to talk her out of getting married?"

Both women laughed, seemingly in surprise. "Of course!" Ms. LeBlanc said. "You see someone, even if you don't know them, driving at top speed in the wrong direction on a one-way street, you try to warn them, don't you?"

I believed there was some point I was missing, so I looked at Mike. He shrugged. It was not my Asperger's Syndrome that was making this situation a confusing one. "I don't understand. Please start at the beginning. You say the two of you met only two months ago?" Amy and Ms. LeBlanc seemed like an established couple in my eyes.

"Maybe a little longer," Amy said. Mike looked at her quickly; I think he had forgotten she was in the room. "I had just found out about the baby, and that's when I came to find Jenny. She's been great to me, protecting me, keeping me here in her house."

"You are living here?" I asked.

"Oh yeah. For about four or five weeks now. Jenny said it would be safe."

Ms. LeBlanc's face became stern again. "It was, until you two showed up."

"We bring you no danger, I assure you."

"Even if you didn't mean to, you will," Ms. LeBlanc responded. "Someone's probably following you."

The deliberate vagueness had begun to irritate me. "What is this danger? Who would be coming after you, and why?"

Ms. LeBlanc looked at Amy, who nodded. "Ollie Lewis," she said. "He's definitely looking for Amy, and if you've been in touch with him, he probably has someone watching you. So once you showed up on my doorstep, he'll follow up. You say you weren't looking for Amy, but you've found her, and that's what he wants."

"I can assure you that Oliver Lewis is definitely not following me," I said. "He is dead."

It was a moment in which I made sure to watch Jennifer LeBlanc's reaction to my statement. If she were pretending to be unaware of Oliver Lewis's death, it would be difficult for her to hide that knowledge now. Still, I was no expert, and some people are better at pretending than others, which is why some people are actors.

It was a problem that I could not watch both Ms. LeBlanc and Amy at the same time, because while Ms. LeBlanc's reaction was probably the more relevant, Amy's would most likely be more genuine. Amy seemed to have very little natural ability to deceive.

But I had to admit, Ms. LeBlanc's reaction was quite telling on its own. It was not what I would have expected under any circumstances.

She laughed.

"You're kidding," she said after a moment during which she seemed to collect herself.

"I assure you, I am not. I was one of the people who discovered his body. He is unquestionably deceased."

Ms. LeBlanc looked toward Amy, so my eyes naturally drifted toward the younger woman as well. Amy was not laughing; she looked stricken. Her face was pale, her eyes were wide and her mouth was open, but not emitting sound.

"Oh honey," Jennifer LeBlanc said. "You can't be that upset about this guy. He's not worth your tears." She stood up and walked to Amy, putting her arms around the other woman and patting her shoulders, which shook a little, although Amy did not appear to be weeping. "If it's true, this makes our lives a whole lot easier."

I took a moment to look in Mike's direction. He seemed not to have moved; he was watching the scene with a face that betrayed no emotion at all to me. It was like looking into the eye of a camera. I began to wish I owned a cellular phone, so I could have called Ms. Washburn and asked her to assess the situation. Mike would have an opinion, I knew, when he drove me home, but it might lack the insight my associate brings to such matters.

"I just ... I was afraid of Ollie," Amy said to Ms. LeBlanc. "I didn't hate him. I didn't wish that he would die. What happened?" I could not see her face, as Ms. LeBlanc's embrace had obscured it from my view, but I assumed the question was directed at me.

"Someone murdered him," I said, and suddenly I was able to see Amy again, because Jennifer LeBlanc had stood up stiffly, straight and surprised.

She turned and looked at me. "You're kidding," she repeated, but this time she did not laugh.

I did not understand why she would believe that I had such a macabre sense of humor, but this was the second time she had insisted my report of Oliver Lewis's death was a joke. "I am assuredly not," I told her.

"Expression," Mike mumbled from his corner of the kitchen. I had actually understood that point, but the expression itself made little sense. Telling someone he or she is kidding is ridiculous; of course the person would know if what was being said was meant to amuse.

"Who did it?" Ms. LeBlanc asked.

"I do not know," I said. "But I have been contracted to answer that question."

"Cindy Maholm hired you to find out who killed Ollie?" Ms. LeBlanc said. "That doesn't sound like Cindy."

"It was not," I explained. "Another party asked me to look into that question."

To her credit, Ms. LeBlanc did not ask the identity of my second client. "That's not what you said when you came in," she said. "You said Cindy had asked you to answer a question."

"She did," I assured her. "But it was not that question. I have not seen Ms. Maholm since before Mr. Lewis died."

"Oh my god," Amy said, seemingly to Ms. LeBlanc. "Do you think Cindy killed him?"

I did not respond, since that question was not aimed at me. But it did open some interesting possibilities, and established a connection I had not previously known to exist. "Do you also know Cynthia Maholm?" I asked Amy.

"Oh, yeah," came the answer. "She's also a wool."

I looked at Mike to see if this was an expression I should have been familiar with, but he shrugged and shook his head. "A wool?" I repeated.

Jennifer LeBlanc looked somewhat sharply in Amy's direction, but the younger woman did not notice or chose not to take the expression into account. "A WOOL," she said, as if it were obvious and she could not understand why I seemed confused. "A Wife Of Oliver Lewis. Like Jenny and me."

146

NINETEEN

It took quite some time—fifty-seven minutes—to sort out the story. Apparently Hazel Montrose had not been accurate nor honest in her accounting of Oliver Lewis's wives. Besides herself and Cynthia Maholm, there had been three more women who had married, and divorced, the dead man.

"We all got to know each other," Amy Stanhope said after a series of rebukes from Jennifer LeBlanc that she was divulging privileged information. Ms. Stanhope had countered with the idea that since Mr. Lewis was dead, there was no harm in revealing the small subclass of women belonging to the exclusive club they had named WOOL. "Jenny started it. She tried to reach out to Rachel—that's Rachel Vandross, Ollie's second wife—to try to warn her about him. But Rachel had already married Ollie, and then there was Hazel, and then there was me, and then there was Cindy... well, you know how that went. We all got together. But you had to be divorced from Ollie to join WOOL, and Cindy was still married to him, so she couldn't come and hang with us." She stopped and considered. "I guess now she can. Does a widow count, Jenny?"

Jennifer LeBlanc, with an air of resignation, waved her hands in a gesture of futility. "What the hell. Maybe Cindy offed the bastard and did us all a favor. Sure, she can come and have a glass of wine."

Mike had spent the past three minutes intermittently blinking in what must have been astonishment. He looked at me, then at Ms. LeBlanc, then at Ms. Stanhope, and then at me again. "There were five of you? You all married the same guy and you all divorced him?"

"Not Cindy," Ms. Stanhope reminded him.

Ms. LeBlanc ignored Mike's confusion and went on. "That's the kind of guy Ollie is—was," she said. "You actually needed a support group after he was done with you. He'd make you feel like the center of the universe, and then he'd leave you by the side of the road without so much as a toothbrush."

The information was coming at me quickly. "Why would he not allow you a toothbrush?" I asked.

"I didn't mean it *literally.*" But I continued to muse over the concept of a figurative toothbrush for a few moments.

When I could focus again, Ms. Stanhope was saying, "It wasn't a regular thing. Like, there weren't WOOL meetings or anything. We just kept in touch and we'd get together for a drink or coffee or something. Not all of us at the same time ever, I don't think. Whoever happened to be around and need some cheering up or whatever, you know?"

"When was the last time you saw Oliver Lewis?" I asked.

It was significant that the two women looked at each other before answering. I wondered if it were necessary for them to coordinate the response, to set their story. But I did not suggest that as it would undoubtedly lead to a confrontation about the possibility of a false answer, and that would not be a productive strategy.

"At least a year ago," Ms. LeBlanc said. "Probably longer. After he's done with you, he's done with you."

"Yeah, at least that," Ms. Stanhope concurred.

We all stared a bit in her direction. "You are pregnant by Mr. Lewis?" I asked.

Ms. Stanhope's eyes wandered up and to the right; she was thinking. "Oh, yeah. So I saw him maybe four months ago. But that was the last time."

At that point I had a decision to make. Calling out Ms. Stanhope on the obvious lie could lead to her confessing the truth, but if Ms. Washburn were here, she would probably say it might alienate Ms. LeBlanc and that would be the price to pay. However, letting the statement go without any expression of skepticism might convince the two women that I was gullible and therefore easily manipulated.

It was hard to make the choice without Ms. Washburn's advice.

"What were the circumstances under which you saw your ex-husband four months ago?" I asked Ms. Stanhope. The question did not betray any disbelief in her statement, and I took pains to say it with the least inflection I could offer. I don't always know when my tone communicates some unintended emotion.

Again, Ms. Stanhope looked to Ms. LeBlanc, presumably for some signal that would convey a possible response, but her compatriot was looking at me, and probably could not have communicated the thought anyway.

"Um ... we had sex," Ms. Stanhope said.

Mike stifled a laugh behind me.

"Did you meet often for that purpose?" I asked.

Her face seemed tense. "No. Just that once," she said.

"So your ex-husband, who you knew had frequently married and left women when he tired of them, left you, but at some point you and he reunited one time to have intercourse?" I confess I would have preferred another word at the end of the question, but could think of none at the time. Given a few more minutes, I might have said, "an intimate encounter."

"I think that's enough," M. LeBlanc said as Ms. Stanhope's eyes pleaded with her for relief. "We've told you everything you're going to find out here. It's everything we know. We had no idea Ollie was dead, so we can't help you with that. And we don't know where Cindy is, so we can't help you with *that*. I'm not going to shoot you and your pal here isn't going to shoot us. So what do you say we call it a night?"

"Yes," Ms. Stanhope concurred. "Go back home and see your mom."

At the mention of Mother, my instinct had me look at Mike, who knew what I was thinking. "It's close to nine," he said.

"I must be going," I told the women. "I am late for dinner."

"No kidding," Ms. LeBlanc agreed.

———

Mother was not upset when I walked through the back door into our kitchen. "I knew you were with Mike," she said. "I was sure nothing bad would happen."

Mike had, as was his custom, dropped me off in the driveway and then driven home himself. He thanked me for "an interesting evening," and was grinning and shaking his head as he backed out of the driveway. I did not have the time to ask him why he was doing that.

Mother opened the oven door and reached in with a potholder. "The plate is very hot, so be careful," she said, removing a heavy ceramic oblong plate with slices of turkey breast separated neatly from a baked potato and green beans. "You must be starving."

I knew she did not mean that I was in danger of having my body attempt to nourish itself on its own tissue, so I did not correct her. Besides, I was quite hungry and sat down at the table to eat.

"Janet called twice while you were out," Mother said. "I'm starting to think it wouldn't be an awful thing if you tried getting a cell phone again."

Three years earlier I had acted against my natural impulse and purchased a cellular phone because Mother had been ill and I did not want to be out of touch in the event that she needed me at any moment. But I had lost the phone after two days, and had not replaced it, confident that the same thing would happen again. I do not pay attention to objects when I am engrossed in a question, and I tend to misplace them.

I chose not to address Mother's comment because the idea of carrying such an easily lost item still made me uncomfortable. "What was Ms. Washburn calling about?" I asked her.

"She heard from Detective Dickinson," she answered. "Something about Oliver Lewis's wives."

I knew Mother was usually much more thorough than that, and concluded that she wanted me to return Ms. Washburn's call, but I was not sure about doing so. "It is almost ten," I said. "Do you think I might disturb her?"

"I'm a lot older than her, and I'm not in bed yet," Mother pointed out, although I did not see the correlation between age and bedtime. It was something that Mother understood, I concluded, and not really worth the time to explore at this moment.

I went to the wall phone in the kitchen and dialed Ms. Washburn's number, which I had memorized. I have memorized the telephone number of every person I have ever called, with the exception of some businesses whose computerized services call Questions Answered on occasion to ask if I am a senior citizen in need of medical insurance or a new mother interested in a diaper service. I call them to ask firmly to be taken off their lists of potential clients.

Ms. Washburn answered on the second ring and said I had made the correct choice by calling and had not interrupted anything important at her home. I did not hear Simon Taylor at all, so I assumed he was not in the room, as he might be otherwise telling his wife again what a poor decision it was to resume working with me. I was a bit intimidated by Simon Taylor, despite our never having met.

"Detective Dickinson called before for a progress report," Ms. Washburn told me now.

"It has only been hours since the last time we spoke," I pointed out. "The detective must be unusually anxious about this question."

"He is. When I told him I'd left you after we'd talked to Hazel and then Roger Siplowitz, he asked about Oliver Lewis's other wives. Did you know he had other wives?"

"Yes. Five in all, I believe. I just left two of them in a house in Fords."

There was a silence of four seconds on the other end of the line. "You went to someone's house in Fords?" Ms. Washburn asked. "How did you get there?"

"My friend Mike the taxicab driver took me there. He served as a very adequate backup when one of Mr. Lewis's ex-wives was holding a gun on me."

Mother's head turned sharply toward me, and she and Ms. Washburn chorused at the same instant, "Samuel!"

"No shots were fired," I pointed out, and told Ms. Washburn— and by extension, Mother—the entire story of my visit with Jennifer LeBlanc and Amy Stanhope. I did not leave out any details, since the one that Mother (and, it appeared, Ms. Washburn) would find most disturbing was the one I had mentioned first.

"What did the detective say besides pointing out Mr. Lewis's rather colorful marital history?" I asked Ms. Washburn when my tale had been completed.

"He mostly grumbled about doing more work on this case—his words, not mine, Samuel—than we are," was her reply. "It's very strange to me that he hired us on this question when he seems to be doing the same things we're doing. Why would he pay for that when he can do it himself?"

"Only one of many contradictions and puzzlements surrounding this question," I agreed. "I wonder if Detective Esteban is really the one doing the work for the Piscataway police department, and our client is merely reporting what she has accomplished as if it were the fruit of his own labors."

"Good question," Mother said. I had forgotten about the dinner she had served for me, and looked at it. I realized I was hungry.

"Well, thank you for the report," I told Ms. Washburn. "I believe I will eat some turkey now."

"Hang on, Samuel," she said. "There was one more thing the detective said that I think you need to know."

"What is that?" I was focusing on the food and had to force myself to pay attention to the voice on the telephone, which now seemed more disembodied because my mind was elsewhere.

"He said the preliminary report from the medical examiner showed that the cut to the throat was not the cause of Oliver Lewis's death. He said Oliver had also been poisoned with something called Metoclopramide, or Reglan, stabbed in the ribs with a smaller sharp object, possibly a scissor or nail file, and probably suffocated."

That stopped my thinking about the turkey for a moment. "Four causes of death?" I said, mostly thinking aloud.

"Technically, the poison was what did him in. They found it in his stomach, not just in his esophagus, which would indicate it had been swallowed and made it into his bloodstream. The others were either inflicted on him after he was already poisoned or maybe someone cut his throat just before he died. That could have something to do with the relatively small amount of blood found on the scene."

"Indeed. Whoever killed Mr. Lewis was being remarkably thorough."

Mother looked at me with a questioning expression, but said nothing. She considers it rude to speak to someone when he or she is talking on the phone, and knew I would inform her of my findings—or in this case, Ms. Washburn's recitation of the findings from either Detective Dickinson or (more likely in my estimation) Detective Esteban.

"Did the detective say what Reglan is?" I asked. I had no immediate access to my Mac Pro, so I could not do the research now.

"It's a medication for nausea," Ms. Washburn said. "Ironic, no?"

I had no idea if that was ironic; the concept is a difficult one for me. "Nausea. Is it a prescription medication?"

"Yes. It's given for acid reflux, for some diabetics, and for a number of other conditions. How can that kill?"

"An overdose of almost any medication, in sufficient quantity, can be fatal, Ms. Washburn." My dinner was now utmost in my mind; my attention was flagging.

"What do you think we have to do next?" Ms. Washburn asked.

"I have to go eat some turkey," I answered. "I believe you should go to sleep. In the morning, we are going to redouble our efforts to find Cynthia Maholm, and I believe I know how to begin."

"How?" she asked.

"We need to find the address at which Oliver Lewis was living before he married Ms. Maholm. Good night, Ms. Washburn."

"Good night, Samuel," she said.

TWENTY

"I CAN'T BELIEVE WE didn't think of this sooner," Ms. Washburn said.

It was the next morning, and we were at the Middlesex County Clerk's office, inquiring after any public records involving the deceased Oliver Lewis. The woman behind the counter, who had informed us her name was Janice (and that her favorite Beatles song was "I'm Down"), had gone off to retrieve what she had assured us would be "not much. The Freedom of Information Act doesn't mean you can find out everything you want about everybody." And off she'd walked.

"No," Ms. Washburn had said quietly. "We leave that to the NSA."

I had not responded to that comment, but now I said, "The issue was not that we hadn't considered it. The issue was that what we had found out had not yet led us to this. This kind of research is a progression, and each step is necessary to that progression."

Ms. Washburn nodded. "So what got us to this? I'm a couple of steps behind."

Janice was still nowhere in sight, so I had time to answer, "The idea is that there were four ex-wives and one current wife when Mr. Lewis was killed," I said. "Clearly, the apartment we had been led to believe was the home for Ms. Maholm and her husband was simply a staged set. So given that he had done this so many times before and had probably not rented a new home every time led to the conclusion that Mr. Lewis must surely have used his own residence for each marriage."

Ms. Washburn's brows furrowed. "Why didn't you just ask Jennifer or Ms. Stanhope where they lived when they were married?"

I broke eye contact, which I do quite readily when embarrassed. "The atmosphere was not an especially welcoming one," I said.

"I'm sorry I wasn't there."

That took my by surprise, but I did not search Ms. Washburn's face. I trusted my ability to read her tone well enough to know she was not being sarcastic. "You have no reason to be sorry," I said. "You didn't know I was going to Ms. LeBlanc's house."

"Even so. I could call her now and ask, if you like. Did you get the phone number?"

I had memorized Ms. LeBlanc's telephone number when I'd found it online, but did not recite it for Ms. Washburn. "The address is not the only data we are here to collect," I said.

Janice arrived back at the counter at that moment, so Ms. Washburn did not have time to ask me anything else. I was glad because I felt I had diminished in her view somewhat, although she had not communicated that feeling directly, so I was relieved not to continue that conversation.

"This is what you can have," she said. "There's a fee." She deposited a rather thick envelope on the counter.

Ms. Washburn paid the fee with the understanding that I would reimburse the expense in her paycheck. I prefer not to handle cash except when necessary—I will do so when I have to—and also have issues about using a debit or credit card, as they are traceable by unscrupulous individuals who can access one's personal and financial

156

information. And by that I do not mean the kind of public data we were now obtaining about Oliver Lewis.

Ms. Washburn and I left the clerk's office and walked into the corridor where there were a few benches. We sat on one and she opened the envelope we had just purchased.

"You sure you don't want to take this back to Questions Answered?" she asked as she pulled out copies of various county documents.

"If this information leads us to an address—and I believe it will—going back to the office would only waste valuable time. What is included here?"

Ms. Washburn, who had no qualms about handling the documents, scanned the top few. "There's an application to register a business with the county," she said.

"Excellent. That should have all the personal information we need, and it adds the data about the business. What kind of establishment was Mr. Lewis registering?"

"Hang on. I've read halfway through the description and I still don't know." Ms. Washburn scanned the one-page document. "There are only two lines to describe the business and Lewis went on for six. He wrote really small too."

"Please read it to me," I said, being careful to include the *please*.

She read, "OLimited will provide its clientele with financial and practical life advice and products generated by multiple suppliers in an effort to increase wealth, generate retirement income, and insure against long-term health care necessities."

"That is certainly a convoluted sentence, but—"

"Wait, there's more. 'Clients will provide some initial seed sources in an effort to multiply opportunities through prudent and bold investments, fiduciary products, and insurance options to diversify portfolio and ensure a secure future.' What do you think that means?" Ms. Washburn asked.

"That he was trying to cheat old people," I said. "Does he list a business address?"

"It's in Milltown," she answered.

"Near Questions Answered. Very convenient."

Within minutes, we were in Ms. Washburn's car heading toward Oliver Lewis's reported place of business. As usual, Ms. Washburn was attending completely to the road, but we continued to speculate (something I usually prefer to avoid doing, but which sometimes allows me to consider the facts I have in my possession in new and fruitful ways) on the information in Lewis's file.

"He listed a home address and a business address," Ms. Washburn reminded me. "Why go to the business first?"

"If I am correct in my assumptions, it makes more sense to go to Mr. Lewis's business first because that is most likely the place in which he was killed," I explained. "I think the apartment we were led to by Ms. Maholm was simply a stage and that even when they were married, neither Mr. Lewis nor Ms. Maholm lived there. So it is highly possible they were living in Mr. Lewis's residence."

"So why do you think he wasn't killed at home?" We were four minutes from our destination, located above a bakery on Main Street in Milltown.

"Because I think Ms. Maholm is still living in the residence, and it seems, although we cannot confirm it, that she was involved in the killing. She would not want to leave evidence in her home because it could be easily tied to her."

"If Oliver Lewis was murdered in his office, wouldn't someone have noticed something at the scene? Co-workers, secretaries, janitors, somebody?" Ms. Washburn was going through the same thought process I had employed in reaching this conclusion; she is very intelligent.

"Not if it is the kind of office I presume it to be," I said.

The building was a two-story commercial structure boasting a sign on its street-level story for a "classic Italian bakery" at which there was currently a fairly robust business. Ms. Washburn parked the car across the street and we walked to the entrance.

"This isn't Oliver's office," Ms. Washburn said. "It was supposed to be upstairs. There must be another door somewhere."

We walked around the building to the back, where indeed there was a wooden door with a window and a mailbox that bore the legend ITALIANO's/OLIMITED. I looked at Ms. Washburn, who shrugged.

"You didn't expect it would be luxurious, did you?" she asked.

"On the contrary. This is precisely what I had anticipated. I was waiting for you to open the door." I did not have a pair of latex surgical gloves with me.

Ms. Washburn did as requested, and we walked into the hallway and then, since the form we'd read indicated the office was on the second floor, up a case of rather suspect stairs. We ascended successfully and came to the only door on that level.

It had no identifying mark on it. I hesitated a moment, then nodded at Ms. Washburn, who knocked four times. There was no answer, so I nodded and she knocked again. Still no response.

Ms. Washburn did not ask; she merely reached over and turned the doorknob. The door swung open.

The room inside was the very description of empty. It would have been like the scene at Ms. Maholm's apartment after everything had been removed, except in this room, clearly intended to be used for office space, there was a thick coat of dust on everything. I hesitated before stepping inside.

"It's just dirt, Samuel," Ms. Washburn said. "You know we have to go in."

I nodded. The thought was not a pleasant one, but it was necessary. I waited for Ms. Washburn to lead the way and followed her into the abandoned suite.

"Did Oliver Lewis *ever* have an office here?" Ms. Washburn asked. "He hasn't been dead that long, and it doesn't look like anyone's been here in a while."

"No," I agreed. "You are quite correct. This space was never intended to be a legitimate office for Mr. Lewis or anyone else. It was an address he could use to show a loss for tax purposes, legal ramifications, and in the event a potential client would ask. But I guarantee that if someone would show interest in the 'services' he was offering, Mr. Lewis would arrange to see the client in his or her home or office. He never brought anyone up here."

We wandered about the room, examining the dust and the floorboards, which were almost all the room had to offer visually. The windows had not been cleaned recently, if ever. The walls had last seen a coat of paint in another decade, and possibly not the most recent one. And the room held the quiet and musty smell of a space that had been neglected for quite a while. When we reached a door marked REST-ROOM, I had to gather my thoughts for a total of seventeen seconds.

"I am not going to ask you to look inside," I told Ms. Washburn. "That would overstep the boundaries of the professional relationship we have initiated. But please give me enough time to—"

Ms. Washburn curled her lip and opened the washroom door. She flipped the light switch but seemed mildly surprised when the fixture over the sink illuminated.

"He had to keep the utility company paid so he could claim to have the business here; it would look suspicious otherwise," I explained. "I'm sure the water in there is operational as well." But I was staring at the light fixture in an attempt to avoid looking at anything else in the small room.

"There's nothing scary here, Samuel," Ms. Washburn said. "It's not pleasant to look at, but I don't see anything that looks like violence occurred here."

She had mistaken my revulsion for fear, but I chose not to explain myself. "Remember that it was probably the poison that killed Mr. Lewis, if our information is correct," I said. "There might not be the kind of gore one would expect."

"But the knife wound," she reminded me.

"Probably administered postmortem," I said. "Not much blood flowing through his veins at that point."

"Makes you wonder why they bothered," Ms. Washburn noted. "Look, there's nothing in here." She stepped out of the restroom and we diverted our attention—thankfully—back to the main office space. "There's nothing out here, either."

I scanned the room again to confirm an earlier suspicion. "I think that might be a premature conclusion," I told Ms. Washburn. "Look up in that corner." Without pointing, I indicated the corner where the ceiling met the wall behind the open door. "But be careful about being too obvious about it."

Ms. Washburn's eyes narrowed. She kept her head down, but turned her body as if to confront me more directly, and that allowed her to look up by tilting her head to make it seem she was asking me a question. "Oh," she said.

There was a security camera mounted from the ceiling—one of three I had noted when looking around the room. "The red light is on," I said.

"Well, he never turned the electricity off."

"That is true, but it is not the point. The camera moved when you came out of the restroom, possibly due to motion detection, but I think not. I believe we are being watched right now."

Ms. Washburn made an odd noise in the back of her throat. "You think Oliver Lewis is still alive?" she said quietly.

"Absolutely not. You saw the body, and it was unquestionably him. But someone is still monitoring this office."

"Why would they do that? There's nothing here."

"That is an excellent question," I said. "I do not have an adequate answer at the moment."

"Well, here's another question," she replied. "What should we do now?"

"Leave, I think."

We did not run for the door, but we were not especially leisurely in our pace, either. When we were settled into Ms. Washburn's car, I instructed her to set her Global Positioning System device to the home address Oliver Lewis had listed on his registration form with Middlesex County. After one minute and twelve seconds, we were on our way.

Ms. Washburn was unusually unsettled as she drove; she shifted in her seat a bit and her mouth twitched while she made a left turn. She did not turn her head, but she did initiate a conversation, which was not typical. "If Oliver was really cheating seniors out of their money the way you say, isn't it possible that one of them killed him?"

"It is possible. Almost anything is possible. But it is unlikely. Mr. Lewis was poisoned, his throat was cut, and he had been stabbed and deprived of oxygen, according to the medical examiner. If those things are true, as a healthy man in his thirties, it is not plausible that an older person by himself could have done all four of those things. And even if that were the case, the idea that the killer then felt it necessary to deposit the body in our offices rules out anyone who was not acquainted with Questions Answered."

Ms. Washburn seemed to consider my argument and nodded her head slightly. "Then by that line of reasoning, the only likely suspect is Cynthia Maholm. She's the only person who had reason to be mad at Oliver Lewis and knew Questions Answered at all. She was the one who went out of her way to bring us to the fake apartment and then keep us away while the body could be brought to the office. It has to be her."

I clapped my hands twice. "Very good indeed!" I said. "Excellent reasoning! But there are other suspects who might have killed Mr. Lewis."

She blinked. "Who?"

"Virtually any of his many wives," I answered. "Keep in mind that all the information we have from any of them, even Hazel Montrose, we have only from their own mouths. It was clear from my perspective—and Mike agreed with me—that Ms. LeBlanc and Ms. Stanhope were lying about at least some of the details of their marriages to Mr. Lewis."

"I wasn't there so I don't know," Ms. Washburn said quietly.

I did not respond because I did not know why that information was relevant. "We still have not met with Rachel Vandross, the one ex-wife of whom we have heard the least. And there is the matter of Terry Lambroux, the person who seems to have introduced all these women to Oliver Lewis without any of them ever meeting him or her face to face. Roger Siplowitz does not seem to have a motive to kill Mr. Lewis, but he did indeed put considerable effort into distracting us from the question and threw us out of his office when he saw he could not accomplish that goal."

"That's seven suspects," Ms. Washburn said.

"At the very least. And we might be about to increase our list by at least two."

Ms. Washburn's brow wrinkled as her eyebrows dropped. "How's that?"

"There are two men in a black Sport Utility Vehicle behind your car," I said. "They have been following us since we left Mr. Lewis's office."

TWENTY-ONE

If I had been riding with Mike the taxicab driver, I could have suggested that he try to elude the Sport Utility Vehicle, a 2012 Ford Escape, as soon as I had noticed it matching us turn for turn, activating a turn signal each time a moment after Ms. Washburn had done so on her car. That is because Mike is a professional driver and a military veteran, and has learned some techniques that he says can prove useful under such circumstances.

I had never had to put such a claim to use until now, but unfortunately Mike was not driving the car.

Ms. Washburn's voice was scratchy. "I beg your pardon?"

"We are being followed. No doubt by the people who were watching us search Mr. Lewis's office. Please watch the road."

Ms. Washburn stopped looking deeply into her rearview mirror. "Are you serious? There are two men following us and you want me to just watch the road and keep going?"

"That is the best way to find out who they are and what they want," I said. "Perhaps we should change our destination, however. There is no sense in leading them to Ms. Maholm if indeed she is where we presume her to be. Do you think it is risky to return to Questions Answered now, or should we stop somewhere for a bottle of spring water? And a diet soda for you?" I knew that was her preference.

"This is hardly the time to worry about soft drinks, Samuel! People are following us! If we just stop and let them approach us, how do we know they're not carrying guns or something?"

It was a legitimate point. "It is likely they are armed," I said. "But I doubt they mean us harm, at least not immediately. They are following us to gain information. Simply injuring or killing us in the street will not secure that data for them."

"You're not making me feel better."

Since that had not been my intention, I was not surprised that I wasn't assuaging Ms. Washburn's anxiety. However, now that she had mentioned it, I wondered if I should have been more empathetic about her worries. What could I say now that would accomplish that goal?

"Perhaps they are going to tell us something we need to know."

"What are the odds?" She probably did not really want to know the answer to that question, but I did calculate the probability and determined that the men behind us were highly unlikely to be interested in aiding our answer of the question regarding Mr. Lewis's death.

It occurred to me at that moment that involving Ms. Washburn in any interaction with the two men in the Escape might bring her into contact with considerable danger. Since I had promised to avoid any such scenarios while she was working for Questions Answered, it would be necessary to abandon my plan to confront our pursuers, or to somehow eliminate Ms. Washburn from the situation.

But I could not decide which was the better plan of action.

Ms. Washburn took a quick glance into her rearview mirror again. "What do you think they're hoping to find?" she asked.

"I have no facts on which to base a hypothesis," I said. "But the only thing it seems logical for them to be seeking would be Ms. Maholm's whereabouts."

She bit her lower lip. "Do you think they're cops?"

The possibility had not been one I'd considered. "I doubt it," I said after thinking it over. "Police officers could simply stop us and ask if they thought we knew where their quarry might be hiding. And the fact is that we really don't know at the moment, so we would have no conclusive information to impart."

"They don't know that."

Weighing possibilities and forecasting outcomes, I was quiet for three minutes.

"Where am I driving to?" Ms. Washburn asked again.

Perhaps there was a way to accomplish both goals. "I think our best bet is to go to the nearest coffee shop," I said. "There is one three blocks south of here on the far right corner."

"You sure?"

"Of course I am. I saw it on our way here."

Ms. Washburn's expression indicated I might have misinterpreted her question, but there was no need to explore that reaction now. She appeared to be thinking seriously, but drove to the coffee shop I had indicated, the Escape staying at what the driver clearly believed to be a discreet distance behind Ms. Washburn's Kia Spectra.

The establishment, with a sign reading Viva Java!, was located in a small strip mall of four storefronts not unlike the one where Questions Answered is located. Ms. Washburn parked her car in a space near, but not directly in front of, the shop.

"What's the plan?" she asked.

"It's very simple. I will enter the coffee shop, buy a bottle of spring water and sit at one of the tables. If we are lucky, the two men from the Ford Escape will walk in, realize I am aware they are following us, and sit down to have a conversation. If we are not lucky, the most likely scenario is that they will stay in their vehicle and wait until I come out, at which time I will have to approach them directly and ask about their intentions. Either way, the meeting takes place in public, away from any areas where they might feel safer threatening me."

She waited for three seconds, which is a longer time in a conversation than it might ordinarily be considered. "And what am I doing all that time?" she asked.

"You have a choice. Either you can lie down on the front seat of your car, or you can go inside the coffee shop and stay inside the restroom until I knock on the door four times."

Ms. Washburn squinted at me. "Samuel, I know you have a sense of humor, but this is hardly the time to be joking with me."

"I am doing no such thing. Those are the two options you have open that will ensure you will be in no danger at any time during the encounter. Which would you prefer? We have very little time." The Ford Escape pulled up to a parking space on the street in view of the strip mall's parking lot, but not entering the lot itself. The driver was clever, if not necessarily the most subtle stalker.

"I did not sign on to work with you so I could go hide in the ladies' room, Samuel. What can I do that will help answer the question?"

"Actually, there is something extremely helpful you can do while you hide in the ladies' room," I said. "Call Detective Esteban on your cellular phone and ask her if there were any complaints filed against Oliver Lewis at the time of his death."

"I can do that from the coffee shop too," she said.

"Yes, but then I will be distracted and will not be operating at peak efficiency if the two men in the Escape walk in. Please. Do as I ask." I adjusted the side mirror on Ms. Washburn's Kia to take in the location of the Escape. The two men sat in the front seat.

"All right," Ms. Washburn sighed, "but don't ever ask me to do this again." She got out of the car and without looking in my direction walked into *Viva Java!*

As I had decided to do moments before, I stayed in the Spectra. I watched Ms. Washburn walk into the coffee shop and then immediately shifted my focus to the side mirror.

The two men were getting out of their vehicle and walking toward the shop.

Before they could reach the front door, I got out of the Spectra and stood in their path. "Gentlemen," I said.

Outwardly I believe I was exuding confidence, but inside I was feeling quite the opposite. More so than when Jennifer LeBlanc was pointing a gun at me, I had a sense of danger as the two men stopped and considered me.

One was tall and thin and wearing "skinny" jeans and a gray t-shirt. The other, shorter but also in obvious athletic trim, wore dark trousers and a navy blue polo shirt. Both wore identical New Balance running shoes. I wondered if they shopped for their footwear together.

"We're in a hurry," the shorter one said. "Get out of the way."

I scanned both of them for signs of concealed weapons. There were no bulges in their armpits, where a shoulder holster might be located, or their hips. I decided that if they were carrying weapons, they were either in the men's shoes, hidden by their trouser legs, or were knives.

"I think I am the person you're looking for," I told them. The two men stared at me for a moment, then at each other.

The taller one looked back at me. "You're Janet Washburn?" he asked.

TWENTY-TWO

Now I was the one who was confused. "You have been asked to follow Janet Washburn?" I asked the two men.

"This is none of your business," the shorter one said, and attempted to push past me.

"No. It is indeed my business. I am her employer," I said.

The shorter man stopped. "You're her boss?"

The conversation seemed to be going in a redundant direction. "Please tell me why you have been asked to follow my associate, or I will be compelled to call the police." The fact that Ms. Washburn was, if she were following my instructions, doing exactly that at this moment felt like something I could avoid mentioning.

"Oh, go ahead and call the cops," the shorter man said. "I'd like to see that."

"We don't have to tell you nothing," the taller man said. I understood that his double negative did not indicate he had to tell me something, but it took an effort not to inform him of his error.

"I don't have to not call the police, either," I said, using a double negative properly. "If you do what you don't have to do, I won't do what I don't have to do."

The taller man squinted. "What?"

But the shorter one had grasped my explanation. "Okay. Tell me why I shouldn't just muscle past you now and go talk to your girl-friend, and maybe we can do some business."

The suggestion that Ms. Washburn and I had some sort of romantic relationship slowed my thinking process until I realized that if she were here, Ms. Washburn would have explained that the man was speaking symbolically.

"If your business has anything to do with Oliver Lewis or any of his ex-wives, I am the person you want to talk to. If your business is about Ms. Washburn's personal life, I can assure you I know nothing at all, but will take every step I can to stop you from infringing on her privacy, including calling the police and filing charges against you. If, on the other hand, your business is in some way to help Ms. Washburn, I can assure you I will be glad to assist you in any way I can. Is that clear enough?"

"It's none of your—" the taller man started to say.

"Also, I have achieved a second level black belt in tae kwon do and 'muscling past' me would be considerably more difficult for you than you might have anticipated. If you are carrying concealed weapons and attempt to use them, I have been trained to subdue you and the list of charges I could press would increase. Now please tell me, why have you been asked to follow my associate?"

"It's a collection problem," the shorter man said.

"I sincerely doubt it," I countered. "Lying to me will be extremely difficult. I have a neurological condition that helps me to detect untruths when they are told to me." That was, of course, a lie itself. Asperger's Syndrome (or autism spectrum disorder) does not help anyone separate truth from fiction. If it did, I never would have trusted the woman who identified herself to me as Sheila McInerney. "So please, do not waste any more of our time."

The taller man looked to the shorter one, who seemed to be in charge of their operation. The shorter man drew in a breath and let it out slowly. "All right," he said. "Let's go in and sit down."

As long as Ms. Washburn stayed inside the restroom, that did not seem an unreasonable suggestion. I was sure to follow the two men into the coffee shop rather than turn my back on them.

Once inside, we sat at a booth on the right side of the room. The taller man sat on one side, while the shorter one insisted on boxing me into the booth. I got in first, and he sat to my left.

"We were hired by someone—and I'm not going to tell you who, so don't bother asking—to keep an eye on the office you just left. It's been a real easy job so far because no one ever goes there. So we've been taking our fee for sitting around eating doughnuts and drinking coffee." The shorter man shifted in his seat, which made me uncomfortable.

"That does not explain why you were following Ms. Washburn specifically," I pointed out.

The taller man straightened up, as if pleased that he could answer a question without prompting. "Her name is the one that showed up when we ran the license plate," he said. "Easier to find out stuff from her when we could use her name. We had no idea who you were."

That told me a good deal more than the man had probably intended. "And what was it you were going to ask when you found her?" I said.

"Mostly, we wanted to know what you two were doing in that office, why you'd come there, and what you think you found out," the shorter man said. "How about you share with us now?"

"We had some questions for the man who owned that business," I answered. "We had no idea the space had been abandoned."

"Abandoned," the taller man repeated, as if it were amusing. That helped confirm the suspicion of mine that Oliver Lewis's business was never intended to be a true running concern. If I could get the taller man to not tell me anything for another ten minutes, I might be able to answer the question with very little difficulty.

"What are your names?" I asked the shorter man.

"I have no reason to tell you that," he responded. "And you haven't really answered any questions I've asked you yet. This was supposed to be an exchange. So start exchanging."

"Very well. Ms. Washburn, at my request, drove me to the supposed headquarters of OLimited. We entered the office, found it empty and neglected, and left to pursue other avenues in our business. That is all I can tell you."

"We knew all that already," the taller man said.

"I have no more information than that," I told him. "My apologies if you expected a fuller explanation."

The two men exchanged an unsatisfied look and the shorter one placed his hands flat on the table, bracing himself to stand. "We're not doing each other any good," he said.

"On the contrary. You have told me quite a bit. You are two off-duty police officers who have been hired by one of Oliver Lewis's ex-wives to find out more about his business dealings, perhaps with an eye toward a more favorable settlement in the divorce. I don't know your names, but that hardly seems to matter, since your interest in Ms. Washburn is based strictly on her license plate number, so I have nothing to fear from you. I do regret that I have no further information to pass along to you, but unfortunately, that is the case. Thank you, gentlemen. You may certainly return to your surveillance of the OLimited offices with no fear that Ms. Washburn or I will be back."

"How did you know…" the taller man said. The shorter one, pursing his lips, had not moved from the spot where he had begun to stand.

"Police officers would have access to motor vehicle information like license plate numbers," I said. "And when I mentioned calling the police, you seemed to find that amusing. You believed you would have an advantage in such an encounter because you are a member of the brotherhood, no? You clearly are off-duty, or you would not be driving in a private vehicle—and I know enough about the workings of government to recognize municipal, county, or state markings and numbers—and wearing your personal clothing. It makes sense that anyone who wanted to keep track of Mr. Lewis's offices would have some dealings with one or more of his ex-wives. There was no business partner listed on his incorporation forms, so his ex-wives would be the only ones to benefit from any of his business dealings. And your lack of interest in Ms. Washburn is evident in the fact that you did not notice when she walked by you three minutes ago and left this coffee shop."

Both of the men turned and looked toward the door, which was predictable but pointless, since Ms. Washburn had clearly gone back to her car and was probably now sitting in it waiting for me to return.

The shorter man appeared to be grinding his teeth; this was probably an indication that he did not care to be told about his shortcomings in front of his colleague, or probably under any other circumstances. "You can count on seeing us again, Sherlock," he said.

Before I could point out that the fictional Mr. Holmes would no doubt have deduced a great deal more from the two men's appearance and mannerisms than I had, both of them were gone from the booth and walking toward the door.

I put two crisp dollars in the tip jar on the counter as I followed them out. The young woman behind the counter, who no doubt knew we had not ordered any refreshments, looked up at me with a surprised expression.

"For the use of the booth," I said.

She nodded her thanks, still seeming a little dazed, and I exited the coffee shop.

Ms. Washburn was indeed seated behind the wheel of her car, whose engine was running. The two men were nowhere to be seen, and neither was their Sport Utility Vehicle. I opened the door of Ms. Washburn's Spectra and sat in the passenger seat.

"Detective Esteban was surprised to hear from me," she reported before I could tell her about the encounter with the two officers. "She said she thought we had answered the question we'd been asked and would be done with the situation."

"Obviously it would be an embarrassment and a breach of protocol for Detective Dickinson to tell her he had engaged us," I said, nodding. "It makes sense he would not mention it. Was she still willing to tell you about Oliver Lewis's criminal record?"

Ms. Washburn, knowing it would unnerve me if she were to start driving while we were having this conversation (since it would unquestionably distract her from the road), left the car in park. It would be best if we kept this conference brief in order to relieve the Kia's overtaxed cooling system.

"Yes," Ms. Washburn answered. "But I don't know why. She just seemed helpful. She said there had been an investigation by the county prosecutor's office into Lewis's dealings, but there hadn't been enough evidence found to merit a grand jury indictment. But there were civil cases pending filed by Jennifer LeBlanc and Terry Lambroux."

That was a surprise. "Really!" I said. "What were the specifics of those suits?"

"We'll know better when we get the documents the detective is sending you in an email," she said. "But the Lambroux one was interesting, the detective told me."

"Interesting in what way?"

"It was a lawsuit filed claiming breach of promise," Ms. Washburn answered, a sly grin crossing her face. She had been waiting to tell me this particular fact. "Apparently Oliver Lewis had been engaged to Terry Lambroux and broke it off before the wedding."

TWENTY-THREE

AFTER OUR TRAVELS TODAY, the Questions Answered office felt welcoming and peaceful, I thought. Ms. Washburn, no doubt still especially cognizant of our discovery of Oliver Lewis's body in this room, did not appear to be quite as comforted by our return.

"So I guess this means that Terry Lambroux is a woman," Ms. Washburn said as I took my usual seat behind my desk and she got a bottle of diet soda from the vending machine.

"Not necessarily," I noted. "New Jersey does have marriage equality now. But it would seem likely that Terry is a female, since that has always been Oliver Lewis's orientation as far as we know."

We had decided after some discussion not to seek out Cynthia Maholm at the last known address for her husband, Oliver Lewis. Ms. Washburn had suggested—and I had concurred—that the two men in the Ford Escape might very well be following us more discreetly, and might be trying to find Ms. Maholm as well. Leading them to her would not be an equitable way to answer the question.

"I think it's a safe assumption," Ms. Washburn agreed. "He's been married at least five times we know about, always to a woman."

I had essentially just said the same thing, but I understood that Ms. Washburn was voicing her agreement. I turned my attention to my computer screen, where deep Internet searches for Terry Lambroux continued to come back without any useful information or image.

"I think we have to at least consider the possibility that Terry Lambroux is an alias," I said. "It is extremely rare for a person in our society to exist with no record whatsoever of her life in a file somewhere online."

Ms. Washburn sat down in her traditional spot, to my right and in front of my desk. "So what can be done to determine her real name if there are no records of her anywhere?" She took a sip directly from the bottle of diet soda. I do the same with my spring water, but I clean the mouth of the bottle first with a paper towel. There are some habits Ms. Washburn has—shared by a great many people—that I have to overlook in order to function outside my own room in the attic, Mother tells me.

"There aren't many scenarios that work under these circumstances," I said, musing out loud. "We have to approach the problem from the perspective of our subject."

Ms. Washburn smiled, but I could not read any thought into the expression. I chose not to ask about it, but filed it away in my mind. New facial looks are always interesting to me because they might become useful at some later date. Asking a person I trust, like Mother or Ms. Washburn, why they look a certain way can alleviate my need to do so with a stranger.

"Our subject?" Ms. Washburn said.

"Terry Lambroux. Given our inability to locate Ms. Maholm, we should focus our attention on Terry."

"Why?" my associate asked. "Why not one of the wives or Roger Siplowitz? How do we know Terry is the key?"

"We don't," I said honestly. "But we have met all the ex-wives except Rachel Vandross, and we will rectify that oversight soon enough. The fact that Terry Lambroux chooses—no, takes great pains—to remain unseen is what piques my suspicion. Please, while I am doing some more research on Terry, use your cellular phone to find an address for Rachel Vandross."

Ms. Washburn nodded and produced the instrument in question from a canvas tote bag she carries with her. She was tapping on the touch screen of the device before I could divert my attention back to my own work.

The trick with Terry Lambroux was to find a chink in the armor of the elusive figure who had somehow introduced Oliver Lewis to all five of his wives. Searches for Teresa, Theresa, and Terrence Lambroux had proved useless previously. It was possible, then, that Terry was a middle name. Trying each letter as a first initial—"A. Theresa Lambroux"; "B. Theresa Lambroux", and so on—had proven just as fruitless for all possible spellings and variations on the name.

The problem was that we had no information at all about Terry Lambroux. Although we could assume the person was a woman, we had not confirmed the fact. We had no stated profession for her, no place of birth, no age or description. A search of marriage records for someone named Lambroux had turned up one record, in Alabama in 1958.

It seemed unlikely, but I filed away the information to confirm at home tonight when I would have more time. There was no baseball game scheduled for the New York Yankees, the team whose games I follow.

Since I was now assuming "Terry Lambroux" was an alias, it made sense to think about the name in reverse, that is, to consider how one chooses such a name when creating an identity for oneself. Perhaps the spelling was the variable. There were more people named "Lambreaux" than "Lambroux." I started to search on those terms.

"I've got something," Ms. Washburn said. "A Rachel Vandross lives in Metuchen, and her relationship status on Facebook reads, 'it's complicated.'"

"Excellent work," I said, standing up to walk around the desk. I stood behind Ms. Washburn and looked over her shoulder at her cellular phone screen. I had to bend to see it even though she was holding it vertically in front of her own eyes. "Do you have a street address?"

"Not yet. I just found her on Facebook, and they don't give you a home address unless the person wants you to know. I'm not a friend of Rachel's, so I don't really have much information about her at all."

I considered the concept of people establishing friendships based strictly on a social media site somewhat comical, but such networks can be useful in discovering more about a person when trying to answer a question. For reasons I can't fathom, some people are willing to share all sorts of personal information in a fairly public setting for the purpose of exhibiting photographs of their pets.

"But you can see who her friends are on Facebook, can't you?" I asked. I don't belong to Facebook, but have searched the site on occasion when doing research.

"Yes. Let me call up the list."

She brought up the Facebook page for Rachel Vandross and maneuvered through it to get to the list of friends. "That's funny," she said.

I had not been able to read the whole page in depth due to my distance from the small screen, but I had seen nothing amusing on it. I waited for the coming explanation, and was not disappointed.

"Rachel Vandross only has four friends on the site," Ms. Washburn said.

Since I have fewer than four people I can reasonably count as friends, I did not understand her concern. "Why is that funny?" I asked.

Ms. Washburn looked at me briefly to see if I was in earnest, and clearly realized that I was. "It's an expression, Samuel. It doesn't mean you should laugh at something; it means that it's odd or unexpected."

"What is odd or unexpected about Rachel having four friends?" I said.

"Well, that's a pretty low number, especially on Facebook, where people you don't know at all can be your friends." Ms. Washburn looked up at me, and I chose not to question the concept of friendships with people one doesn't know, which makes no sense. It was more important for her to explain the odd element involved here. "For example, I have two hundred and thirty-eight friends on Facebook."

"So four would be a very low number, then," I said. "I don't really see how that tells us anything we can use."

"The four friends are all of Oliver Lewis's other ex-wives," Ms. Washburn said.

That *was* unusual, but once she said it, I realized it was not entirely unexpected. "So the members of WOOL have a Facebook page?" I asked.

"Not exactly. They don't exist as a separate entity on the site. But they probably communicate through it. I'm getting the feeling these ladies know each other better than we might have been told." Ms. Washburn scrolled through the phone's Internet browser. "Let me see if I can get an address on Rachel."

After fifteen minutes, which I spent making a few unsuccessful inquiries about Terry Lambreaux, we were in Ms. Washburn's car, driving to Metuchen, which was not far, to meet Rachel Vandross, the second wife of the deceased Oliver Lewis. The drive took only seven minutes. During that time, Ms. Washburn seemed distracted but never to the point that I was concerned for our safety. She wrinkled her nose three times, making me wonder if something nearby smelled distasteful (I have a rather untrained sense of smell), but I did not ask. We were at Rachel's home before a conversation of any significance could begin.

I made a point of vigilance during the drive to be sure the two off-duty policemen were not following us to Rachel's house. They were not.

The house was small, not new, but in good repair. The roof had recently been replaced and there were still a few loose shingles piled on one side of the driveway. The front door was painted brown, the vinyl siding was tan, and the windows were open. It was not the home of an especially wealthy person, but one who had a steady job and could manage her budget well.

Ms. Washburn parked in a space two houses to the east of Rachel's and we walked to the front door. Recalling the reception I had gotten at Jennifer LeBlanc's home, I ran briefly through some tae kwon do training mentally as we approached. And I remembered to stand back an extra three feet from the front door after Ms. Washburn rang the doorbell.

It took twenty-seven seconds for the door to be opened, and the woman who revealed herself behind it was not what I would have expected, having met Oliver Lewis's four other wives.

She was about fifty-two, slim and small, but confident, head held high, back straight. I would likely wager her favorite Beatles song was "Sgt. Pepper's Lonely Hearts Club Band." Anything military would fit her nicely.

"Can I help you?" she asked. It was the proper question. She could have had no idea if it were possible for her to be of assistance to us. Usually, people mean "*may* I help you," which is more a question about beginning a process.

"That is what we are here to find out," I said. I identified myself and Ms. Washburn and asked if she were Rachel Vandross. She nodded, still looking somewhat skeptical or inquisitive. I said we were inquiring about her ex-husband Oliver Lewis.

"Yes, I heard that Oliver had died," Rachel said. "I wish I could tell you I'm upset about it, but I'm not."

Ms. Washburn, knowing my preferences, asked if we could come inside, and even though she stepped aside and gestured us in while apologizing for what she called bad manners, I could tell Rachel Vandross was not happy about having people enter her home.

She ushered us into her living room, which was decorated spartanly—no movie titles or musical selections were displayed in the built-in bookshelves. There were not even many books, but what there were appeared to be about either military history or architecture. A saber hung on one wall and a rifle that appeared to be an authentic specimen from the American Civil War decorated another.

Rachel sat on an armchair near the front door while Ms. Washburn took another facing Rachel's, and I sat on the loveseat where I could see both their faces, but not at the same time.

"Why are you not upset about your ex-husband's death?" I asked when we had all settled into our assigned seats.

Rachel, military bearing intact, barely moved except for an arched eyebrow. "The word *ex-husband* in that question should tell you everything you need to know," she said. "There are reasons people get divorced."

"What was your reason?" I said.

Ms. Washburn winced, just barely perceptibly, at the question. I wondered if my tone was too confrontational.

It did not seem to bother Rachel Vandross, however. "He lied to me on a regular basis," she said. "He married me under false pretenses, and then he lied to me every day after that until I filed the papers."

I assumed the papers to which she referred were a petition for divorce. Ms. Washburn took out her notepad and began to write in it. "What do you mean when you say Oliver Lewis married you under false pretenses?" I asked. That was something none of the other ex-wives (except Cynthia Maholm, who had told me she didn't know the man she'd married at all, which turned out to be a falsehood itself) had claimed.

"He told me he loved me and that I was the only woman he'd ever loved," Rachel answered. "He said he'd never been married before, and that was a lie. Pretty much everything he ever told anyone was a lie."

I needed to clarify her statement. "But you are not suggesting that Mr. Lewis told you he was someone he was not, or married you while he was still in a marriage with Hazel Montrose, are you?" I asked.

Her eyes took on a confused look. "Who's Hazel Montrose?" she asked.

Ms. Washburn looked up, startled, then wrote on her notepad. She and I exchanged a look and she showed me what she'd written. It read *ANOTHER ONE?*

"Are you not a member of the informal group known as WOOL?" I asked Rachel. "Jennifer LeBlanc identified you as a member."

"Sure, I know Jenny and Amy and Cindy and Slim," she said. "Who's Hazel Montrose?"

"Who's Slim?" Ms. Washburn said.

Rachel's expression indicated that we must both be mad. "Slim McInerney," she said, as if it were evident and we should have known all the time. Then she shook her head and laughed lightly. "That's her nickname. Her real name is Sheila."

That made no sense. Sheila McInerney was the alias Cynthia Maholm had used when she came to Questions Answered and hired me to provide some validation of her marriage to Oliver Lewis. But Rachel had mentioned Cynthia when she listed the WOOL members and had added Sheila McInerney as if they were two separate people.

"So who's Hazel Montrose?" she asked again.

Ms. Washburn and I explained our belief, based on what we had been told, that Hazel Montrose had been Oliver Lewis's first wife, that

182

she was second, and had been followed by Jennifer LeBlanc, Amy Stanhope, and finally Cynthia Maholm, posing as Sheila McInerney.

Rachel shook her head. "No. You got it right that I was second, and you got Jenny and Amy right, but Cindy was last under her own name. His first wife was Slim, or Sheila. I know she was first because Ollie always used to tell me how I wasn't as good a wife as she was, and I kept asking him how come he divorced her if she was so great. It was one of the things that split us up."

I found myself concentrating so hard on the question at hand that I was not paying attention to my physical being, which meant my hands were moving rapidly, albeit lightly, at my sides. The "stimming" was once quite pronounced, but now even when it was completely involuntary, it was not as noticeable. Rachel did not react, but Ms. Washburn touched her cheek casually, a visual reminder. I nodded and stopped the movement, letting my hands fall into my lap.

"Have you met Sheila McInerney?" I asked. "Through WOOL or privately in some way?"

"Sure. I saw Slim for a drink once or twice, and after I divorced him too, we got to be friends, sort of. Veterans of the same war from different platoons, you know?"

The military metaphor was not a complex one, so I nodded. "Can you describe Sheila McInerney to me?" I asked.

"Well, her nickname is Slim, and it's not ironic," Rachel answered. "She's about five-eight and really slender—not skinny, but just angular, almost. It's the first thing you notice about her. She has dark hair and blue eyes, which might be colored contacts, I don't know. And she has very long legs, which makes her popular with guys. Probably the thing that got Ollie after her to begin this whole merry-go-round." She laughed without mirth.

I did not feel like laughing because I felt like Sheila McInerney had taken me in with a false story once again. What Rachel told me increased my sense of frustration and made me question the validity of my qualifications to answer questions on a professional basis.

The woman she had described was undoubtedly the one Ms. Washburn and I knew as Hazel Montrose.

TWENTY-FOUR

"You have Hazel's number," Ms. Washburn said. "Call her and ask her out. When she shows up, you can either confront her with what you know or try to lead her into a discussion about Oliver Lewis. She'll slip up somewhere."

We were once again in the Questions Answered office. Ms. Washburn would be leaving in a few minutes; I had told her I'd call Mike for a ride home as I had on the previous evening. She needed to get back to her husband for tonight, I felt, because there had been a tension surrounding her that one's spouse should be able to alleviate. If I noticed it, it must have been fairly obvious.

"I do not intend to ask Hazel Montrose or Sheila McInerney out socially," I said, not for the first time. This discussion had been going on since the drive back to Piscataway. We'd called—that is, Ms. Washburn had called and I had spoken on speakerphone—Detective Dickinson and informed him of what I could not reasonably call "our progress." He informed us that there was no record of Sheila McInerney using the name Hazel Montrose, only that Cynthia Maholm had been using the name Sheila McInerney since she had married Oliver Lewis. The swirl of names in the research of this question was becoming quite thick and difficult to understand.

"I don't know what I'm getting for my money so far," Dickinson had noted, although it was true that he had not yet paid Questions Answered any money at all. "All you keep doing is calling me for information that I've gotten myself."

It is not good business practice, Mother has explained to me, to argue with a client, particularly about the value of the service being offered. But since I felt the information offered would be more reliable if it had come from one of two sources, it did seem reasonable to me to say, "Have you gathered the information, or has Detective Esteban?"

Ms. Washburn winced a little, which told me my question might not have been communicated in the manner I had intended. And when Dickinson's voice came back over the speakerphone, it was deeper, with a bit of a gravelly tone to it. "It's official police information I shouldn't be sharing with you, Hoenig. Keep that in mind."

Now I had a problem: Dickinson's tone convinced me I'd said something wrong, but he had failed to adequately answer my question. Pressing the issue would probably be seen as rude, but I had to know if Detective Esteban was the source of the data, in which case it would be considered trustworthy, or if it had been Detective Dickinson, which would at least make me wonder about its accuracy and depth.

I looked at Ms. Washburn, who was driving and not available to make eye contact. I could have muted the call, but that would have required touching the phone, and since it was a model with which I was not terribly familiar, I was not sure which button was the correct one for the function. Ms. Washburn stole a very quick glance in my direction, and I believe she shook her head horizontally to indicate I should not press further.

"I appreciate that, detective," I said. Ms. Washburn nodded slightly in approval. "But I need to know who I should thank for the privilege."

That seemed the flattering way to approach the question, and I have learned over time that people respond well to being told they are owed appreciation for something, even if they had little to do with it.

"Just thank me and I'll pass it along," Dickinson said, and that gave me the answer I needed. The data about Hazel Montrose was from Detective Esteban, and therefore could be assumed more reliable. That was good, because it was useful information, but troubling, since it indicated Hazel had been lying to us. And her appearance at Questions Answered seemed even less coincidental, and more worrisome.

"I'm not saying you have to marry her," Ms. Washburn continued now, back in the Questions Answered office. "But you can ask her out. She seemed interested in you; you were certainly interested in her. Even if you don't find something out, you might have a pleasant evening. Is there something wrong with that?"

I could think of numerous things wrong with it, but there was the possibility that a person in a social setting might be more relaxed, and therefore more apt to provide useful information because she would be less guarded about her words. But it seemed somehow dishonest to use a social invitation as an excuse to interrogate a subject about a question. It was a difficult dilemma.

With such things, I usually rely on Ms. Washburn's judgment, or Mother's. Since Ms. Washburn was the person pressing the idea, I decided to ask Mother about it when I returned home. "I will consider it," I told Ms. Washburn before she left the office. She gave me an odd look when I said that, which I interpreted as a combination of skepticism and disappointment. I did not understand the expression, and knew I would not be able to adequately describe it to Mother at dinner. It was a lost opportunity.

Once Ms. Washburn left, I sat down to finally focus on the elusive Terry Lambroux. The many variations on the name had proven to be a dead end, but I felt that with the proper amount of concentration, I could find a thread to pull on, to use a common investigative expression, that would eventually unravel the mystery surrounding the person, if indeed Terry Lambroux existed.

The last time I had searched, it had occurred to me to think of the type of person who would invent the name Terry Lambroux as an alias. As there were no records of arrests associated with the name, it was not one that had been assumed strictly for criminal purposes, or the criminal assuming it was crafty enough never to have been arrested.

It was not a typical, unobtrusive name. It would be easy to hide with an alias like Robert Mason or Susan Wells. The person using the name Terry Lambroux was adopting something with a more distinctive tone, one which through use of the "oux" suffix might be related to the Cajun or Creole regions in Louisiana. That might be a place to start.

On the other hand, the name "Lambrou" seemed, after a fairly thorough search, to be one originating largely in the United Kingdom or Australia. If Terry were interested in covering her British roots, she might have altered the spelling on her last name to something more closely associated with the American South.

Then I thought the name might be an anagram. I do not have a special talent for anagrams, so I consulted a very helpful source meant to be used for something considerably more devious: An Internet site devoted to helping people cheat at Scrabble and related games. I will not repeat the name, but it proved to be an invaluable resource in my efforts.

Even with its help, however, the best I could do was "MORTUARY LERX." That was not terribly helpful. It seemed to me, anyway, that criminals rarely try to put their mark on a false identity by making it from the letters in their real names. It would seem counterproductive.

This perplexing problem was raising my level of frustration, not a terribly rare thing in those whose behavior is classified as being on the autism spectrum. The circumstances of this question seemed to be extending in every direction, with no discernible pattern and therefore no logical path to follow toward a successful conclusion.

Oliver Lewis had been asphyxiated, stabbed, and poisoned and his throat had been cut. His body had been left in my office specifically for me to discover. The slightest investigation into the dead man indicated he had been married at least five times, never for long, to women who found him charming at first and then cold once he had married them, apparently finding the pursuit of his prey more interesting than having caught each one he chased.

He had been operating a business, ostensibly from an empty space over a pizzeria (not unlike the office I kept in such an establishment that had closed the year before). The purpose of OLimited appeared to have been to entice people to invest in nonexistent companies offering insurance policies that did not pay back on the event of their holders' deaths.

Two men in a Ford Escape had followed Ms. Washburn and me from Lewis's office to a coffee shop. They had claimed to be operating some kind of surveillance on the OLimited office, but had offered no explanation as to why watching an empty suite would be necessary, or who was paying for their services.

Of the four ex-wives Oliver Lewis had at the time of his death (Cynthia Maholm, who had engaged my services while calling herself Sheila McInerney, was a widow, not an ex-wife), one, Hazel Montrose, was unknown to another, and the last for us to meet was apparently really named Sheila (although sometimes called "Slim") McInerney, which brought me back full circle (as Mother would say) to my musing about the many contradictions in this question.

All that, and Terry Lambroux was still nowhere to be found, in person or online.

The keys, because they were so mysterious, appeared to be Lambroux, whoever she might be, and Cynthia Maholm, who had first engaged my services and then vanished almost the instant Oliver Lewis had been murdered.

And now Ms. Washburn was suggesting I call crime scene cleaner Hazel Montrose and ask her on a date. That was perhaps the most unnerving of all the elements of this matter.

I decided not to let Terry Lambroux get the best of me. Mike knew I would call whenever I was ready to leave, but there was time before Mother would consider me late for dinner, something I assiduously try to avoid. It is rude to Mother and unsettling to me, as straying from routine is not something I enjoy doing. It allows for too many unexpected occurrences, which I accept only when absolutely necessary.

The only thing left to do was determine what I knew about my quarry, and work backward from that. Terry Lambroux was probably female, although that fact had yet to be confirmed. But operating under that assumption, her breach of promise lawsuit against the dead man was especially puzzling. It was somewhat antiquated as a concept—the idea of a woman going to court because the man she intended to marry had canceled the wedding. And that scenario broke with Oliver Lewis's usual pattern of intense interest in a woman *until* she married him, at which time he was likely searching for the next object of his desire.

Detective Esteban had faxed the filed suit papers to Questions Answered, so I now had them on my desk. I picked them up and read them in six minutes.

The suit hinged, as well as I could extrapolate the legalese, on the idea that after a prenuptial agreement had been signed between the two parties, Oliver Lewis had called off the planned marriage three days before it was scheduled to take place. Terry Lambroux (and the legal papers listed her as "Terry," and not any longer form of the name) had asserted that even without the wedding, she was entitled to the amount of money specified in the prenuptial agreement to be paid to her if the couple were to divorce.

That seemed odd; there was no contract signed joining the two people together other than a document meant to secure each one's interests for the period after the wedding, which had not taken place. I am not an attorney because I have never sat for the bar exam in New Jersey, but any rudimentary knowledge of the law would indicate Terry Lambroux had no standing—she could not be awarded money for a divorce if there had never been a marriage.

Still, the suit had been pending in civil court in New Brunswick until the day before Oliver Lewis married Hazel Montrose, when it had been withdrawn.

What made the document more interesting and more relevant to Detective Dickinson's question, however, was not the odd nature of the suit. There were two elements of the document that bore immediate interest: First, a prenuptial agreement included as evidence in the suit specified that Terry Lambroux, should she and Oliver Lewis divorce, would be awarded sixty percent of his total estate. That by itself was fairly interesting, as the percentage seemed high for such an agreement, but it was not glaringly odd.

But the amount of the estate's estimated worth demanded more attention: The man with the empty office in which no phone was connected, no employees were stationed, and no clients were served had admitted in a legal document to holdings worth seventeen million dollars.

That was surprising enough, but to add an air of mystery to an already perplexing question, the attorney who had filed the suit on behalf of Terry Lambroux was Roger Siplowitz, the dead man's supposed friend.

The office door opened and Mike walked inside, hands on his hips. "I've been honking for five minutes," he said. "What are you so engrossed in?"

"I'm sorry I didn't hear you," I told him, although I did not see how I could have avoided the problem, since I had not ignored his car horn intentionally. "I have been considering how to locate a person whose only known address is from a lawsuit filed more than two years ago. I checked, and the address is a false one—a Dairy Queen actually stands on that spot, according to Google Earth."

"Oh no, Samuel," Mike said. I had no idea to what he was referring. "I'm not taking you anywhere but home tonight."

I waved a hand to indicate he was mistaken. "I have no intention of going anywhere else," I said. "But the problem has been weighing on me."

"How do you find a person who doesn't want to be found?" Mike leaned against the doorjamb and crossed one leg in front of the other, the very picture of relaxation.

"Usually the person leaves a trail," I answered. "Documents, business transactions, marriages, births, deaths. This person, Terry Lambroux, has not left any of those things as far as I can discover on my own."

We agreed Mike would drive me home, but Mike would listen to my ideas along the way. He is a skilled enough driver that I can have a conversation from the back seat of his taxicab and not be distracted by thoughts of automobile crashes. I locked the door to Questions Answered, got into the taxicab, and strapped on my safety harness. Mike started the vehicle and began to drive toward Mother's house and my home (Mother holds the title to the house, and I live there).

"Is this Terry a guy or a girl?" Mike asked as he made a right turn onto Stelton Road.

"She is female, according to court documents."

Mike nodded, as if that made sense in his estimation, which I did not understand. "The cops can't find her?" he asked.

"Not yet."

"Well, can't you ask her friends? Somebody must have been at her house at one time or another."

I had already asked the only friends of Terry Lambroux I knew of, the members of WOOL. "They all said they'd never met Terry anywhere but at a party, and most of them knew of her only by name, had never actually met her, and could not confirm her gender."

"This is somebody trying very hard not to be found," Mike observed.

"Indeed."

"So it seems to me that the best way to find her is to get her to come looking for you," he said.

It was the best idea I'd heard all day. The first thing I did when I got home, after greeting my mother and having the dinner she'd cooked, was to call Hazel Montrose and ask her out to dinner the next night.

She agreed.

TWENTY-FIVE

"You took my advice," Ms. Washburn said. She sounded surprised.

We were in her car, driving toward Oliver Lewis's most recent address in what I feared would be a futile attempt to locate Cynthia Maholm. I was taking a great deal of care to be sure that the black Ford Escape with the two off-duty policemen in it was not following us, and so far, it certainly was not.

"I often take your advice," I reminded her. "I find your advice invaluable. Why do you consider this instance to be unusual?"

"Because I was advising you to do something you really didn't want to do," she answered. Her Global Positioning System indicated we would be in the car for another fourteen minutes. "And then you went ahead and called Hazel Montrose for a date. I know that's very frightening for you, so it does surprise me that you did it."

"I was operating on Mike's suggestion that we find a way to get Terry Lambroux to come to us because we have not been able to find her as yet," I explained.

"Mike is the cab driver?"

"Yes."

"What's his last name?"

"I don't know," I said.

Ms. Washburn's eyebrows undulated a bit. "You don't know? This guy comes and drives you home a few times a week and you don't know his last name? That's very uncharacteristic of you, Samuel."

"Mike has never given me any reason to mistrust him," I said. "He comes whenever I call him, and he drives me wherever I need to go. I don't need to know anything more than that."

"You do have a valid driver's license," Ms. Washburn reminded me.

"As a means of identification and for use in extreme emergencies," I answered. "I got it because Mother was worried about her health and felt I might need to transport myself if something incapacitating happened to her. I accepted her reasoning and did as she asked. But I never use the license. You know that."

"You should keep in practice in case you need it. Maybe I should let you drive the car once a week or something."

The idea of it led to a band of perspiration at my rear hairline. "I don't think so," I said.

We sat silently for forty-one seconds. "How?" Ms. Washburn said.

"How?" I echoed.

"How does your buddy's saying you should get Terry Lambroux to come to us lead to you asking out Hazel Montrose?"

"Ah! That is the interesting part." Ms. Washburn turned onto Route 22, one of the most notoriously dangerous roads in New Jersey, and I refrained from speaking for fear of distracting her. She did not ask me to explain myself, understanding my concern, for the seven minutes and eight seconds we remained on the road.

When she turned off again, I resumed my thought. "Since Terry Lambroux has been so careful about maintaining her anonymity, it was clear that she has some involvement in the death of Oliver Lewis, or in some matter that she prefers no one discover. 'Smoking her out,' as

Mike would say, is difficult. And since whoever sent the two men in the Ford Escape after us certainly did not want to be identified, we might put Terry on the list of possible suspects for that."

"That doesn't get to your date with Hazel," Ms. Washburn noted.

"Not yet, but consider this: Assuming that Terry is the person who sent the two men—or at least who is having Oliver Lewis's business watched—the only contact, however indirect, we have had with her is through them."

Ms. Washburn said nothing. That sometimes means the other person is waiting for you to speak. I realized I had not yet explained the connection to Hazel, which was certainly indistinct, but undeniable.

"Add to what I've said that Hazel is the only member of WOOL who Rachel does not know, and of whose existence Rachel seems ignorant. According to Rachel, there is no such person as Hazel Montrose, but there is such a person as Sheila McInerney. Clearly, Hazel is the crux of this deception, even if she herself is not aware of it."

"I said that very thing before," Ms. Washburn reminded me as she stopped the car on a suburban street in Manville, the last address Oliver Lewis had registered as a residence.

"Yes, but now it is part of an effort to find Terry Lambroux," I answered. "When I meet with Hazel in public, I will be sure at least one other WOOL member knows it, and that, we can probably assume, will lead to it being common knowledge among them. I think we can assume our two stalkers in the Ford Escape will be in the area as well. If I can make it look like I'm getting new information from Hazel, Terry Lambroux will be forced to reveal herself and we can start to make real progress toward answering Detective Dickinson's question."

Having turned the car's engine off and applied the parking brake, Ms. Washburn removed her seat belt and turned toward me, making sure I was looking into her face. "You wanted to ask out Hazel Montrose," she said. "Why not just admit that's why you're doing it?"

This was puzzling. Clearly she had been listening when I detailed the reasons for my action, and yet she was assuming another motivation entirely was responsible for the plan. "I assure you, my interest in Hazel is entirely within the context of the question," I said.

A moment passed, then Ms. Washburn opened the driver's side door. "Okay," she said. "Let's go talk to Cindy Maholm."

I considered it extremely unlikely we would, but that was the purpose of our visit, so I got out of the car and followed Ms. Washburn to the house.

It was a ranch style home, all on one level, appearing by the architecture to date to the 1960s. The house had been maintained, but not improved, so the casement windows and the original siding, which was probably made with asbestos, were intact. I hesitated for a moment, thinking about the danger of inhaling near the exterior of this house, but the fact is that asbestos is probably most dangerous when being removed, and we had come for a reason. I waited for Ms. Washburn to press the doorbell button, but she did not.

"Go ahead," she said, pointing to the button. "Push it."

I did not understand. "Why?" I asked.

"Because sometimes I won't be here and you'll have to. Go ahead, Samuel. Nothing bad is going to happen to you." She pointed at the button once more.

"Honestly, I would rather not." The thought of what could be living on that device was enough to make me rethink the whole trip. I am not a germaphobe, but I do like to minimize my exposure to illnesses. I do not enjoy being sick, and Mother says I am an especially bad patient.

"It's not about what you'd rather. It's about what you need to know you can do." She crossed her arms. This is a signal in body language that one is firm in one's convictions and unwilling to bend on the subject.

Finally it became a choice between what was more disturbing: pushing a button or prolonging my exposure to asbestos. I reached into my hip pocket, pulled out a handkerchief, and covered my finger with it, pressing the doorbell button, which initiated a sound inside the house.

Ms. Washburn did not smile smugly, and I appreciated that.

We waited for thirty-seven seconds, during which Ms. Washburn said, "I'm glad you did that, Samuel. If I'm not there, you know now that you can handle it."

I did not respond, but my mind was racing through possible scenarios under which Ms. Washburn might not be present. The most obvious, of course, was a decision to stop working at Questions Answered because her husband, Simon Taylor, disapproved. But people in films and on television sometimes speak of situations in which they might not be present when they know they have a short time to live. I did not want to consider that possibility for Ms. Washburn.

Before I could ask her about it, however, she looked at me and said, "I don't think anybody's home."

"Certainly no one who wishes to let us in," I acknowledged. "Would you try the doorknob, please?"

Ms. Washburn seemed to consider the question and nodded. "This time," she said quietly. But when she tried to turn it, the doorknob would not move. "Locked."

"Perhaps a back door." I started around the left side of the house, where the driveway extended from the street to the back yard. Ms. Washburn, understanding my desire for thoroughness, walked around to the right side of the house, where there was grass.

I did not encounter any promising signs, and there was no back door, but there was one on the side of the house, where Ms. Washburn joined me. This door was also locked, and she told me there was none on the opposite side. It appeared the front door and this one were the only entrances.

"I don't suppose you know how to pick a lock," I said as a joke. It would never occur to me to enter someone's house without permission; that is the very definition of rudeness.

Ms. Washburn, apparently thinking I was serious (something that happens to me quite often when I'm trying to amuse), shook her head. "No. Sorry."

It would be pointless and perhaps insulting for me to tell her I had not been in earnest, so I simply looked up at the house. "Perhaps we should try the doorbell again."

"Yeah, or maybe we could do this." Ms. Washburn walked to the left of the door and reached for the window, which was not high off the ground. She raised the screen meant to keep insects from flying into the house, and lifted herself from the concrete step to the windowsill before I could protest. She let herself into the room just inside the entrance, which appeared to be a sunroom or an enclosed patio, and vanished.

I was dumbfounded. I could not even call her name for fear of being discovered. I felt my hand reach up to touch my nose. How could I get inside and keep Ms. Washburn away from any danger that might confront her? What if something were happening to her right now? Should I climb through the window? Wouldn't that be a serious breach of social interaction, in addition to being illegal?

Standing paralyzed by indecision was no answer. I took one step toward the window, telling myself I did so just to examine the window more closely and determine if Ms. Washburn was inside and safe. But I did not have time to consider that, or even to take another step.

Ms. Washburn opened the side door from the inside of the house and beckoned to me. "Come on," she said in a low volume. I had no decibel meter, but I could tell it was not as loudly as she might normally speak from this distance. "It's okay."

I walked to the door and shook my head. "That was an extremely reckless action," I told Ms. Washburn. "We should leave before the police come and arrest us for breaking and entering."

"We haven't broken anything. I even put the screen back down. And you haven't entered yet. But this is the way you can find out if anything fishy is going on in Oliver Lewis's house." She turned back and headed inside the house, then stopped and looked at me. "Well? Come on! *Oliver*'s not going to file a complaint, and anybody else who's in there is just as guilty as we are." She walked inside without looking back again.

Ms. Washburn had made some salient points, but the fact remained that walking into the house would be an illegal act. The real question was whether the information I might gain from entering would be valuable enough to justify the risk. And there was no way of determining that ahead of time.

In short, I walked into the house and followed Ms. Washburn, largely to keep my promise to shield her from any possible dangers.

Under analogous circumstances, Mother might say that was my story, and I was sticking to it. Although one doesn't actually stick to a story, as it is not a physical object.

Ms. Washburn was waiting for me in the sunroom, which was bordered on one side by windows that could be insulated to make the room usable during the winter. Now they all had insect screens pulled down. They were also, with the exception of the one Ms. Washburn had used for entry, closed, and it was stuffy and warm inside the room. The other three walls were bare except for one bookshelf, which held nothing but six compact discs, all by bands that were not the Beatles.

"I didn't see anything important in here, but maybe you'll notice something," she said as soon as I was near enough to hear. This was, I understood, Ms. Washburn's way of starting the conversation and refraining from teasing me about coming inside when I believed it to be the wrong thing to do.

The room was unremarkable except for being somewhat under-furnished. If Oliver Lewis had lived here, either he had not lived here long, or he had not used this room very extensively. There was an old, somewhat threadbare sofa under one bank of windows, a standing pole lamp next to it and a stereo system, covered in dust, opposite. Hardly the kind of place a man with seventeen million dollars might live.

"This is certainly not the hub of activity for a man living here anytime recently," I said, mostly to myself. Ms. Washburn's notebook was out and she was writing in it. "Oliver Lewis might not have been using this as his residence, but if not, it was somewhere other than the apartment in Edison where Cynthia Maholm staged his escape. That was never a residence for either of them."

I moved through the room, taking in each angle, although I knew Ms. Washburn, a photographer by trade before she became my associate, was using a small digital camera she carries with her to preserve the site just as we saw it. She does not trust photographs taken with cellular telephones, she has told me. "Something that's not made expressly to take pictures doesn't take very good pictures, Samuel." It seemed logical.

Similar sights awaited us in a small dining area with no table but a chandelier, a kitchen with nothing in five of the six cabinets (the sixth held three cereal bowls, a plate, two beer mugs, and a box of Kellogg's Frosted Flakes of Corn), and a living room with a somewhat incongruous large-screen high-definition television with impressive surround-sound speakers, a reclining chair, wall-to-wall carpet that appeared to have been vacuum cleaned recently, and a photograph on the mantelpiece of Oliver Lewis and Cynthia Maholm at what must have been their wedding.

In the photograph, Oliver Lewis smiled toward the camera. He wore a dark blue suit with a red tie and a white shirt. "He looks like a walking American flag," Ms. Washburn observed. I did not agree, since flags are flat and the suit had no stars or stripes, but I understood she was being sarcastic.

The Cynthia Maholm in the photograph was the Sheila McInerney who first walked into the Questions Answered office. She appeared stunned, her eyes a little red and unfocused, as if drugged. She could easily have been unaware of her surroundings or the proceedings apparently taking place around her.

"Except for all that has happened since our first meeting, I would believe this woman's story about marrying a man she didn't know, possibly against her will," I told my associate.

"I see what you mean. Do you want to go back?" Ms. Washburn pointed toward a passage to the far side of the kitchen, which undoubtedly led to the bedrooms, since none had been evident on our walk to this spot.

I nodded, and Ms. Washburn led the way. The hallway was paneled, which gave it a look similar to the exterior of the home, dating back to the mid-twentieth century. It was not, in my opinion, attractive.

There were three doors on the left side as we walked around the kitchen toward the rear of the house, where the bedrooms were situated. The house, I had noticed since we'd entered, was oddly quiet—more quiet even than would be expected from an empty residence.

The first bedroom we encountered had clearly never been used for sleeping. There was an acoustic guitar on a stand in one corner, two amplifiers on the opposite side of the room, and some sound-mixing equipment on the far wall under the window. There were no chairs and no bed, nor any other instruments.

"Maybe the house was being used for recording," Ms. Washburn said. "Was Oliver Lewis a musician?"

I shook my head negatively. "This would be a very poor room in which to make a recording," I said. "There are two windows that would brighten the sound and bring in noise from the outside, and no soundproofing on the walls. In fact, the room is barely absorbent of sound at all. The area rug on the floor is the least soundproof of any floor covering we've seen here."

Ms. Washburn took some photographs of the room and we moved out into the hallway, then to the next door, which unlike the one to this bedroom, had been closed. She waited for me, then wordlessly looked at the doorknob. I turned it with my handkerchief, careful to keep the same side touching the knob as I had used before.

When the door swung open, Ms. Washburn gasped.

The room was certainly a place for someone to sleep; it had a queen-sized bed on the far wall, with a nightstand on either side. On the far nightstand was a paperback book of crime fiction, placed spine up to keep the page open. On the near nightstand were a prescription bottle, closed, a plastic bottle of Poland Spring water, a small bracelet, and a cellular phone. The wall to the right of the entrance had a dresser with four drawers, each of which was closed.

On the bed was Cynthia Maholm, and she was dead.

TWENTY-SIX

"How DID YOU GET into the house?" Detective Arthur Eastbrook of the Manville police department asked, left eye slightly more squinted open than the right.

It was a tricky question. We had called the police immediately after finding Cynthia Maholm, eyes wide open, mouth equally so, and her skin discolored and cold, on her bed. It had taken six minutes to get through to the proper dispatcher in Manville, but only four once the call had gone through for the first police cruiser to arrive.

But the fact was that we had entered the house illegally. Ms. Washburn had in fact crawled through a side window and let me in the side door. If we were called to testify in a trial, should the death be ruled a homicide, it was possible anything we said would be disallowed because of our improper method of entry.

It was also possible that we would be charged, right on the spot, with breaking and entering and taken to jail, where we had already been once in the course of this question. I was sure neither of us had any desire to be put back into that position.

"The door was unlocked," Ms. Washburn said. "We came to see if Cindy Maholm was here, and when we called and rang, we discovered the side door was unlocked. We found her exactly that way when we came in."

It was a lie, of course, but I saw no immediate reason to contradict Ms. Washburn's statement. Detective Eastbrook, with a battery-powered voice recorder in his hand, simply nodded.

"And what did you touch in this room?" he asked.

"Nothing," I could say truthfully. "I had used a handkerchief to open the door, and we touched nothing once we saw Ms. Maholm's body on the bed."

The detective's eyebrows met in the center of his forehead. "Why did you use a handkerchief to open the door?"

"Mr. Hoenig has Asperger's Syndrome," Ms. Washburn explained immediately. "One of the ways that shows itself is in his … reluctance to touch objects he knows other people have handled." I thought that was an excellent way to explain my feelings, and I added nothing.

But Detective Eastbrook seemed unsatisfied. "Uh-huh," he said as Ms. Maholm's body was wheeled out of the room behind us. Ms. Washburn chose to look away; I watched, but gained no useful information. "So you were here looking for Cindy and you just found her like this?" It is not unusual for detectives and police officers to ask the same question in a number of varying ways, trying to elicit something other than the uniform response.

"That's right," I said. "She was in exactly that state when we arrived. How long do you estimate she has been dead?"

"About six hours," a medical technician behind me answered, perhaps believing I was part of the investigative team. "I can't be a hundred percent sure, but no more than twelve. I'd bet my job on that."

Detective Eastbrook looked annoyed, possibly because the technician had answered to me and not to him. "You just did," he said.

The technician stopped, frowned, and left the hallway where we were standing, presumably for the front door and his vehicle.

"Do you honestly believe, detective, that we came here, somehow killed Ms. Maholm, inexplicably stayed in the house for up to twelve hours, and then called the police?"

"Honestly? I don't know what to believe, but I'm willing to bet the door wasn't unlocked when you got here," Eastbrook said. He glanced at Ms. Washburn, who continued to avert her glance. "There are footprints in the dirt near the side window and the screen in that window is a little bit crooked, like someone put it back down in a hurry."

"Very well. We did gain entry through that window," I admitted.

Ms. Washburn looked at me. "I want my lawyer," she said to the detective.

"You have to wait until I arrest you," he answered, "and I'm not doing that. Your pal here is right. It would be stupid for you to kill Cindy and then call us to come and get you. I've seen it done, but you're not the type. I think you're just nosy and you needed to find out what was going on. You found out, and you let us know. We'll have more questions over the next couple of days, but as of right now, you're free to go."

Ms. Washburn immediately turned to leave, but I stayed put and made the effort to look Eastbrook in the eye. "Do you have a suspicion as to Ms. Maholm's cause of death?" I asked.

He smiled a bit. "Yes. I do." But he said no more.

Ms. Washburn took me gently by the arm, and we left the house. "I'm not sure it was a smart move to tell him we broke into the house," she said quietly to me as we walked.

"It was the truth."

"It can get us thrown in jail," she countered.

"I doubt it will. If this is an issue with your husband—"

Ms. Washburn stopped walking and held up her hand to stop me. "My marriage is not an appropriate topic of conversation between us, Samuel," she said. "Am I making myself clear?"

I must have stood silent for a long moment because her apparently angry suggestion had caught me unexpectedly. "Yes," I said when I had considered a number of alternative responses.

"Good."

The technician who had answered my question about Ms. Maholm's time of death was loading a black station wagon with equipment not far from where we were standing. When he saw me nearby, he walked toward us.

"Was Detective Eastbrook serious?" he asked. "Is my job really on the line on this call?"

I thought quickly about how to answer him honestly without revealing that I did not work for the Manville police department. "I believe the detective was simply expressing some irritation, but I'd be very surprised if your job was in jeopardy," I said.

Ms. Washburn smiled faintly. I was doing well, apparently.

"That's a relief," the technician said. "I don't know what got him so mad."

"It is a perplexing case," I said. "Can you make a guess about the cause of death?"

He hesitated. "I don't want to get myself into any more trouble."

Ms. Washburn put a hand to her mouth, perhaps stifling a small laugh.

"I promise you," I said, "anything you say will stay between us. I will never mention it to Detective Eastbrook."

That seemed to relax the young man. "If I had to guess, I'd say she OD'd," he said. "But whatever it was hit her pretty fast and pretty hard. Her eyes were open and she looked surprised. There's just one thing."

That is always significant. "What?" Ms. Washburn asked.

"The pill bottle on her bedstand was for thirty pills. There were twenty-eight pills in the bottle. She didn't OD on that."

"So it might have been something else," I suggested.

"Could be almost anything," the technician answered.

"What is your favorite Beatles song?" I asked him.

He didn't hesitate, the sign of someone not easily unnerved by a question he did not expect. "'Doctor Robert,'" he said.

Workaholic.

———

"This makes it much more difficult to answer the question," I told Ms. Washburn as we drove to the Questions Answered office.

"The fact that she's dead?" she asked. "Doesn't it suggest some pattern to you? Something that can bring us closer to figuring out who killed Oliver Lewis?"

"It suggests a number of possibilities," I answered. "I meant that Ms. Maholm's death makes it much more difficult to answer her question about Mr. Lewis."

"I think that ship has sailed, Samuel." It was a metaphor. She was not referring to an actual ship. I'd heard the reference before, and Mother had explained that it meant some things were simply too late to reverse. Death does that.

"I suppose so," I said. "Our focus should now be firmly on Detective Dickinson's question."

"You said Cindy Maholm's death suggested a number of possibilities," she reminded me.

That was true; I'd said that. But it seemed that Ms. Washburn was expecting some sort of response. After seven seconds, she added, "What are those possibilities?"

"Two things seem clear," I answered, grateful for her intuition and understanding of my train of thought. (That is also a metaphor, but one that visually makes sense to me—thoughts do travel in a linear fashion from one to the next, as a train travels on a track but can be diverted when someone throws a switch. I had a special interest in train travel when I was six years old.) "First, it appears that Oliver Lewis's marriages and his business interests were in some way intermingled. Both were certainly unconventional and provided motives for someone to want him dead. Second, Cynthia Maholm, who approached me as Sheila Mc-Inerney, must have been closer to the center of the intrigue than the other ex-wives, since she is the one someone decided to eliminate."

"Do you think it's possible the other WOOL members are in danger?"

"I do. And that is one of the reasons I am glad I will be seeing Hazel Montrose later today."

Ms. Washburn, even in profile, could not hide her smile.

When we arrived at Questions Answered, Detective Dickinson was waiting in the parking lot. He got out of his car when he saw us arrive, and approached us as I unlocked the office door.

"I saw the bulletin from Manville," he said. "Why didn't I hear it from you first?"

"We were being questioned by Detective Eastbrook," I explained as we walked inside. "The case is outside your jurisdiction, detective. I'm not sure what the information would have told you."

"The *information* is enough to make me think it's linked to Oliver Lewis's murder, don't you?" Detective Dickinson said. His voice had a confrontational tone I found difficult to hear. I resisted the impulse to put my hands to my ears in an effort to muffle the sound.

Ms. Washburn must have seen me wince. "I'm sure Mr. Hoenig agrees," she said. "But you got everything off the dispatch you would have gotten from us, I'm sure. Now, we can give you a report if you like, but we don't have an answer to your question yet." She motioned toward the client chair, but Detective Dickinson was not showing signs of calming down.

"One of the key witnesses, a woman we've been searching for since the body showed up on your floor, just died, possibly murdered, and you want to give me a report but you don't have an answer?" he bellowed. I could no longer resist and put my left hand up to my ear. "It's been *days*!"

"Could you please lower the volume of your voice, detective?" I asked as I began to walk the perimeter of the office. I had not exercised enough times today, and there was the added benefit of being farther from the detective as I walked most of the room.

"What are you doing?" he demanded. He did lower his voice by a factor of approximately one third.

"I am exercising to maintain my health," I told him. "Now, here is what we know: Oliver Lewis was a serial monogamist who seduced women, possibly with date rape drugs, married them and then ignored them until they filed for divorce. He might be the father of Amy Stanhope's child, but we have no proof of that yet. After posing as Sheila McInerney and contracting me to discover who the man calling himself her husband really was, Cynthia Maholm claimed she was being threatened by her husband, set up a strange scene for Ms. Washburn and myself to witness, then insisted we be arrested for trespassing on her property.

"She vanished, and now has been discovered in Oliver Lewis's home, dead in the bedroom from what appears to be a drug overdose, although quite likely not an accidental one or a successful suicide attempt."

"It was definitely a murder?" Detective Dickinson asked. "That wasn't in the dispatch."

"It is not confirmed, but it is probable," I told him. "And the most likely person to ask about it is Terry Lambroux or the real Sheila McInerney, neither of whom we have yet been able to locate."

"That's not a great report," Dickinson groused. "The only thing I know now that I didn't know a minute ago is that Cindy Maholm was probably murdered, but the MO is different from Lewis's murder. I don't know what to make of that."

"Neither do we," Ms. Washburn said.

"Don't worry," I told them both. "We should know more by tomorrow morning."

"You have a plan?" Dickinson asked.

"No. I have a date."

TWENTY-SEVEN

"How did you choose this restaurant?" Hazel Montrose asked.

We were seated in a booth at Applebee's on Centennial Avenue in Piscataway, not far from the supermarket, the bagel store, and the nail salon. The waiter, a man in his early twenties (probably a student at nearby Rutgers University) who told us his name was Tyler and he would be taking care of us tonight—a rather bizarre declaration I chose not to question—had taken our dinner orders and retreated to the kitchen.

"It is part of a chain, so the food is predictably of the same quality at every location," I explained. "The menu can be found online before leaving one's home, so there will be no surprises other than the daily specials, which can be avoided. For me, that makes a great difference."

Hazel, who was wearing a blue top with a white skirt, nodded understandingly. I had not told her about my Asperger's Syndrome, since I believe the word *syndrome* tends to lead people to the incorrect assumption that I am in some way ill or damaged. I am not. My personality has features that do not conform to the accepted definition of "normal," and enough people are different in this way that it has acquired a label. So Hazel's nod was in all likelihood an acknowledgement that she had noticed some "quirks."

"There is a certain comfort in predictability," she said. "You can concentrate your thinking in other directions."

I had not mentioned the death of Cynthia Maholm. When I had told Ms. Washburn that I intended to avoid the topic unless Hazel brought it up, she'd smiled and suggested it was because I didn't want to spoil the occasion. I'd responded that I simply wanted to determine if Hazel had already heard the news, and Ms. Washburn smiled and said, "Of course." I had not extended that part of the conversation.

When I had told Mother of my intention to go to dinner with Hazel, her first question was a practical one: "How will you get there?" But Hazel had already offered to drive, and she had picked me up at Questions Answered, since she had already visited the office and knew its location.

Then my mother had asked me if this was a social dinner or one related to my business, and I had been unable to answer that question completely. "It's business," I finally decided, "but in the guise of a social occasion."

Mother's voice took on a slightly scolding quality. "Are you leading that girl on, Samuel?"

I was not sure what that expression meant. I was certainly not leading Hazel anywhere physically, as she was driving. "Leading her on where?" I asked.

Mother's tone softened a bit, as if often does when she needs to explain an idiom to me. She sometimes forgets that I take such expressions literally on my first exposure to them. "It means to deceive someone by making them believe you have a romantic interest in them, when your real intentions are … not in that area."

That was simply absurd. "I am not 'leading on' Hazel Montrose," I said through the phone. I was in the office and Mother was at home, probably in the kitchen because she insists the reception on the wall phone there is the clearest in the house, even though the signal must logically be the same to each extension. "I am going to dinner with her to ask her about Oliver Lewis and Terry Lambroux."

"You usually don't take people to dinner just to ask them questions," Mother pointed out. "You just ask the questions."

"It is meant to relax Hazel so she will answer more honestly," I explained.

"You're not going to ply her with alcohol," Mother admonished. Then she caught herself as my mind raced. "That means offer her drinks until she loses some control over her decisions and her behavior."

"Did Oliver Lewis ply you with alcohol?" I asked Hazel as Tyler retreated to the bar.

She laughed quickly, apparently taken by surprise. "You get right to it, don't you, Samuel?"

"I am merely asking because some of Mr. Lewis's other ex-wives have suggested that he might have induced them to marry him by encouraging them to drink more than they would normally have on their own, or possibly with cocktails laced with drugs." The late Cynthia Maholm had suggested that, as had Rachel Stanhope.

"No, Samuel. As far as I know, I was completely sober and consenting when I married Ollie. Just as I was when I divorced him." At that moment Tyler returned with a glass of water for me (no lemon) and a martini for Hazel. He retreated immediately, saying our dinners would be out "real soon."

"I am glad to hear it," I said once Tyler was gone. "I'd hate to think you had been married to a man you didn't care to marry."

"No, I definitely wanted to be married to Ollie when we met," Hazel said after a sip of her martini, which she had described as "dry." The concept of a dry liquid is still one I have difficulty understanding. I did comprehend the existence of dry cleaning fluid because I had once researched a question regarding the operation of a process called Martinizing.

"In the beginning, Ollie made me feel like a princess, something I never thought I would like, but it was fantastic. His attention was completely and totally on me. I felt pampered and important and loved."

"But you divorced him," I pointed out. I had an odd feeling of resentment toward Oliver Lewis, a man I had met only once. I could not explain it.

"Sure. After he married me, I became an accessory. He introduced me to his business contacts to show off that he was married, I guess. Some of them were real family values guys who wouldn't have been crazy about two unmarried people living together. So Ollie wanted to get married fast. I only knew him a couple of months before we were at the justice of the peace in Darien, Connecticut, vowing all sorts of stuff I never really thought about." She shook her head in seeming disbelief at her own naiveté, then took a larger sip of her drink.

"Is that why he married all the others?" I asked. I was attempting to find a conversational path toward Terry Lambroux and the real Sheila McInerney, but I had to do so gently. Scaring off Hazel Montrose would be a serious setback for the research on Detective Dickinson's question.

Hazel shrugged. "I can't tell you why he married anybody else," she said. "I can't even really tell you why he married me." Another sip. It seemed there would be no reason for me to ply Hazel with alcohol; she was doing it herself.

"Well, what about Sheila McInerney? Did you meet her?"

Hazel shook her head. "I wasn't really friendly with any of the others. I know Jenny LeBlanc likes to pretend there's this club of the five of us, but I didn't really keep up with any of them. Maybe they have meetings or something, but I've never gone." She looked up and caught Tyler's eye, pointed at her empty martini glass, and nodded when he acknowledged her order.

"So you are not a member of WOOL?"

Hazel sputtered a laugh that was part amusement, part surprise, and part disgust. "No," she said firmly. "There's no monthly newsletter or anything, you know. And it isn't my nature to wallow in the past like that. I married Ollie, I divorced Ollie. Once the papers were signed, it was over. You move on."

"What kind of settlement was included in your divorce?" I asked.

Hazel blinked. "I beg your pardon?"

I worried now that I had violated some social protocol. "I'm sorry," I said. "Was that an inappropriate question?"

"Samuel, it's considered rude to ask people about their finances, so yes, that was inappropriate."

"My apologies." How could I get the information if a direct question was not considered allowable? "I merely believed that you might have become wealthy if you now own part of OLimited." This was calculated to estimate Hazel's divorce agreement along with the viability of Oliver Lewis's business.

She shook her head. "I'm not rich. I don't think anybody got rich off Oliver Lewis." She looked up as Tyler brought her second martini to the table. "Oh thank you," she said. She took a sip and looked at me. "Can we talk about something else?"

I scanned my mind for alternative topics of conversation. "Did you know that the original title of 'Yesterday' was 'Scrambled Eggs?'" I asked. I consider that fact to be common knowledge, so it gives me information when other people are unaware of it.

Unfortunately, I did not get a response because a young woman dressed in the same style as Tyler appeared from the kitchen carrying a tray with our dinners on top of it. She opened a collapsible stand for it, put the tray down, and placed our orders in front of us. She did not tell us her name, nor did she announce that she would be taking care of us today.

Hazel drank more from her martini before beginning to eat her dinner. I examined mine, determined that it was slightly under-cooked, and beckoned to the young woman. I told her of my concern and she apologized (although I doubted the problem was at all her fault) and removed the plate, saying she would have an appropriate one back to me as soon as possible.

I noticed a closed, observant look on Hazel's face when I returned my attention to her. "You're very particular about some things," she said. "A lot of men would have let that go."

It was difficult to know what to say; I did not want to bring up the subject of an autism spectrum disorder at this moment. "There are some issues that are difficult for me to overlook," I said. "Food is one of them." That was true.

She nodded. "I understand. I can't leave the house unless I'm wearing earrings." I did not see the relevance of that statement, but apparently Hazel was trying to draw an analogy between my food preferences and her insistence on decorating her earlobes. It was probably best not to dwell on that.

The young woman returned with my order, and it was now satisfactorily prepared. I thanked her and she apologized again, although I still could not understand the need. There was an interval during which the conversation lagged as both Hazel and I satisfied our appetites. She was, I noticed, still paying a good deal of attention to the second martini. If she decided to order a third, I might consider calling Mike for a ride home for both of us if I could find a public phone; they are very difficult to locate in the age of the cellular telephone.

"The thing is," Hazel said suddenly, "Oliver was not a real businessman." She slurred the *s* in *business* slightly. "He was trying to get money from old people without giving them anything."

Perhaps there was an advantage to this idea of plying with alcohol. "How did it work?" I asked her, trying to keep my voice impassive, which is the way some people believe I sound all the time.

"It was simple," Hazel said after another sip. "Ollie would get names of people whose spouses had just died. They had to be over seventy for him to contact them. Then he'd call up and ask about their insurance. He'd convince them traditional life insurance wasn't worth the money for someone of their age living alone. And he said the way to really provide for your children and grandchildren when you go is to make these really smart investments that his company OLimited would find for them."

"It is not unusual for people to invest in mutual funds and corporate interests," I said. "How did Mr. Lewis make money that way, more than any other investment counselor would do?"

Hazel pointed at me with her knife, which was momentarily alarming. "That's the thing: there never were any investments. Ollie would get these people to sign contracts that basically said they were giving him all their money to do with as he pleased. It said *if* he wanted to invest the money, he could, but in any event, it was in his name. So he invested in Ollie Lewis, that's what he invested in."

"So you must have benefited, as his wife and then ex-wife, from the seemingly illegal and certainly misleading business he was conducting," I suggested.

Hazel took a bite and chewed it while she spoke, which made me avert my gaze to my own food. It now seemed less appetizing than before I'd seen Hazel chewing.

"I never saw a dime of it," she said. She took another sip; the glass was almost empty again. "The fact is, Ollie never really made much on the scheme. He underestimated the old people. Most of them aren't that stupid—they read the contract and threw him out on his ear. It was only a few that bought in on this scheme, and they didn't have all that much for him to glom onto, so he ended up with very little."

I ignored the use of the word *glom*, which does not actually exist in the English language, and pressed on while the martinis were still loosening Hazel's mind and lowering her verbal resistance.

"But he supposedly had millions. Was that his only source of income?"

Hazel's lips vibrated and she made a sound I've heard referred to as a "raspberry," despite it having no relationship to the fruit. "No," she said. "Ollie always had a scheme. He just never had a good one."

"What about Sheila McInerney and Terry Lambroux?" I was playing a hunch, which is not my habit. I do not approve of guesswork, but this question had left me with little of substance to use, so I provided a stimulus and waited for the response.

"I told you, there is no Terry Lambroux," Hazel said. "I don't know anything about Sheila."

She was, I believe, about to add something to her statement when some movement outside the window next to our booth distracted her. "What's that?" she said, and her shoulders seemed to tense.

"I did not see anything unusual," I said.

"They've found me!" Hazel reached for her purse, which was on the seat next to her. "We have to go!"

"I don't understand," I told her, trying to hold her gaze and wondering what I should do about paying Tyler for the dinner, or whether Hazel and I should divide the check by two and pay half each. The fact was, Tyler had not yet given us the check, so for the moment the point was moot. "Who has found you, and why are you so upset? We have not finished—"

Hazel stood up, seemingly sober after one second. Her eyes were focused and intent on the restaurant entrance, where a young woman named Tasha (according to her nametag) had opened the door and greeted us when we'd arrived. "There's no time for it now, Samuel. We have to get out of here!"

I gestured toward Tyler, who had no doubt seen Hazel stand and was already approaching. He handed me the check and I paid it, adding a twenty percent tip because servers have a very difficult job. I would settle with Hazel about her half later, I decided, since she seemed very agitated about leaving immediately and was already walking toward the door.

A glance toward the table as I hurried after her revealed that her martini glass was now empty.

I did consider calling Mike, but there was no public telephone nearby and Hazel was a few strides ahead of me and obviously had no intention of stopping to wait for a taxicab. I noticed that the white skirt she was wearing was very attractive on her, but that did not seem important at the moment. Perhaps I should let her drive away and then find a way to get in touch with Mike or Ms. Washburn or Mother.

"Come *on*," Hazel insisted, getting into the driver's seat of her car. I increased my speed to show her I was serious about her insistence that we were in some sort of danger, but I stopped at the driver's side window, which Hazel opened.

"Would you like me to drive?" I asked. "I do have a valid driver's license." I felt it was best not to mention that she had been drinking alcohol and might be violating New Jersey state law by operating a motor vehicle.

"Get in!" she shouted, not ceding the controls of the car.

It was a difficult decision, but with no other means of transportation home, I sat in the passenger seat and immediately fastened my shoulder harness.

Hazel engaged the car's engine and backed out of the parking space at an alarming rate. I'm not sure I didn't let out a yelp involuntarily. She headed for the exit very quickly.

"I believe you are exceeding the speed limit," I noted.

"You ain't seen nothin' yet," she answered. It took me a moment to untangle the double negative, but when I did, I felt my hand on my nose.

The car spun out of the parking lot and onto Centennial Avenue, but without the tires squealing and spinning as they often do during chase scenes on television and in films. I could see the speedometer from the passenger seat—it lit up in large numbers on the dashboard—and the message it gave was extremely unsettling.

I had to choke out words. I could feel my head shaking. "Why are we going so fast?" I asked.

Hazel actually took her eyes off the road (at this speed!) and regarded me with a withering look. "To keep them from catching us, of course," she spat out.

I dared not turn around to see through the rear window, but I could barely force my eyes toward the passenger side mirror, expecting to see the black Ford Escape in hot pursuit. But there was no obvious pursuer behind us. The Escape was not there, and other vehicles were doing their very best to stay out of Hazel's path.

"Who?" I asked when I could speak again. The speedometer had gained eight miles per hour.

"Them!" she shouted, as if that were an adequate answer.

She made a right turn onto Stelton Road, the opposite direction from the Questions Answered office, at a very high speed, and I held my breath for fear the car would turn over on its side and we would be injured or killed. But it did not do that, and Hazel seemed to take it as a signal that she should increase our speed further. I made a choking noise in the back of my throat.

"We have to get away!" Hazel insisted.

I forced my jaw open. "Please let me off here. I will find another ride home."

"I can't stop! They'll catch us!"

There was no rescue in sight. I would have thought a Piscataway police cruiser would have stopped Hazel's car by now, but there was none behind us. I had only myself to rely upon, and that was not comforting.

My hands were flapping, my brow was coated in sweat, my head was shaking at the neck, and my voice was out of control. I could hear myself vocalizing without making any conversational sounds. It sounded like, "uuuuuuuuuuuuuuuuhhhhh ... "

"Cut that out," Hazel said. "You're helping them find us."

There was no choice. Ms. Washburn was not here finding a way to refocus my thoughts. I had to do it myself. I closed my eyes, trying to block out the increasing whine of the engine as it accelerated.

"Hazel," I said, "there is no one chasing us."

She started as if shocked. "There isn't?" she asked.

"No. I would see them if they were there. And no, there is no one so clever that I wouldn't see them following this car if they were doing so, especially at the speed you are driving. Please. Believe what I am saying, and slow the car down."

Hazel, eyes wide, looked into her rearview mirror, then the one on the driver's side. She moved spastically, quick, darting movements of her head that made her look oddly like Elsa Lanchester in *The Bride of Frankenstein*, a classic film made in 1935. It also starred Colin Clive, Boris Karloff, and Ernest Thesiger. The film was directed by James Whale and distributed by Universal Pictures.

Mother says I sometimes offer too much information on a topic.

The car began to decelerate as Hazel's face looked less frantic and more worried. "I was so sure," she murmured as the speedometer showed a speed only slightly higher than the posted limit for this area.

Normally I would be concerned in a vehicle only slightly exceeding the legal limit. Now I felt positively relieved.

"Why did you think someone was following you?" I asked when Hazel appeared to be breathing normally again.

"Someone's been following me for days," she answered. "Two men in a black—"

"A black Ford Escape?" I asked.

She looked over at me, which caused my right hand to flutter a bit, but then she turned her attention back to the road. "How did you know that?"

"They followed Ms. Washburn and me as well. I believe they work for someone with an interest in Oliver Lewis's business, perhaps Terry Lambroux." I watched her face for any reaction at the name I'd mentioned, and I got one.

Hazel scoffed waving a hand. "I don't think there's such a person as Terry Lambroux," she said. "You keep hearing about him, but nobody ever sees him."

"Terry Lambroux is a man?"

Hazel shrugged. "Far as I know. Everybody always says 'him' when the name comes up. But I don't think there is such a person."

That was when I spied the black Ford Escape behind us, which opened a debate in my mind: Tell Hazel and have her drive wildly and dangerously again, or say nothing and risk putting both of us in danger?

Then I remembered the men in the Escape. So I said to Hazel, "Would you pull over at that parking lot, please? The excitement has me feeling a bit light-headed."

Hazel pulled in her lips, but she did as I asked, and in forty-three seconds we were safely parked in the lot for a Dunkin' Donuts. I told Hazel I wanted to get some air, and let myself out of the car.

The Escape pulled into the lot at the other end and parked, its lights turned off.

I bent over a bit, pretending to be gasping for air. Hazel opened the window on her side and asked if I was all right. I nodded, but said I'd like to walk around a little. She should stay there, I told her, I would be right back.

Still a little stooped, I did not wait for an answer and walked in a somewhat indirect path toward the Escape. At one point I walked to the door of the Dunkin' Donuts, although I did not want to buy a doughnut. I stopped, pretended I had thought of something, and walked away from the door, approaching the Escape.

Once near the Ford, I waved my arm in a greeting and approached the driver in his seat. "Gentlemen," I said. "We meet again."

"Hoenig," the taller man said. "What are you doing here?"

"He was at the Applebee's with Montrose," the shorter one answered with a slightly annoyed tone. "Don't you ever pay attention?"

"I wonder why you are now following Hazel Montrose if you are, as you said, not interested in the murder of Oliver Lewis," I said, paying no attention to their bickering. "Could it be that you were not entirely truthful with me?"

That was sarcasm. It did not come to me naturally, but once I grasped the concept, I was able to utilize it almost immediately.

The smaller man exhaled, indicating this was more effort than he had anticipated or desired. "What do you want, Hoenig?" he asked.

"I want to know who asked you to follow Hazel Montrose and why."

"And why should I tell you anything?"

"Because I will pester you until you do. This way you can avoid the aggravation easily. I have Asperger's Syndrome, sir. Believe me, I can irritate you in ways you have not yet imagined." I did not exactly know what that meant, but I was willing to bet the man in the Escape didn't know, either.

Clearly, he did not. "All right. There's no harm in it. First of all, there is absolutely no chance I'm going to tell you who hired us. But I was asked to see where Montrose went because someone thinks she might have had something to do with Oliver Lewis being, you know, dead."

Beyond that, the man in the Escape told me very little. His employer, he said, was interested in what had happened to Oliver Lewis for "business reasons," and if Hazel was involved in the murder, there was money to be made, he insinuated.

"She was the one of his wives who hated him the most, but she was also the one most closely tied to the scam," he said.

"What do you know about Terry Lambroux?" I asked. The man looked at me without saying anything. Then before I could ask another question, he had raised the automatic window on his vehicle, engaged the engine, and driven away.

I walked back to Hazel's car, where she was listening to a song I did not recognize on the radio. She turned off the music when I sat back in the passenger seat. "Are you feeling better?" she asked.

"Yes." I nodded. "Thank you." I know it is proper to thank someone at a moment like that, but am not sure if one is expressing appreciation for the idea that the other person hopes you are feeling better—which was not stated explicitly—or for simply asking, which seems odd, given that it is an inquiry based on the situation. No one thanks me when I ask questions as part of my research. As with many items of social protocol, it is not logical.

Hazel engaged the car's reverse gear and backed out of the parking space. She stared straight ahead as she pulled out of the parking lot and then onto Stelton Road again.

"So what did the guy in the black Escape tell you?" she asked. She did not look at me to gauge a reaction.

"He said he is employed by someone who believes you to be the most likely suspect in Oliver Lewis's murder," I responded. There was no sense in lying to Hazel about the conversation. She had already determined that I'd spoken to the man, and I would not have been able to create a believable story that would leave out the pertinent information. Besides, Mother often says it's easier to tell the truth because you don't have to remember the lie.

Hazel seemed unfazed by the information. "He didn't say who?"

"No. He has refused to name his employer on a number of occasions. He also does not respond when I mention Terry Lambroux."

Hazel shook her head slightly. "I told you, I don't think there is a Terry Lambroux."

"Someone sued Oliver Lewis for breach of promise," I pointed out. "Whoever that was used the name Terry—not Terrence or Theresa—Lambroux. Can you explain that?"

"No. But it seems weird to me that nobody's ever seen this person."

"I agree. But strange circumstances surrounding a person do not necessarily mean there is no such person."

Hazel seemed to consider that idea. "You must have thought I was crazy when I started driving like that. Does it make you feel better to discover we really were being followed?"

"No."

She laughed. "I don't blame you. I guess I'm asking whether you still think I'm crazy."

I took a deep breath; this moment is always awkward for me. "I have Asperger's Syndrome, Hazel," I said. "I think *everyone* is crazy."

She laughed harder but did not move to pull the car over, which made me slightly nervous. But she did manage to drive safely and controlled herself after eleven seconds.

"You're probably right," Hazel said.

She dropped me off at my home three minutes later, but we had not continued our conversation. I opened the car door, and Hazel said, "This was fun, Samuel. We should do it again sometime."

I thought the idea of going to dinner, driving wildly into the night, and being followed by unsavory characters was hardly something I would care to repeat. So it took me a moment to realize that

Hazel meant we might like to see each other on a social basis at some other time.

What do men say at such moments? "Yes. I will make a point to call you." It was a variation on what I have heard in films and on television.

I walked into the house and called to Mother, who was in the den watching television. She walked into the kitchen, where I was taking a pitcher of water out of the refrigerator (I do not use plastic bottles at home, and have considered renting a water cooler at the office, but it would not be possible to get a cooler of diet soda for Ms. Washburn). Mother wasted no time. "So?" she said.

"I do not believe that dating is necessarily my strongest activity," I said. "But I have gained some useful information toward answering the questions."

"Questions?" Mother asked. "Are there more than one?"

I poured some water into a glass and sat down at the table after I returned the pitcher to the refrigerator. I nodded after taking a drink, which felt good. "Of course. There is Detective Dickinson's question about the death of Oliver Lewis, and Cynthia Maholm's question about her husband."

"But Cynthia is dead, poor thing," Mother reminded me.

"That does not absolve me of my responsibility. She asked me a question, and I am obligated to answer it, even if she is not alive to hear the answer."

Mother sat down opposite me and searched my face as if for the truth in some strange puzzle. "What information did you get tonight?" she asked.

I told her about my dinner with Hazel, and how it was cut short by her odd insistence that we hurry out because there were assassins on her trail. And I told her how I had spotted the men in the black Escape and had a conversation with the one who seemed to know more than the other.

"I believe I am getting very close to answering the question for Detective Dickinson," I told Mother after assuring her that I was perfectly all right and was not even sure that, aside from Hazel's erratic driving, I was ever in any true danger. "Hazel's repeated declarations that there is no such person as Terry Lambroux indicates that there must be such a person. Everyone else involved in the question insists there is, although no one can identify Lambroux or conclusively state if that person is male or female. There is no reason for anyone else to lie about it, so I must assume that Hazel has a reason to deceive me on the subject."

"What do you think the reason is?" Mother asked.

"The most obvious is that Hazel *is* Terry Lambroux," I suggested.

TWENTY-EIGHT

"Man, you go out on one date with a girl and you're already accusing her of all sorts of deceptions." Ms. Washburn was undoubtedly kidding with me, but I did not understand the humor of the insinuation she was making. It was not worth clarifying, but I noted it and moved on.

"We have no physical proof," I admitted. "That has been the problem with this question from the beginning—it has been impossible to verify, so we have had to rely on the testimony of the parties involved. That makes the question considerably more frustrating than most to answer."

We waited outside the Piscataway police department on Hoes Lane in the town's municipal complex. Sitting in Ms. Washburn's car, we were waiting for a glimpse of the officer to whom we wanted to talk, and at Ms. Washburn's suggestion, had turned the car's engine (and the air conditioning) off and opened the windows. That is not my favorite environment, but I do understand the importance of using less fuel for the sake of the planet's ecosystem. I was, however, noticing some slight perspiration and itching on my right triceps.

"If we don't have any proof, how can you have a theory?" Ms. Washburn asked.

"I do not have a theory. I have a series of assumptions. If they are correct, we are well on the way to answering the questions. If they are incorrect, we could be acting irresponsibly and impetuously. But I will confess I have no other ideas at this moment and would love to hear a suggestion of another plan of action if you have one."

"I'm sorry I don't, Samuel." Ms. Washburn's voice had a slight tinge of hurt in it, so I thought over what I had said to see if it might have been misconstrued. It was possible.

But there was no time to make my apologies and explain myself. Detective Esteban walked out of the police station, and I had one of the first lucky breaks I'd experienced since this question was first posed: She was alone.

"Remind me to tell you something later," I said to Ms. Washburn as we got out of the car and approached the detective. We reached her around the side of the building before she could find her car. Ms. Washburn called to her, and the detective turned. She looked surprised when she recognized us.

"Look, I'm not in the business of answering your questions," she said.

"I am," I told her. "But I don't expect you to do all the research for us. I have only two things to ask, and I expect they will be very easy for you to answer. This will not take much of your time."

Detective Esteban's eyebrows dropped a little. I could not interpret that expression but she said, "What's the first question?"

"What is your first name?" I asked.

There was no hesitation, as there often is when I ask a question someone is not expecting. "Alicia," she said. "What's the other thing you want to know?"

"What is your favorite song by the Beatles?" I asked. I did not look at Ms. Washburn, because we had not discussed this moment. I had asked that question spontaneously.

"'Let It Be,'" she said, again with no moment to think about what I might want to hear rather than what she actually believed. *Values stability. Believes in positive outcomes.* "Is that it?" She turned to walk to her car.

"No, detective," I said.

"You told me you had only two questions." Detective Esteban did not turn back to face me, but she did stop walking.

"I'm afraid I was mistaken about that," I said. "There is one more thing. But first, could you go back inside and retrieve one item from your evidence locker?"

"I still don't understand why you didn't go to Dickinson about this," Detective Esteban said. "He's the primary on this case." She was still unaware of my association with her partner since he had insisted on secrecy, and we were honoring that promise.

"I will be completely honest with you, detective," I said. "I trust your skills more than I do Detective Dickinson's."

Ms. Washburn looked away from the blackboard displaying the menu. The Bagel Bazaar was not fancy, but it was just far enough from the police department that Detective Esteban would not be seen by her partner or her colleagues and besides, it was her lunch hour. Ms. Washburn's expression indicated that my statement was bolder than she had expected it to be.

"Dickinson's just going through a slump," his partner said. "It happens to everybody."

"I do not dispute that, as I have never been a police officer," I said. "But I have never had a slump before. I do not understand the inability to answer a question, and this one baffles me. I believe you can help with some information you probably know without having to refer to notes."

"I'm waiting for a turkey sandwich on a seven grain bagel," Detective Esteban said. "You said you have one more question. Ask it, because when that sandwich comes, I'm taking it back to my desk and our meeting here is over. *Comprende?*"

I did not see why we might now be speaking Spanish, but Detective Esteban did not elaborate. "I understand," I said. "Here is my question: Did the preliminary medical examiner's report show a puncture mark, as for an injection, anywhere on Cynthia Maholm's body?"

"Yes," she answered. "How did you—"

"Someone injected her with Reglan. Do you believe it is possible that Hazel Montrose, Terry Lambroux and Sheila McInerney are all the same person?"

Ms. Washburn, while ordering ham on a pumpernickel bagel, was watching the detective closely. I had not ordered lunch, as Mother would be expecting me in forty-five minutes. But I was carefully examining the detective's face as well.

Her reaction was exactly as I'd hoped: She looked angry.

"How did you know that?" she asked.

After a good deal of discussion, I was able to convince the detective that I had not in fact hacked her office computer (although I probably could, but had no desire to do such a thing) and had not been in touch with any other members of the Piscataway police department. She said there would have been no advantage to doing so, because even her partner, Detective Dickinson, was not aware of her findings yet.

"The trail just kept coming back to those three names, but not one of them was like a complete person," she said, confirming data I had already collected through Internet research. "Hazel Montrose is as close as she comes to having a whole profile, with an address, a Social Security number, and several credit cards in that name. But she doesn't seem to have a birth certificate, she doesn't file taxes because her income is supposedly too low, and her bank accounts have virtually no money in them."

"How did she manage to obtain a marriage license with Oliver Lewis?" Ms. Washburn asked. It was the next question I would have put to the detective.

"You don't need a birth certificate for a marriage license in Connecticut," she said. "Just a driver's license. And she has one of those."

I asked if the detective had what I had asked her to retrieve, and she said she did.

Detective Esteban reached into her pocket and pulled out a small plastic bag. Inside the bag was a cellular phone. She took it out carefully and laid it on the counter next to me. "Why did you need this?" she asked. "I got it from the Manville police to analyze because of the possible connection to the Lewis murder."

"I assume it has been examined and is not needed as evidence as of yet."

She nodded. "That's right, or I wouldn't have removed it. Why should I give it to you?"

"You are not giving it to me. You are, if you choose to do so, lending it to me because I believe it will be helpful in answering the question of Oliver Lewis's death, and perhaps Cynthia Maholm's as well."

Detective Esteban's eyes narrowed. "Do you think it's going to find Terry Lambroux?"

I shook my head. "How did you tie the name Terry Lambroux to the other two?" I asked.

"That was the most interesting one," Detective Esteban admitted. "There seemed to be no record of such a person as Terry Lambroux,

Terrence Lambroux, or Theresa Lambroux anywhere, and that's just not possible in this day and age."

"Exactly," I said. "How did you find a link when I could not?" Immediately, I heard Mother's voice saying with a loving but ironic tone in my mind, "It's always about you, isn't it, Samuel?"

"You don't have access to police records," the detective answered. "It's not a public record when a juvenile is involved in a crime, particularly if the record is expunged after the offender does the time or goes on probation. So don't feel bad, Mr. Hoenig—only a cop could have found that one."

I tended to disagree, but people don't seem to like being told they're wrong, even when it is clearly the case. Ms. Washburn rescued the silence (which lasted only five seconds) by asking, "So Terry Lambroux had a criminal record, but someone with some clout got it expunged?"

"It was a relatively minor offense, but an interesting one," Detective Esteban said, nodding. "I won't tell you the charge, but suffice it to say it was not violent and involved cheating people out of money when she was only twelve years old."

But that was not the interesting part of the detective's news. "Who was it who could make the charges disappear off the record?" I asked.

The detective allowed herself the slightest smile. "Her father, Judge Henry T. McInerney."

"And that's what leads to Sheila," I said.

She nodded again. "I believe that is her birth name. But she had it legally changed at eleven, when her mother remarried a guy named Lambroux. 'Terry' came later as an aka in the file, a name she was only using when she was scamming."

"So they *are* all the same person," Ms. Washburn said, shaking her head in wonder. "But does that really lead anywhere? I mean sure, she's shifty, but does that necessarily lead to the conclusion that she murdered her ex-husband?"

Ms. Washburn's sandwich was delivered and we moved from the counter to a table on the opposite side of the establishment. Detective Esteban took the seat away from the door to better conceal herself if one of her colleagues should wander in.

"Not definitely," she told Ms. Washburn in answer to her recent question. "But when there's a lot of smoke, you have to figure there's a fire someplace."

I had heard the idiom "Where there's smoke there's fire" before and had it explained to me, but this was a new configuration; I had to consider it for a moment before grasping the meaning. I nodded. "It is always a mistake to overlook coincidences," I told Ms. Washburn. "They are rarely what they seem. The idea that Hazel has three identities is certainly reason for concern."

"How did you figure it out, Samuel?" she asked.

"Last night Hazel was acting like someone who had something to fear," I said. "It was clearly just that—an act—but she decided to begin it just when I was asking about Oliver Lewis's somewhat illicit businesses and how they might have benefitted her as his ex-wife. The question was innocent enough, considering there were, theoretically, four other wives and an ex-fiancée, but it seemed to alarm Hazel.

"At first I assumed I had gotten close to some financial scheme in which she and Mr. Lewis might have been in collaboration. But I had asked about that before. It was when I grouped together the names of Sheila McInerney and Terry Lambroux that she felt most threatened and initiated the melodrama that ensued."

"That's a pretty big guess," Detective Esteban said. "You mention two names and you decide she was both of them and herself at the same time?"

"There was the fact that no one had seen the fictional Terry Lambroux, and that Sheila McInerney was a name the other members of WOOL had clearly heard, since Cynthia Maholm had used it as her own. That was when things began to happen, which indicated to me that the name was a signal, a sore subject, for someone. Cynthia was doing the same thing I did—she used the name Sheila McInerney as a stimulus." I sat back. "I think it worked, and somehow Oliver Lewis ended up murdered."

"And so did Cindy Maholm," Detective Esteban said. "In Manville." She sounded oddly melancholy that the crime hadn't taken place in her jurisdiction.

"Yes. That suggests Ms. Maholm was somehow breaking ranks. She was the one who came to me first, then set up the elaborate drama in the apartment in Edison. She went out of her way to keep Ms. Washburn and me away when Oliver Lewis was being murdered, probably in his office, then taken to mine. It is still a wild coincidence that Hazel happened to be in the Extra Safe Cleaning van. Detective, is it possible for you to see if she is indeed on that company's payroll?" I checked my watch; Ms. Washburn would have to being driving me home in five minutes if I were to be on time for lunch with Mother.

"I'll call, but I'd also like to get a warrant for physical evidence for that van. The problem is convincing a judge," the detective said. "Everything we have is guesswork or circumstantial."

"That is true, but there have been two murders, and there is a very strong possibility one of the victims was transported in the van or Hazel Montrose's car trunk."

Ms. Washburn looked up from her sandwich, which she had almost finished. "Is there a way to get into the car and the van without a warrant?" she asked.

"Only with the owner's permission," Detective Esteban said.

"Well, the van isn't owned by Hazel, so the company might be willing to give you permission," Ms. Washburn noted. "And Hazel might let you into her car, either because she didn't do it, because she didn't put Oliver in the car, or because she wouldn't want to appear guilty by refusing."

"That is excellent logic," I told my associate. "Excellent work."

"I'm already staying with the company, Samuel," she reminded me. "You don't have to butter me up."

That phrase conjured up such a disgusting image that I chose to think about the next point immediately. "It is worth a try, detective," I said.

"Maybe." Detective Esteban stood. "I've got to get back. Dickinson will be asking me where I was so long, and you don't seem to want him to know you came to see me. I certainly don't want him to know you gave me some ideas about the case."

I nodded. "It is in both our better interests to keep any consultations to ourselves for the time being," I said. "Thank you for the help, Detective Esteban."

She nodded slightly. "Thank you, Mr. Hoenig. Ms. Washburn." And with that she turned on her heel and left the building.

Ms. Washburn looked at her cellular phone, which displays the time. "We have to get you back home for lunch," she said, picking up her purse.

I followed after her, leaving a tip on the table.

"Was that much help?" Ms. Washburn asked me as we left.

"It was certainly a step in the right direction," I answered. "We are getting closer to answering the question."

"Yeah, but Detective Dickinson is our client," she reminded me. We walked toward her Kia Spectra. "Isn't this a little devious, going behind his back?"

"Our client has been very clear about not wanting to do the research himself," I said. "We are gaining information without asking him to do so, just as he would have approved."

"I don't know how I feel about working for him, Samuel."

"You are not working for him. You are working for me."

I got into the car and sat in the passenger seat as Ms. Washburn took her place behind the steering wheel. "What I mean is, I feel bad about working to give Dickinson the collar when his partner is doing so much of the work," she said as she started the engine.

"That would be unfortunate," I admitted.

"So what's our next move?"

"I believe we should call a meeting of WOOL."

TWENTY-NINE

It was not as easy as it sounded.

In order to get all the surviving ex-wives of Oliver Lewis in one room together, it was necessary to plan carefully. As far as we knew, a full meeting of all the ex-wives had never taken place before, and the invitation coming from outside the group would easily have been considered suspicious by the guilty party we were trying to unmask.

"There are a number of suspects in this crime that must be investigated if we are to answer the question," I said to Mother and Ms. Washburn. Mother had served herself and me turkey sandwiches, and had expressed her displeasure with Ms. Washburn for paying for lunch when she could have eaten with us. ("Just consider yourself invited for lunch every day, Janet.") As it was, Ms. Washburn sat with us at the kitchen table and simply watched as Mother and I had lunch.

"Yeah," she said. "And most of them are Hazel Montrose."

Mother looked concerned. "Isn't that the young woman you were out with last night, Samuel?"

"It was a business dinner, Mother," I explained. Again.

I chose to phrase the last sentence in a way that seemed to express some consternation, but it was for comic effect. I was not upset with my mother.

"Nonetheless, the WOOL members are only some of the people who might have had a hand in Oliver Lewis's murder," I said, attempting to change the subject. "There is also Roger Siplowitz, who claims to have known Mr. Lewis only slightly, but whose name shows up on Terry Lambroux's civil suit against Mr. Lewis. He is clearly hiding something."

We had called Siplowitz's office again, twice, and had not been granted access to him. Another visit would undoubtedly have resulted in the same outcome and would have used up valuable time.

"And if Terry Lambroux really is Hazel Montrose, he might know something about the whole crazy setup," Ms. Washburn suggested. "I see where you're going, Samuel."

"It might not be necessary to have Mr. Siplowitz in the same room as the ex-wives for this meeting," I theorized. "That would seem too coincidental; perhaps we should see him separately after we see the WOOL members."

"It's a silly club name," Mother said.

"They've never all met before at the same time," Ms. Washburn reminded me. "How do we get them all to show up without rousing their suspicion?"

"We need only worry about one of them," I said. "Hazel Montrose."

"That's three of them," Ms. Washburn noted.

There was no reasonable response, so I went on: "While there is no direct evidence linking Hazel to either murder, she is the only one of the ex-wives who has said she never met any of the others."

"Do you believe her?" Mother asked.

"I do not have enough proof to form an opinion, but she does have a rather varied history of lying to us, so I am wary. Still, there is some reason to question each of the ex-wives again."

I had finished the sandwich I was eating and told Mother I would clear the table myself. She has some issues with her knees and had prepared the meal, so I felt it was the least I could do to save her the time and effort to clean up.

Ms. Washburn offered to help, but since she had not partaken in the meal, it seemed unfair to accept the offer.

I turned toward Ms. Washburn. "Is there some need in women— obviously not all women, but enough that it would be considered unremarkable—to have a protector, a man who is meant to stand guard or deal with imposing danger?"

Mother and Ms. Washburn exchanged a look that I could not decipher. "It's a really old instinct," Ms. Washburn said after a moment (two seconds). "The stereotype is that women are helpless physically and need men to serve as a ... buffer, I guess, against dangers. It's a view that's changing, but it's still there. How did we get to this?"

"It occurs to me that both Cynthia Maholm and Hazel Montrose have attempted to cast me as the male protector, and I think I have failed to play the part both times," I said. I noticed Ms. Washburn had put the plates and utensils into the dishwasher and decided not to bring it up, assuming she had not forgotten my declining her offer and simply did what she had decided she would do. Ms. Washburn often acts in ways I don't understand intellectually, but comprehend on an almost instinctual level. "I wonder if it was meant to distract me from the facts surrounding the question we are attempting to answer."

"Distract you?" Mother said. "When you called me from jail, I got the impression you thought the whole ruse was a means to get you out of the way."

I began cleaning the table with an antiseptic wipe. "Yes. And perhaps that was Hazel's intention last night as well, to remove me and herself from the Applebee's, but somehow I think my intended response was supposed to have been to see myself as her hero, her protector, and therefore not suspect her in the murders."

Ms. Washburn looked at me and exhaled. "You took her to an Applebee's?"

"It is possible dating is not one of my stronger skills."

"It will be when you find the right girl," Mother suggested. Mother is something of an optimist where I am concerned.

"Nonetheless, our focus now should be on assembling the members of WOOL without them knowing we have done so." I took Cynthia Maholm's cellular phone from my pocket, getting a knowing smile from Ms. Washburn in the process. "Perhaps Ms. Maholm can lend some assistance. Please show me how one sends a text message with this phone."

Ms. Washburn took the phone from my hand gingerly, as if afraid she would damage it or contaminate its ability to operate as evidence through touching it. "Are you sure it's already been fingerprinted and everything?" she asked.

"Quite sure. Don't worry." I gestured toward the phone. "How is it done?"

"It's really easy." Ms. Washburn showed me the proper sequence of movements that would identify the person receiving the message, and then how to compose and send it. The technology was, as she had said, quite simple. "I could just do it for you."

"Perhaps I should learn how to do these things myself," I said, and identified Jennifer LeBlanc's cellular phone number among Cynthia's list of contacts. I began composing a message.

"You already have the phone numbers," Mother pointed out. "Couldn't you just send these from Janet's phone?"

"I believe the message will have more impact if it comes from beyond the grave," I said.

I sent the first text message to Ms. LeBlanc, then started composing one for Amy Stanhope. Ms. Washburn sat next to me at the table and looked puzzled.

"Why aren't you sending them all at once?" she asked.

I stopped what I was typing. "How does one do that?"

It took only two minutes for Ms. Washburn to instruct me in the proper way to create a list of contacts and then send them all the same text message, but in that time, a reply had come back from Jennifer LeBlanc.

WHO IS THIS?

Ms. Washburn smiled. "It's working the way you want. Should you answer her?"

"In a moment. Let me send the message to the other women. Ms. LeBlanc can wonder for a little while longer."

"This seems cruel, somehow," Mother suggested.

"Do you think I should stop?"

"No."

Amy Stanhope, Hazel Montrose, and Rachel Vandross each received the text I had sent, which read:

EMERGENCY MEETING OF WOOL. TONIGHT 6 P.M. OLimited OFFICES. Then, before the others could reply, I sent a second message to each and added Jennifer LeBlanc's cellular phone number to the list. The second message read: I'M NOT DEAD. That was true, as I was not dead. But the message was intended to seem like it had come from Cynthia Maholm.

Within seconds, Cynthia's cellular telephone began to ring, but Ms. Washburn and I had agreed we would not answer, as that would immediately spoil the illusion. We would respond to text messages if it would help expedite an agreement to attend the meeting. If it were simply an inquiry into the sender, the message would receive no response.

Mother was right; it did seem cruel. I confess there was a certain satisfaction to that, as one of these women had probably been responsible for the difficulty this question had posed since the beginning, and at least one death. The others, I'm afraid, were to be classified, as the military would deem them, "collateral damage."

WHY AT THE OFFICE? Ms. Stanhope texted back after a number of pleas for the sender's identity had been ignored.

That seemed a reasonable question, and one that would help bring her to the scene when she was needed, so at Ms. Washburn's suggestion, I sent back the message: SCENE OF THE CRIME.

We could not be certain that Oliver Lewis was murdered in his offices; in fact, our inspection of the space had found no evidence at all that it was the location in question. But only the murderer would know that, and Ms. Stanhope was not at the top of my list of suspects, although she could not be ruled out entirely.

I HAVE AN APPOINTMENT. That was from Jennifer LeBlanc. Again after consultation with the two women in the room with me, she was given the (probably unsatisfying) response, BREAK IT.

Rachel, the least visible of the WOOL members, did not respond at all to the text, although one of the unanswered calls to Cynthia's cellular telephone was from her number. Hazel Montrose, however, did respond, and her message was probably the most disturbing to me.

I know who you are.

"She didn't mention your name," Ms. Washburn said. "It's a bluff."

I am aware of the term; it comes from poker, a game with which I am only passingly familiar. But I was not sure Ms. Washburn was correct. "Suppose she does know who is sending the messages?" I posited.

"Does it matter?" Mother asked. "The key is getting them to show up."

That was true, but not the point of my concern. "If Hazel is the killer and she knows I'm the one sending the messages, she also has one vital piece of information: where I live." I decided I would no longer respond to text messages and put Cynthia Maholm's cellular phone into my right hand pocket, where I would check on it every few minutes to be sure I had not misplaced it. I had promised Detective Esteban she would get the item back unharmed.

Ms. Washburn and Mother looked at each other for nine seconds. That is a relatively long look.

"I don't think you have to worry, Samuel," Mother said. "She knew you were looking into the murder before, and nothing happened."

"It is three hours until the meeting. Ms. Washburn and I should be there early, so we should leave in less than two hours. I am not comfortable leaving you here alone, Mother," I said.

"I could come with you."

I thought that over and shook my head negatively. "In a room that might very likely have a killer in it, my thinking about your safety as well as Ms. Washburn's would be a dangerous distraction. We have been through that before." There was a time when Mother's life was threatened because of a question I was researching, and that was much too upsetting an experience to risk again.

"You could call your pal Mike," Ms. Washburn suggested.

I did not have to consider that long. "That is an excellent idea," I said, and got up to use the telephone on the wall. After all the use of Cynthia Maholm's cellular phone, it was both strange and comforting to be working on a landline again.

Mike agreed to come by and stay in the house with Mother until Ms. Washburn and I returned. I did briefly consider asking him to come with me and having Ms. Washburn stay with Mother, but the idea of leaving both of them out of sight with danger lurking was not acceptable. I could do more to ensure Ms. Washburn's safety if I could see her and not worry about Mother at the same time—Mike agreed, and said he would be at the house within an hour.

He was as good as his word, and I relaxed when he walked in, gave Mother a hug, and told me he was being careful—which meant, I knew, that he was armed in case of an emergency. I introduced Mike to Ms. Washburn, who seemed to find him interesting. She asked about his work driving the taxicab and his military background. Mike smiled and answered the questions, and I made a mental note to remind him that Ms. Washburn was, using Mother's phrase, "another man's wife."

We left shortly thereafter in Ms. Washburn's Kia Spectra, after Mike offered me a spare firearm he carries in his taxicab and I declined. I am not licensed to carry or use a gun, and I have no desire to misuse one and endanger myself or others.

The drive was unusually devoid of conversation; apparently both Ms. Washburn and I had our own thoughts about the upcoming confrontation to keep our minds occupied. I did not want to share them with her—not because I dislike Ms. Washburn at all, but because they would not have been constructive—and she seemed to sense that. The only talk in the car was about directions provided by the Global Positioning Satellite device (although we had been to the office before) and the amount of time it would take to make the trip.

I had brought with me two large rolls of duct tape and an aerosol can of black paint, but I did not have a crowbar or other such implement, so it was a bit of a problem when Ms. Washburn and I discovered that the door to the OLimited offices was locked, which it had not been on our last visit to the building.

"Now what?" she asked. "They'll be here in a little over an hour, assuming they don't show up early."

"The only course of action is to go to the roof," I said. "Luckily, it is only a two-story building." I started up the metal ladder that led to the trap door opening onto the roof of the pizzeria and office structure.

"Wait. What?" Ms. Washburn was four seconds behind me.

We reached the roof—the access door had to be kept unlocked for fire code purposes—and were standing on the flat tar paper structure shortly thereafter.

"I don't see how this helps us," Ms. Washburn said. "Unless you're really Spider-Man and can swing down to the right window, we're even more stuck than we were before."

Of course, Spider-Man is a fictional character from comic books, but I understood the reference. "Super powers will not be necessary," I assured her. "But it is helpful that we have left ourselves enough time to prepare."

She squinted at me, and not because of the imminent sunset, which was behind her. "Prepare for what?" she asked with a tone I believe signaled suspicion.

It took eleven minutes to fashion a sixteen-foot triple-ply extension made of duct tape, twisted into a tighter configuration able to bear more weight than it would be it if it were flat. We secured one end to a structure on the roof, very near the edge, which had no doubt once housed a fire extinguisher or some other emergency supplies. It had a hook-like handle on its door that fit the width of the duct tape improvisation quite well.

"Now I will secure the other end to my waist and legs, and lower myself over the edge to the nearest accessible window," I told Ms. Washburn.

She did not look terribly confident in the plan. "Have I mentioned that this is incredibly dangerous and you shouldn't do it?" she said.

"Yes. Seven times, including this one." With the "rope" of duct tape wrapped securely around me, I moved cautiously to the roof's edge.

"Samuel!" Ms. Washburn shouted, causing me to start and turn toward her. "Maybe ... maybe I should do this. I weigh a lot less than you; the tape is more likely to hold me."

"I will not risk your safety," I said. "I have calculated the physics, and the strength of the tape should be more than sufficient to bear my weight for the short drop. I will be careful. Believe me, Ms. Washburn, I have no desire to plummet to the ground, but even if I do, the fall will probably not be life-threatening."

"You can't imagine how much that doesn't make me feel better."

I had no response, so I beckoned to her, and Ms. Washburn walked to me immediately. She looked up. "Samuel?" she said.

"Yes."

"What do you want to say?"

I did not know what she might have meant, so I answered honestly. "Please watch the point where the tape meets the edge of the brick, here." I pointed at the area most likely to suffer from stress once I was suspended over the roof. "Tell me if it starts to fray."

Ms. Washburn's eyes seemed to move in an unfamiliar way. They appeared to widen horizontally rather than vertically, although that is not physically possible. "Couldn't we just ask the people in the pizzeria if they have a key?" she asked.

I smiled. "I doubt they would be amenable to letting someone break in above them. Please don't worry." I put my right leg over the side of the building that bordered an alley between two businesses. I would probably not be seen from the street.

"This is a bad idea," Ms. Washburn said.

"No doubt." I held on tightly to the bricks with both hands and lowered my left leg over the side.

Ms. Washburn made a sound I would not classify as communicative.

With my legs dangling, it was difficult to look down and see the gap between my feet and the second-flood ledge below them, which I had estimated at about four feet. Once I would let go of my grip on the bricks above me, I would drop that amount. The key would be to steady myself once my feet hit that ledge, and not slip down below it, which would probably create too much stress on the duct tape and drop me to the pavement at street level.

"Don't let go," Ms. Washburn coaxed. "Pull yourself back up."

My voice sounded strained when I heard it coming from me. "I believe you have too much faith in my upper body strength," I hissed.

"I'm afraid," she said quietly.

I was too, but there was no alternative. I extended myself as completely as I could, stretching to the limit of my height, approximated in my mind what the distance would be to the ledge, took a breath, let it out, and released my grip on the upper edge of the brick.

THIRTY

I FELT THE ODD sensation of having no control over my body's position, but only for a very brief moment, less than one second. My feet hit the ledge and because I had made a conscious effort to relax my legs, I did not slip off. I did feel my head pull back on my neck, and had a horrid sensation of falling backward, which could have been disastrous even at this relatively low elevation. But I had anticipated the move, and forced my hands to push forward. I saw the window in front of me, and my fingers found the inside edges of the window frame. I grabbed them and hung on very hard.

"Samuel!" Ms. Washburn shouted from the roof. I did not look up. It seemed more important to regain my balance.

"Yes?"

The response came after a pause, but I did not calculate the time. "Is everything all right?"

It seemed an odd moment to ask that question. Evaluating one's total experience when under stress is a concept popularized by the myth that one's entire life flashes before one's eyes (something that is physiologically impossible) when facing an untimely end. I had not experienced that phenomenon, and so had not considered every aspect of my existence in the time it took to drop four feet to the ledge and hold on.

"I am uninjured," I said, since I believed that was the real intent of Ms. Washburn's question. I pulled lightly on the duct tape harness; it was intact. "Is there great stress on the tape up there?"

"No. It looks pretty secure."

"Good," I said. "Wait two minutes and then walk down the stairs to the door of OLimited. I will admit you."

"Why the two minutes?" Ms. Washburn asked.

"In case I encounter any difficulty in getting inside, like slipping off the ledge," I said.

Her voice was much lower in volume when she responded: "Oh."

But there was no obstacle to my progress. I reached down and opened the window to the OLimited office from the outside, then had barely enough slack on the makeshift rope to get inside before I disentangled myself safely and walked to the office door. Nothing appeared to have been disturbed since my last visit.

I opened the door and Ms. Washburn stood in the hallway. For a moment. Upon seeing me inside, she reached over and embraced me tightly with great speed. Normally I resist such contact with others— it is uncomfortable and has a great number of unspoken rules I do not understand about what is and is not appropriate—but under these circumstances I allowed Ms. Washburn as much time as she needed (six seconds) to control her emotions.

"I was very worried," she managed. I believe she might have wiped her right eye when she relaxed her arms and we separated.

"There was no reason to be concerned. The strategy worked as planned. We should be very pleased indeed if the same is true of our other strategies for this evening."

Ms. Washburn half smiled. "Of course."

I began my preparations by asking Ms. Washburn for the can of aerosol paint she had put into her bag. In rapid succession, I sprayed paint over the lens of each security camera mounted in the office suite. I was careful to be sure the lenses were covered completely and that the black paint was thick enough to block any images the cameras might have recorded from this moment forward.

"That should keep the two men in the Ford Escape from seeing anything that goes on here tonight," I said when I had completed the task.

"But they'll know we're here," Ms. Washburn countered. "Won't that bring them here to find out what's going on?"

"I am counting on it." I looked around the empty room to assess it in context of the situation I expected to unfold here shortly. "It's too bad we didn't think to bring a few folding chairs," I said. "We'll all have to stand for the duration."

"That's the least of our worries."

"It is five thirty-two," I said. "We should be expecting the members of WOOL soon. Would you like to go downstairs for some food?"

Ms. Washburn regarded me with a look that indicated I was making an odd suggestion. "This is a gathering of murder suspects, Samuel," she said. "I don't think catering is necessary."

"I meant to ask if you wanted something for yourself."

She smiled. "I'm a little too nervous for food right now. But it was nice of you to think of me." I had considered asking Ms. Washburn to purchase a bottle of spring water for me, but this was hardly an atmosphere in which I would be comfortable eating.

We sat down on the floor after I had found a broom and cleaned off a large enough area. Then we waited.

I went over the list of possible suspects in the murders of Oliver Lewis and Cynthia Maholm, and determined through the observations I'd made when I'd met each one that Rachel Vandross would be the third to arrive. The first, I surmised, would be the duo of Jennifer LeBlanc and Amy Stanhope, who would arrive together because they were living in the same house.

The last to enter the office, I believed, would be Hazel Montrose, because I assumed that Hazel was at this moment watching the entrance to observe everyone else as they entered, and that she would want to enter only after she could be certain the others had arrived.

At five fifty-two, I heard footsteps on the stairs outside the office. As we had discussed earlier, Ms. Washburn and I stood up and walked to the office restroom, which we—to be fair, mostly Ms. Washburn—had cleaned to the degree that I would be able to stay there.

We had left the office door unlocked. There would be no point to listening in on the WOOL meeting if the women involved were not capable of entering the room. I had no idea if any of them owned a key to the OLimited offices, although someone did. The door had not been locked on our first visit and had been locked when we'd arrived today.

Ms. Washburn quietly closed the restroom door. The walls were thin enough that hearing any conversation would not be an issue. Keeping our presence secret might be more of a challenge, as the walls were indeed porous and there was very little space to maneuver in the small restroom. It would be necessary in this old building to stand very still in an attempt to avoid leaning too heavily on an unstable, creaky floorboard.

I leaned on the sink, with a handkerchief between my palm and the surface. Ms. Washburn, less visibly alarmed by our surroundings, sat on the lid of the toilet. We were as stable and silent as would be possible under these circumstances.

As I had suspected, the first voice I heard after the squeak of the office door was that of Jennifer LeBlanc. "—doesn't make sense that it's Siplowitz. He'd just call if he needed to talk to one of us, and he wouldn't need us all in the same place at the same time. It's got to be the cops."

Amy Stanhope, who must have entered with Jenny, answered in a tempered, quiet voice. "Wouldn't the police just arrest us if they thought we'd done something?"

"It doesn't work like that."

"How does it work?" Amy asked.

Ms. Washburn looked at me with a quizzical expression. I shrugged, largely because I did not know what she meant, and could not speak. I assumed that, since she had never met Amy, she was wondering about the younger woman's naïveté.

"They have to have evidence before they do anything. They don't have any evidence that I know about, so they can't just arrest anybody." Jenny spoke to Amy as if to a child, and she did not speak to others that way, in my experience. Amy did invite that sort of treatment. But others have sometimes spoken to me that way because of my Asperger's Syndrome, and I know how it feels. It is not the way I would address another person, not even a child.

"Well, that's good," Amy answered. "I wouldn't want to see anybody get arrested."

"Neither would I." More footsteps, this time in high heels if I was interpreting the sound accurately, were audible in the room, and the voice was that of Rachel Vandross. "Hello, Jenny. Amy." She, too, spoke as if to a small child, drawing out the long "a" in the younger woman's name.

They had indeed met before, much as I'd expected.

"Rachel!" Amy's voice rose three full tones and there was a scuffle of feet, no doubt evidence of an embrace between the two women. "Excuse my belly. I'm getting big."

"Yes, you are, aren't you?"

Ms. Washburn made a spinning motion with her right forefinger extended, expressing the wish that the ladies would get to a more relevant topic.

"Hello, Rachel," Jenny said in a noticeably less joyous tone. "You want to take a guess at who's sending us all mysterious texts?"

"I figured it was Terry Lambroux," Rachel suggested. "It would be in character for that mysterious bitch."

Ms. Washburn tilted her head slightly—so Rachel *didn't* know who Terry Lambroux really was! I didn't know if that was a relevant fact, but it certainly seemed like one. Hopefully the ensuing conversation would clarify matters somewhat more.

"Oh, Rachel." Amy giggled. "Such language."

Perhaps more talk would not be as enlightening as I hoped.

"I don't think it matters as much who called this meeting as *why*," Jenny said. "Is someone trying to blackmail one of us?"

I nodded; that would be a logical supposition if I did not already know who had summoned the women to this spot and why. Ms. LeBlanc was clearly one of the more intelligent members of the group.

But the most intelligent—and potentially most dangerous—was just entering the room now. "Blackmail?" Hazel Montrose said. I heard the office door close behind her and saw Ms. Washburn's shoulders tense just a bit. "I don't see how there can be blackmail when there's no evidence of a crime."

"Slim," Rachel said.

"Maybe there *is* evidence," Ms. LeBlanc suggested. "Maybe somebody's found something. Maybe the fact that there are now two bodies instead of one was a mistake."

Just that—the idea that they were discussing among themselves that killing Cynthia Maholm could be a tactical error—sent a chill up my spine. I put my finger to my nose without thinking about it. I had not considered this possibility, but I realized that was simply an error in arithmetic getting in the way of my process. I had made a very grave error indeed.

My hands started to flap at my sides. Ms. Washburn's expression became one of concern, but she could not say anything to calm me down, nor could she make a move beyond very small gestures without attracting attention. I was becoming, rapidly, a liability.

I felt my head begin to shake, or more accurately, to vibrate. I was trying desperately to contain the anger with myself and the disappointment in my mind for placing Ms. Washburn in such a dangerous situation because of a simple miscalculation. And I was compounding the problem by threatening to give away our position and place us in a terrible situation.

"Two bodies?" Amy asked. "What do you mean, two bodies?"

That was an interesting response. In retrospect, had I been thinking along my normal patterns and not in a growing state of panic, I would have processed it more quickly.

"Ollie and Cindy," Hazel told her. "That's two."

"Cindy's dead?" Amy sounded shocked. "What happened?"

"She OD'd on some Reglan," Hazel said. "Can you imagine? She must have been *really* nauseous." And she laughed lightly.

I was shaking from head to toe now, furious with myself for increasing the danger to Ms. Washburn and knowing I was about to reveal to the women outside that we were secreted in the restroom. Ms. Washburn looked over at me and flattened her hands, pushing them toward the floor, urging me to calm down. But it was too late for that.

"Sheila!" Amy scolded. "How can you say that?"

The information was coming quickly now and in my present state, I was aware that I could not absorb it rapidly enough to act upon it. That increased my sense of failure and frustration, which made me clench my teeth hard and shake more violently. I could not control my movements, especially those of my hands, which flapped wildly at my sides in the narrow restroom. Ms. Washburn's eyes moved from side to side rapidly; she was trying to think of some strategy to return me to a more rational state. And I could tell she was coming up with no useful tactics to apply.

I tried to stop the shaking by shoving my hands into the pockets of my trousers. It did not stop the shaking. I pulled my left hand out and looked at it; perhaps concentrating on that could provide the necessary calm. It did not. My right hand was my last chance. I put it in my pocket.

"Sheila?" Rachel asked. "Who's Sheila?"

"The real point here," Hazel interrupted, "is that Samuel Hoenig got us all to show up. Now, why do you think he'd want to do that?"

I felt my knees get weak. If I fell to the floor, our plan would be exposed and Ms. Washburn would be exposed to danger far beyond anything I would have anticipated. I should never have accepted this question. Perhaps I should never have coaxed Ms. Washburn back to Questions Answered.

I should never have opened that business at all. I was a failure.

"What makes you think it was the retard?" Jenny asked. "That guy's got something wrong with him."

Hazel blew out some air. "He's the only one who would have thought of it, getting us all in one room so someone would confess. Well, it's not gonna be me."

I felt a scream catch in my throat. I could not control my limbs. There was pressure inside my head that felt like it would cause a hemorrhage. I could not stand another second of this.

"The only way that works would be if he was in the room to get the confession," Rachel said. "He's not here. But what I want to know is why Amy called you Sheila."

"I don't know about that," Hazel said. "But I'm willing to bet Hoenig has some recording device in this room. So watch what you say. He's a retard, but a smart one."

That was the moment I lost my battle. My knees buckled and I hit the filthy restroom floor. Pieces of linoleum tile scattered where

I fell. I heard a scream emanate from my throat but had no control over my voice. My head struck the sink in a glancing blow—hard enough to bruise but not to draw blood. I saw Ms. Washburn look around the restroom, see me fall, and pick up a piece of two-by-four that had been discarded in the room.

"Samuel," she said quietly. "Stay down."

The door flew open seconds later, but I was too distraught to count the time. I saw only feet at first. But after my head began to clear, with the distant sound of Ms. Washburn's voice repeating, "Stay down. Stay down," I felt the scream stop. I was breathing heavily. And I could see there were three pairs of women's feet in the doorway.

When I could, I angled my eyes upward. And there I saw Jennifer LeBlanc, Rachel Vandross, and Hazel Montrose staring at me in the doorway. I knew Ms. Washburn was behind me, armed with the two-by-four.

But Hazel was holding a pistol.

"This isn't good," Ms. Washburn said, and I heard the two-by-four hit the restroom floor.

THIRTY-ONE

I FOUND THAT I do not respond well to being tied up.

Using the second roll of duct tape I had brought with me, Hazel supervised while holding the pistol on Ms. Washburn and me as Jenny secured my hands behind me on a support post in the center of the OLimited offices. The tape was uncomfortable, sticky against my skin, and the angle at which my arms were being held required a flexibility that even my twenty-seven exercise sessions each day had not brought to my shoulders.

"It hurts," I said to no one in particular.

Rachel was securing Ms. Washburn to a similar post less than seven feet away. Ms. Washburn, looking angry, was not speaking at all, and I could only assume her anger was directed at me for involving her in this question. I did not blame her for being angry.

"Shut up or we'll tape your mouths," Hazel said. "I'd prefer not to, but I will."

Amy stood to one side, holding her pregnant belly, her left thumb curiously close to her mouth. In my mind's eye I felt she should have been holding a red helium balloon. She said nothing and her face was devoid of expression.

"How can the rest of you cover for her?" Ms. Washburn asked. "Look what she's done. Look what she's doing. She killed one of your own. How can you just stand by?"

I shook my head. "That tactic will not be effective, Ms. Washburn," I said. "There is no point. Not one of these women will ever testify against any of the others, and they have good reason not to."

"Didn't I tell you to shut up?" Hazel demanded.

"My apologies, Hazel," I said. "Or should I call you Sheila? Or Terry? How do you decide which name to use on any given day?"

"That's it," Hazel said. She looked to Jenny. "Tape his mouth."

But Jenny did not follow her instructions. "You're Terry?" she asked. She seemed genuinely surprised. "I thought there was no Terry."

"She's not Sheila?" Amy asked at the same moment. "I'm confused."

The only other one of the women who seemed not the least bit fazed was Rachel. "Why are we tying them up?" she asked. "What's the point? So they heard us talking. Doesn't mean anything."

My hand, if it were free, would no doubt have begun flapping again. Had I not been so "cautious" as to paint over the surveillance cameras, the two men in the Ford Escape might be heading up the stairs to the OLimited offices at this very moment. It was, actually, somewhat curious that they were not, given that they must have seen me block the camera lenses.

"You'll see." Hazel, seeing Ms. Washburn and I were securely incapacitated, lowered the gun and walked to Rachel. "Just keep your eye on the spaz." She handed the pistol to Jenny. "Use this if you have to."

My failed attempts at self-control in the restroom had left me discouraged. My forehead hurt. I felt the urge to flap both hands and my jaw tightened. The same thing was happening again, but this time I was tied to a post and at the mercy of a woman who had no doubt killed before.

Ms. Washburn, her face serious and angry, stared at Hazel. "You went out to dinner with him last night," she said. "Didn't you understand who you were with?"

Rachel looked at Ms. Washburn, then at me, and grinned. "You went on a date with *him*?" she said to Hazel.

"It wasn't a date," Hazel said from across the suite. I could not turn sufficiently to see her, but I could hear her voice. I felt anger swelling in my stomach and my head begin to shake. My upper lip curled into an unintentional sneer. "It was a way to get the idiot off track, and it worked."

My failure was complete. I had intended to use the social occasion with Hazel to get information from her, and she had used it to successfully manipulate me. Now Ms. Washburn was going to be hurt or killed because I had been blinded by … what? An attraction to Hazel Montrose? Was that what had happened? I wanted to scream in anger, but I knew it would be met with derisive laughter and I could not let that happen.

Ms. Washburn, however, changed her expression to one of smug satisfaction, if I read it correctly. "That's what you think," she said.

Hazel walked back into my sightline carrying some dusty newspapers she must have collected elsewhere in the office suite. "What's that supposed to mean?" she asked, trying to sound casual and failing to the point that I could easily read her inflection.

"It means Samuel knows everything. He knows who killed Oliver Lewis and who killed Cindy Maholm and he knows it because you weren't nearly as clever as you think you were." Ms. Washburn smiled a knowing smile at Hazel. "Maybe the *spaz* is smarter than you."

Hazel regarded her and her face showed something other than complete confidence. That gave me the moment I needed to gather my thoughts. Ms. Washburn had stepped in at the crucial moment and found the way to calm me down, just as I should have known she would.

261

It clarified my thoughts. My hands stopped trying to flap. My breathing became regular and even. My jaw relaxed. I knew what was necessary.

I had to buy time, and not much of it. Just a few minutes would be enough. Luckily, I had just enough accurate, irrefutable data to fill the time.

"I really don't think so," Hazel said.

Amy, who still seemed baffled by the rapidity of the events before her, squinted as if she were looking from far away. She said nothing, but she was watching Hazel and then me in succession. She appeared to be trying to determine which one of us she should believe.

Jenny, her face unhappy, walked to Hazel. "This is pointless. We should cut them loose and get out of here."

"That's not the plan," Hazel told her.

"There was no plan," Jenny said.

"There is now."

Hazel began taking sheets of the dry, yellowed newspaper and crumpling them, then dropping them on the floor. And in that moment I knew her plan. Fighting the fear that was welling in me, I blurted out, "All four of you killed Oliver Lewis."

Jenny, her face white, turned toward me in one jerky motion. Rachel, who was walking toward the window, stopped dead in her tracks. Amy opened and closed her mouth three times.

Hazel did not react at all, but kept dropping crumpled newspaper sheets on the floor. The next one landed within eighteen inches of my right hand.

"They did?" Ms. Washburn asked. She looked quite surprised indeed.

"Yes. I should have seen it earlier, but I was counting incorrectly. There were four assaults on Mr. Lewis's body—the cut throat, the knife wound to the ribs, the suffocation, and the poisoning."

"That doesn't prove anything," Jenny argued.

"There are four of you and four separate methods of murder, even if the poison was the one that actually caused Mr. Lewis's death. If I had not been counting six scorned women because of Cynthia Maholm and the elusive Sheila McInerney, I would have realized each one of you had a signature modus operandi. No doubt it was Hazel with the razor cutting his throat. I'd guess Amy held the knife, based on the fact that it was a shallow wound. Ms. LeBlanc probably held the plastic bag over his head to suffocate him. And that leaves Rachel Vandross to administer the poison that actually killed Mr. Lewis."

"Ha," Hazel said. Nothing more.

Amy's hand went to her mouth. More and more, she looked like a pregnant child. And I knew then that I'd gotten two of the perpetrators wrong, but I did not correct myself.

In films and television programs, heroic characters who are bound to a chair or other object always manage to wear away their bonds or find a sharp object to saw through them with what appears to be an extremely uncomfortable motion. I could not move my hands enough to erode the duct tape, nor did I have a jagged piece of glass or pocketknife to cut it. Clearly, I was not a heroic character, and it was bothering me. But I saw flaws in the armor of the women, and if I could keep them talking long enough, I could prevail.

Unfortunately, that seemed unlikely.

Hazel had dropped all the pages of newspaper she'd been holding, and the bulk of the debris was now scattered close to Ms. Washburn and me on the floor. Given that the OLimited offices had not been swept (other than by me), let alone cleaned, in months (a rough estimate), it was not difficult to determine her intention, and it was not a pleasant one.

"Everybody out," she ordered. "You're not going to want to be here for this."

She pulled a book of matches from her purse.

Ms. Washburn gasped.

"Won't you at least explain why Cynthia Maholm had to die?" I pretended to beg. "That is the one part I haven't surmised on my own." I actually had, but if I could get Hazel to pause for a minute or two, it might be enough.

"I don't see any reason to tell you," she answered. "You're not going to be alive in fifteen minutes." She opened the book of matches.

I decided to proceed as if that last exchange had not occurred. It's difficult in human behavior to ignore anyone who is speaking, and that might be sufficient to stop Hazel for the vital time period.

"Oliver Lewis was running illegal operations with this office as his front," I said. I noticed the other women had not yet followed Hazel's instructions, and were staying in the offices. They, at least, seemed to be listening, and Rachel in particular was intent on what I was saying, eyes narrowed to slits. "It was apparently making more money than any of you acknowledged, and was keeping you all in fairly comfortable life-styles without, except for Hazel, a visible source of income. Your divorce settlements naturally could not include illegally earned funds, so all of this money was coming to you without the need to pay taxes, which only made the operation more lucrative in practice."

"I never thought about the tax thing," Amy noted.

"Amy!" Jenny shouted again.

"Mr. Lewis's mistake was in marrying and divorcing so often, and in not keeping his business interests secret from his wives. He corrected that last mistake with his final wife, Cynthia Maholm, but as the marriage went sour, as you knew it would, you contacted her and told her about his intentions. You came up with the idea of contacting me as a witness, told Cynthia it would be a staged 'suicide' that would scare Mr. Lewis, and then you killed him. But Cynthia hadn't expected that and she balked. So you found a way to dispose of her too." I was certainly taking more time than Hazel wanted me to, but I heard nothing outside yet, and was becoming discouraged.

"I didn't even know Cindy was dead until tonight," Rachel protested. "Don't blame me for that. I didn't want to have anything to do with any of this."

"Yes, you did," Jenny snorted in response. "It wasn't your idea to kill Ollie, but you were sure fine with it once the plan was brought up."

"You were all there, or was it here?" I asked. "I thought there might be some sign of the event when we first entered these offices, but in the rubble of the place, we were unable to find anything."

"We went to Ollie's house," Amy said obligingly. "But you don't understand. He was a really bad person."

Before Jenny could object again, Ms. Washburn, who was not straining against her bonds (probably assuming correctly that it was a futile waste of energy) kept the conversation going; she knew what I had in mind.

"Well, he certainly didn't treat any of you ladies well," she said to Amy. "Is that what you mean?" It is always a good idea under such circumstances to ask a question. It requires an answer and that provides extra time.

"Oh, that was just the beginning." Amy actually sat on the floor next to Ms. Washburn, which was a serious mistake considering the difficulty she would have standing up again. She folded her hands under her chin. "He made you feel like the center of his universe, but then he cheated on us. He stole money from us—with all he was earning, can you imagine? He would come around with new girls even while we were still married!" She regarded Ms. Washburn. "Are you married?"

"Yes," Ms. Washburn admitted.

"Well, how would you feel if your husband did something like that?"

Ms. Washburn's faced blanched a little. "I ... I'm sure I'd be very angry."

I nodded in her direction; she was doing well.

Hazel must have seen the nod. "Get up, Amy!" she shouted. "We have to set the place on fire and leave!"

"Oh. Sorry." Amy reached her hand up, and Jenny helped her stand, gingerly. Amy dusted herself off. She looked back at Ms. Washburn. "I'm really sorry we have to do this."

"You don't," Ms. Washburn told her.

The idea seemed to be a revolutionary one for Amy. "Sheila says we do."

"She's the one you shouldn't trust," I told the other three. "Hazel is the most devious of you. She managed to infiltrate a crime scene cleaning service so she could see what I had surmised after Oliver Lewis was left on the floor of my offices. She might have had the original idea to kill Mr. Lewis in the first place. And she is the one who killed Cynthia Maholm." I knew that was not true, but I needed confirmation on a theory.

Again, they stopped and stood still. Hazel had me in her gaze, and I averted my eyes; her look was one of terrifying anger.

"You have no proof," she said. "None."

It has been observed that people who are guilty, when confronted with their guilt, first defend themselves by saying there is no proof. But I knew Hazel was playing the role of the killer now and I had to see my plan through.

"That's because there is none," I responded. "I was lying about that."

Ms. Washburn gasped slightly but said nothing. She looked at me. I had to look away. It is difficult for me to admit mistakes. I especially dislike being seen as imperfect to Ms. Washburn, who seems to believe I am especially intelligent, although my IQ is barely in the genius range.

What was important, however, was to observe the other women when I said, "One of the others killed Cynthia. Was it because she was threatening to tell the police about what happened to Oliver Lewis?"

"Of course not," Hazel answered. "Now, enough. I have to burn you up and then get on with my life." Once again she reached for the matches.

Having observed, I had one last tactic to try: "So it was Amy. I had suspected, but until this moment, I did not have it confirmed."

Hazel stopped her motion and the other women looked at her.

"Cynthia Maholm died of an overdose of Reglan, a drug commonly given to pregnant women for nausea. The person who would obviously have had access to that would have been Amy. And when I suggested that you were not the culprit, Hazel, each one of you stole a glance at Amy."

"Amy?" Ms. Washburn was clearly shocked.

"Yes. Interesting how appearances can be deceiving, but I pay little attention to appearance. It made sense that all the women had a stake in Oliver Lewis's illicit fortune, and each one had a grudge against him," I explained. "But when Cynthia Maholm was killed, it was a panicked act, something unplanned, by one of the WOOL members who did not consult the others. Hazel did not mention Cynthia's death when we went to dinner last night. If she had known, she would have said so, if only to distance herself from the crime. She didn't know it had occurred."

Hazel stopped and moved her mouth but said nothing.

"Amy was the real mastermind, wasn't she? I'll bet Oliver Lewis isn't even really the father of her child."

Amy walked over to me, looked me in the eye, and in a voice unlike the one she had been affecting since I'd met her, said, "Of course he wasn't. But that's enough. Light them up, Hazel."

I believe this time there would have been nothing I could say that would have distracted Hazel from her task, but the sounds I had expected throughout this entire ordeal became audible from the stairwell outside the OLimited offices. Loud footsteps were getting louder as they approached. From my position I could not see the window, but I did see blue and red lights reflected on the walls of the offices.

Ms. Washburn drew in a long breath. "Finally," she said.

The four WOOL members looked around the room in disbelief as a voice came from the direction of the door: "Police! Open the door!"

"We are in here, officer!" Ms. Washburn shouted.

Amy turned toward Jenny and said, "Shoot them."

Jenny looked at the pistol, then at me, then at Ms. Washburn, then back at Amy. "Forget it," she said. She handed the gun back to Amy.

I wished she hadn't done that.

But Amy seemed more astonished and angry at Ms. LeBlanc than intent on shooting Ms. Washburn and myself. "What did you say?" she asked. Clearly, she knew what Jenny had said, but the question is sometimes asked as a pejorative, a way to disagree with the statement just made. I believe that was what Amy was doing at that moment.

Jenny did not answer, and Amy raised the pistol in her direction.

"She's got a gun!" Ms. Washburn shouted.

In less than a second, the door to the offices opened forcibly, and behind it was a police officer in uniform, his leg still raised from kicking the creaking door in. I expected the door had been unlocked and could have been opened easily, but police officers do enjoy some drama, I have observed.

Two officers, both in uniform, both with guns drawn, entered the offices. They were not wearing bullet-resistant vests, but were holding their service weapons out in front of them, taking Ms. Washburn's warning seriously, as well they should.

They were the two men from the Ford Escape.

"Drop the gun!" the shorter one shouted. "Now!"

Amy looked at him and immediately lowered the weapon to the floor. When instructed to by the officer, she kicked it toward him. The taller one reached down and picked it up with a pencil from his pocket. He put the gun in an evidence bag while his partner held his own weapon on the four women.

"What took you so long?" I asked.

THIRTY-TWO

"IT WAS THE NUMBER of wives that confused me," I told Officer Ron Carbona.

Carbona ("Magical Mystery Tour"), the shorter (and, it appeared, more intelligent) of the two policemen who had doubled as the men in the Ford Escape, was sitting behind a desk at the police station after the WOOL members had been arrested and taken away and Ms. Washburn and I had been unbound and brought in to make statements. "That would confuse anybody in this case. But you knew how many wives there were," he said.

"Yes, but in my mind, there had always been one extra because I had not immediately associated Hazel Montrose with Terry Lambroux and Sheila McInerney. I was counting five when I should have counted four, and that meant the four methods of murder became the most telling clue. The members of WOOL had killed Oliver Lewis almost in a ritualistic fashion, each one taking part in her own way. I should have thought of four ex-wives, but I was assuming Cynthia Maholm, the current wife, had a role, and that Sheila McInerney was a separate person."

Carbona stared blankly for three seconds. "Uh-huh," he said.

Ms. Washburn, sitting in the other chair on my side of the interrogation table—the only open space to take our statements was in an interrogation room, and Carbona had eschewed police procedure in not separating us—told the officer, "What Samuel means is that he was miscounting the number of ex-wives because Sheila McInerney had taken on so many aliases."

Carbona nodded. His partner, Officer Pasquale, was in another interrogation room with one of the members of WOOL, although it was unclear in the shuffle which one he'd be questioning. "There are enough loose threads on this case to make a three-piece suit," he said. That conjured up a jumbled image in my mind, and I ignored it.

"How did you and Officer Pasquale become involved with surveillance of the OLimited offices?" I asked.

"It was authorized by the county prosecutor," Carbona answered. "They knew there was something fishy going on there, and they wanted two cops who want to make detective and don't mind sitting through hours and hours of blank footage. We fit the bill."

"You must have thought you'd hit the jackpot when we showed up," Ms. Washburn said. "But why didn't you show up faster tonight? Samuel had to keep those crazy women talking for what seemed like an hour."

"It was eleven minutes," I noted.

"We weren't watching the feed," Carbona answered. "We were on duty on the streets. It wasn't until we got your nine-one-one call that we knew what was up and we hustled over there."

Ms. Washburn looked at me. "You dialed nine-one-one?"

"I had Cynthia Maholm's cellular phone in my pocket," I told her. "I thought you saw that when we were in the restroom."

"But you didn't say anything."

"When the emergency line is activated, someone is sent immediately," Carbona said. "It's assumed that the person calling might not be able to talk."

"I couldn't have explained it better myself," I told him.

Carbona gave me another look that indicated some puzzlement, but he was intent on understanding the arrests he had just made. "So let's sort this out. All four ladies killed their ex-husband? That's new. He must have been a beaut."

"They did it mostly for the money," I told him. "There was quite a bit of it, apparently, and Oliver Lewis was holding out on the amount he'd told his ex-wives they would get. Each one had taken out an insurance policy on him while they were married that was not revoked in any of the divorces. So his death would pay off nicely in at least two ways."

"Plus, they seemed to really hate his guts," Ms. Washburn added.

"Why dump his body in your office?" Carbona asked. "They barely knew you."

"It was a public place," I said. "Cynthia Maholm had been told only that the WOOL members were planning to scare Oliver Lewis into paying up his share. She came to Questions Answered to cover their activity, establish Lewis's pattern with his wives, and determine if I would be able to get close enough to get their ex-husband agitated. I did. He showed up in my office, and that established a certain credibility I, as a disinterested outsider, could provide to the police.

"But when the ladies, minus Cynthia, murdered Mr. Lewis, it frightened her enough that she retreated to his house to decide whether she would turn in her fellow WOOL members. Not long after, Amy Stanhope managed somehow to give her a large overdose of a drug for women experiencing excessive nausea in pregnancy, and it killed her."

"Where was Lewis getting all the money, and how much?" Carbona asked. "It had to be millions to get all those women mad enough to kill him."

"I never found out," I said.

"Sometimes money isn't the only thing that gets women angry," Ms. Washburn told the officer.

Carbona shook his head. "All those wives."

"He had a lot of love," Ms. Washburn said. I do not believe she meant that to be taken sincerely.

"So great," Detective Andrew Dickinson said. "You answered my question, and gave the collar to a couple of uniforms."

"It was not under my control who responded to the nine-one-one call," I said. "It seemed more urgent to save Ms. Washburn's life and my own than to assign credit for the arrests."

"Well, that doesn't improve my close rate," Dickinson noted. "I have nothing to add to the collar; I know nothing about anything that the uniform cop doesn't already know. I don't know about Oliver Lewis's shady business or where he hid his money. I've got nothing. I'm not going to pay you."

We were standing in Dickinson's "office," which was a cubicle set up in a larger area of the police station. Because we were standing, I could see the top of Detective Esteban's head in her adjoining cubicle, but I could not see her face. She was sitting at her desk.

"Yes, you will," Ms. Washburn told him. "The agreement was that Samuel would answer the question. He has. There was no provision that you had to get the arrests on your record."

"We're done," Dickinson said. "If you want to sue me, Hoenig, you feel free." He sat down and very ostentatiously began writing on a pad on his desk. He did not look up.

"Oh, we'll sue all right," Ms. Washburn said. "I don't get my life threatened more than once, almost get burned to a crisp after having a gun waved in my face, and then not get paid for it. You'll hear from our lawyer." She turned on her heel and left the cubicle.

I stopped to see that Dickinson was in fact drawing a cartoon picture of a police officer on his pad.

I followed Ms. Washburn, who was walking quickly, toward the main entrance of the Piscataway police department when Detective Esteban appeared to my right and held up a hand. She spoke quietly. "Do you have a minute, Mr. Hoenig?"

The question is one I have heard before, of course; it is of common usage. But it always takes me a moment to consider—does any of us know how much time we have?

"Do you have a question, detective?" I asked.

"Not one I need you to answer professionally," she said. "Please." She gestured outside the building, so I walked outside, where Ms. Washburn was waiting on the sidewalk.

Once outside, Detective Esteban walked to the side of the building; apparently this was to be another of our clandestine conferences. "I just want to clarify something," she said, still not raising the volume of her voice to a level a passerby might hear. "You were clearly answering a question about the Oliver Lewis murder, is that right?"

If that were the extent of the detective's question, this would not be a difficult question to answer. "Yes, it is," I said. I nodded at the detective and took a step toward the parking lot where Ms. Washburn's car was now parked. Officer Carbona had allowed us to drive to the police station in the civilian car rather than a police cruiser, which was a courtesy.

"Hang on," Detective Esteban said. Perhaps this was not going to be so simple after all. "I'm just wondering who might have asked you about that murder."

That was the problem. Detective Esteban was curious about our involvement, and she was intelligent enough to know that Detective Dickinson was possibly our client, which probably violated a number of department policy guidelines, if not laws.

"I'm sorry, detective," I said. "I am not at liberty to divulge my client's name."

Ms. Washburn shook her head slightly. "I don't think that applies, Samuel." She turned toward the detective. "You want to know who paid us to find out about Oliver Lewis being murdered? It was—"

"Detective," I said, "we may not disclose that information, even if we want to. Our clients pay us for confidentiality." I looked at Ms. Washburn. "And they will get it."

Detective Esteban considered that for a moment, then nodded. "You're a man of integrity, Mr. Hoenig. I respect that. Thank you for your help." She nodded again as a way to indicate the conversation had ended, and took a step away.

Ms. Washburn's lips pushed out a little. "I get it. I don't like it, but I get it."

"Detective," I said. She stopped walking and looked at me. "If anyone asks you, Oliver Lewis was selling fraudulent bonds and stocks that did not exist, chiefly to senior citizens who would often die before the scheme was supposed to pay off. He made at least nineteen million dollars doing that and indulging in insider trading as well as other violations. And he would have lived much more opulently, but he had agreed to pay three million dollars to each of his ex-wives. And if he had done so, he might be alive today and we would not have met."

Ms. Washburn smiled, slowly. She looked at Detective Esteban.

The detective, without taking notes, waited and then nodded once more. "Just so you know, I got the warrant and there was some blood in the back of that cleaning van. We were looking for Hazel Montrose before you called. You should have let me know where you were going."

"I regret that I didn't, believe me," I said.

"And we got a call from a Roger Siplowitz. Says you're harassing him about a lawsuit that was withdrawn."

Ms. Washburn let out a breath. "If two phone calls constitutes harassment, I guess we were, but we'll stop now."

Detective Esteban laughed lightly. "I told him to go away."

"I appreciate it," I said. "The lawsuit was meant to goad Oliver Lewis into marrying Hazel Montrose, and it worked. And that set this whole unfortunate affair into motion."

"But I thought Siplowitz's problem was with the wedding pictures, that he didn't want us to see those for some reason," Ms. Washburn said. "What was in the pictures, Samuel?"

"Nothing. Mr. Siplowitz was concerned we would discover the lawsuit with which he was involved, and he thought it was the key to the scheme Oliver Lewis was perpetrating," I explained. "He was wrong, but his anxiety led us in the right direction."

Detective Esteban regarded me for a moment. "You wouldn't make a bad detective," she said.

"I have no such ambition, and I believe I would not be as skilled as you are," I answered.

"Thank you, Mr. Hoenig," she said.

"I believe the expression is, 'no charge,' detective."

Detective Maria Esteban smiled and turned away. She walked around the corner, presumably back to the police station to begin making phone calls to verify what I had said.

Ms. Washburn walked over to me and linked her arm through mine. Since we were both wearing long sleeves, there was no contact, which she knew would have made me uncomfortable. We started toward her car.

"I thought there was all that stuff about upholding the contract no matter what, even if the client refuses to pay us," she said as we walked.

"Ms. Washburn," I said, "I told our client I would answer his question, and have answered it. There was nothing in the agreement that said I would tell him *first*."

THIRTY-THREE

"THE WOMAN HAD THREE names." Mother sat in her traditional easy chair at the Questions Answered office and shook her head, still disbelieving what had been proven. "Why would she do that?"

I looked up from my work on the question at hand, which dealt with the probability that global warming would create a new west coast of North America somewhere in Utah within seventy-five years.

"Ms. McInerney found it best to have a few identities behind which she could hide," I said. "It was convenient to have separate credit card accounts, for example, when she overspent her limit and could not make payments. Once she decided—and it was she who decided—that Oliver Lewis should die, being able to not be Sheila McInerney was quite helpful, I'm sure. She could even send Cynthia Maholm here under that name and create what I believe is called a 'smokescreen' for herself."

"It still doesn't make sense that Cindy would come to us at all," Ms. Washburn said. She was doing her best to organize the files of questions I had answered in her absence. I'm afraid my filing system, particularly with hard copies, was not efficient. Ms. Washburn said she was also in the early stages of creating an advertising campaign for Questions Answered that she hoped would generate enough business to pay her salary, as she put it.

"It does from the perspective of a woman who thought she was going to scare her husband," I said. "And from Hazel Montrose's viewpoint, it was a very efficient way to enforce unity among the other WOOL members. The deeper they got into the plot, the harder it would be to break ranks."

Mother clucked her tongue a bit and shook her head again, I think to herself, without thinking. "That was a strange group of wives. But who am I to judge?" My father left us when I was four years old and had not contacted Mother or me since. Mother doesn't say so, but I think the difficulty of raising a child who wasn't like other children was a factor in his decision to abandon his wife and son.

"You're not judging, Vivian," Ms. Washburn said. "You just never know what's going on in someone else's marriage." Her voice got fainter and she was not looking at either of us when she added, "You're lucky if you know what's going on in your own."

Mother appeared to find some significance in that remark, as she stood and walked to the vending machine and stood admiring the selections. I knew she was not going to buy a diet soda or a mineral water—she never has—and she had no money with her; her purse was back at the chair.

She was giving Ms. Washburn and me a chance to talk privately. The difficulty was in determining exactly what the issue might be.

Ms. Washburn looked at Mother a moment and clearly understood what her gesture had meant. She turned to me and said, "I don't want to talk about it."

Since I was not sure what the implied topic might be, I nodded. "All right."

"I mean, you knew there was trouble in my marriage." Apparently, despite her protestations, Ms. Washburn *did* want to talk about it, and the subject was her marriage.

I thought. "I knew what you told me," I said. That seemed safe.

"Well, I didn't tell you everything, and I'm not going to now, either." I'll admit to some relief at that declaration. "But it's very possible that I'll be getting a divorce."

Mother's shoulders rose and fell quickly.

I was trained in social skills from the time of my "diagnosis" at sixteen, so I had a response ready. "I'm very sorry to hear that." I was not terribly sorry, as I had never met Simon Taylor and only spoke with him on two unpleasant occasions, but that is what one is supposed to say. "But you will be staying on at Questions Answered?" I did not especially care if the timing was appropriate; I needed to have the information.

Ms. Washburn smiled. "Yes, Samuel. I'll probably be needing the job more than ever. Don't worry."

She seemed about to reach out to me, perhaps to embrace, but she stopped herself. It was possible she thought the gesture would make me uncomfortable. I'm not sure whether it would have or not.

"Then everything is all right," I said.

Ms. Washburn shook her head slightly and smiled with an odd expression. "Yes, Samuel," she said. "Everything is all right." She paused. "So. What's next on our agenda?"

"I believe I would like to purchase a cellular telephone," I said.

THE END

ABOUT THE AUTHOR

E.J. Copperman is the author of the Haunted Guesthouse series (Berkley Prime Crime), with more than 100,000 copies sold. Jeff Cohen is the author of the Aaron Tucker and Comedy Tonight mystery series. He also wrote two nonfiction books on Asperger's Syndrome, including *The Asperger Parent*.